Blue, like don't forget about me

A Wildflowers of Deliverance novel
by

Sarah B. Elisa

This is a work of fiction. Similarities to real people, places, or events are entirely coincidental.

BLUE, LIKE DON'T FORGET ABOUT ME

Written by Sarah B. Elisa.
Edited by Ember Hood
Cover photo by Josh Allard, @alljos on Pexels
Interior art by Sketchify, Canva

ISBN: 979-8991930222 (ebook)
ISBN: 979-8991930239 (paperback)
Library of Congress Control Number: 2025904323

First edition. March 26, 2025.

This one is for the girls, the gays, and Coleman. Hope you like it. Hope you find something to carry with you out the other side. Hope you live and live and live and live.

Table of Contents

CHAPTER ONE

In memory

Some days Nash is all too aware that his funeral clothes see more action than his good blue jeans. If he's not in scrubs or sweatpants, he's stuffed into black slacks with worn knees and frayed hems, a black button-up with too-tight cuffs, and his only necktie. Black, if you were curious.

"Nash Owens!"

He looks up from his contemplation of the flower arrangements and searches the crowd for the source of the warbling voice. He spots Cheyenne first, a pink beacon in her scrubs, with a scowl that could wilt carnations at twenty paces. In front of her, waving from one of Cherished Hope's shitty manual wheelchairs, is Darla Biggins.

He fights a frown.

Darla is the smallest of his residents—positively dainty with thin wrists and a frail poof of white atop her head—but she's the liveliest. It settles on him all wrong, seein' her mobility restricted when he's accustomed to her zipping anywhere she pleases with the turn of a joystick. He gets it; power chairs are a bulky pain in the ass to transport. He'd have done it though.

He musters a wave and a smile in return, and they come easy enough. Smiles aren't a difficulty when faced with Darla's unabashed delight, and she seems awful tickled at catching him out and about off the clock, even though she sees him five days out of seven and he told her Sunday he'd be here to say a last goodbye to Geraldine.

It's one of the easier goodbyes to make. She'd been ready for a while now. Dementia is a heartbreaker.

He meets them beside the stained glass panels that wash the room in lifeless indigo and has another smile pulled out of him as he clocks Darla's signature sunshine-yellow Crocs peeking from under the hem of her dress. She evangelizes comfortable shoes, regardless of the occasion, and has made it her life's work to infuse the world with a little more color.

She hasn't converted him yet. Someday he'll be of the age he can grocery shop in his house slippers and no one will bat an eye, but he ain't quite there yet. That said, her commitment to being unabashedly herself quiets the usual twinge of unease that comes with using his cane around folks from work. It's less shame of his disability, and more a bone-deep fear that it could be used to uproot him from his career. He works very hard to perform at least as well as his fully-abled coworkers, despite his obvious limp without his cane.

"Nash Owens," Darla grins up at him through smeary lenses, "I swear it's been a month'a Sundays since I been blessed with your smile."

He's already tucking his cane in his armpit and digging a lens cloth from his pocket as he says, "It's good to see you too, Ms. Biggins. I can give those a scrub if you'd like."

"Oh, bless your heart." She doffs her glasses and hands them to him as she dabs her eyes with a soggy tissue. "Would you believe velvet makes for a terrible cleaner? Though, I suppose, the dress isn't entirely to blame; it has pockets, you know! Leave it to me to forget to fill 'em with anything of use. Oh!" she digs in said pocket and retrieves a heavily scribbled sticky note— "Get this in that book of yours. I don't want that mealy-mouthed man preachin' over me when I'm gone. Didn't understand near a word he said!"

Cheyenne lifts her eyes to the rafters, but Nash ignores her judgment and trades Darla her clean glasses for the note.

"I'll do what I can."

Darla pats his wrist with a cold hand. "You are truly a blessing, Mr. Owens."

He closes his hand over top of hers and squeezes. "It's just Nash. I'll see you tomorrow afternoon, alright?"

"Western Wednesday!" she cheers as Cheyenne releases the brake on the chair, eager to be gone. "I'll be damned if I let Walter shoehorn us into that Hays era claptrap again. I reckon if I made it to this age, I'm entitled to see some chest hair, damn it."

A smile splits Nash's face. "That's a fight I'll be stearin' clear of."

She cocks her head, eyes twinkling. "Ain't you a peach for thinkin' I need a champion."

Cheyenne turns her and starts for the door without a parting word, not that he's expecting anything. As well as he and his residents get on, he's never had an easy time with his peers.

Undeterred, Darla raises her fist and calls back, "I'll get his head on a pike my own self, best you believe it!"

"I wouldn't dream of doubting you, Ms. Biggins."

He takes the little black notebook from his back pocket and tucks Darla's sticky note in the spine of a dog-eared section towards the middle. Due diligence done, he returns to the page marked with the ribbon, scans the few remaining items on his list, and gets back to work.

Nash hangs 'round the lobby 'till most everyone is cleared out. The funeral parlor is a squat little building with threadbare carpet, wood paneling, and a dusty smell that lingers under the gardenia plug-in fragrance. It's kept neat and orderly, but there are folding chairs in the chapel and mice in the basement. Which is to say, if he were challenged to select a single establishment to represent Buford Hills, it would be a top contender.

"Nash Owens, you still hangin' 'round?"

He turns and finds Henry Velure drying his hands on a spotty kitchen towel and eying him from under thick, wiry eyebrows.

Henry shakes his head. "I swear I see you more often than I do my own kin."

Well, that's not surprising considering Henry's daughter moved to the coast half a decade ago and only returns for Christmas. Meanwhile, he and Henry have… complementary careers.

"Thought I'd make sure your back isn't stuck clearin' these chairs again. Where's your nephew?"

Henry snorts and slaps his towel over his shoulder. "Who can tell with that boy? He ain't due 'round 'till late though."

Nash frowns at the near-empty parking lot through wavy blue glass. Most everyone is at or on their way to the burial by now. If he takes his time, he'll miss the scripture and the worst of the crowd, but if Henry's got another service coming in, he might get caught in a new one.

"You got another on the docket?"

"Meant to. Rescheduled for tomorrow morning last minute. Something about a nephew stuck in Minnesota." He cracks a smile and slaps at Nash's bicep. "Somethin' 'bout nephews, eh? Ah well, weren't no trouble and that Mrs. Spinoza was mighty grateful."

Nash's stomach lurches like he missed a step going down the stairs.

"Spinoza?" His voice echoes out of him as though from a long way off.

Henry ticks his head. "That's right. You know 'em?"

"I… Maybe."

It's been so long since he thought about— But surely there are more Spinozas out there: nephews, missuses, and all. But in Buford Hills? Why would they come back here? It's been decades.

"Well, here. I got the pamphlets in the other room. Can't

for the life of me remember the feller's name what passed. Started with a D... Or maybe a T. Similar letters, those."

A sick feeling wells in the back of his throat, and he doesn't lean on his cane as much as he should as he falls in behind Henry's long strides. He hardly clocks the pang of his hip through the pitched whine swelling between his ears.

Henry flicks on the light in the little office tucked near the bathroom and the old fluorescents buzz to life, washing the room in pale light.

"Darren Spinoza," he declares as he swipes a glossy pamphlet off the stack on his desk. "That ring any bells?"

With steady hands, Nash accepts the pamphlet and stares down at the face of the man who was more of a father to him in the six short years he knew him than his own father ever was.

Cane in his armpit, Nash jiggles his key in the lock until it finally turns and lets him into the quaint little ranch he bought thinkin' him and Jo would be sharing it when she finished her degree. Technically, they do, but during these long trips away he gets to feeling like he sees more of people like Henry than he does his own sister.

Seems to be a sentiment going 'round.

He kicks the door shut behind him and flips the switch to bring the lights on in their dingy living room and the strip of laminate they call a kitchen. Hints of Jo pepper the space even though she's been out of town for weeks now: the helmet and pads hanging from the coat rack, her roller skates dropped half-atop his nice boots, and her fleece blanket heaped at the end of the couch where she normally sits.

He hangs his cane opposite her helmet and the time-worn crochet sleeve sags to reveal faded and peeling stickers on the shaft. The entire thing has seen better days. Upon spotting him with it outside of work, his craftier residents have begged him to allow them to crochet a new sleeve and the derby team's been threatening to bedazzle over the old stickers for years now, but he likes it how it is. Beat-up, worn, and faded, yes—but also comfortable, familiar, and swaddled in memory.

He hesitates to add the "In Memory of Darren Spinoza" pamphlet to the mail organizer on the counter nearest the door. It doesn't seem right to slot him in with former residents who lived full lives, even if they weren't always happy ones. Instead, he elects to leave it face-up on the counter and unlaces his dress shoes.

Tomorrow.

It's hardly any time at all to come to a decision. He should go, he knows he should, but just thinking about it gets his heart pounding and his palms damp. He'd never forgive himself if he stayed away, 'specially since this is a lesson long-learned. He runs his thumb over the inked spot of skin on his chest and resolves himself. It ain't about him. Not really. Whether it all goes belly up or... Well, he can't think how else it'll go, but his point is, it's all comin' out in the wash regardless. Ain't no way to make things worse, so he may as well get his goodbye in.

Once he's in his sweats and his funeral clothes are hanging in the center of the closet for easy access, he settles on the couch in front of a card table dominated by an old sewing machine, fabric scraps, and straight pins. Then he

sets himself to the task of sorting out where he left off in the
pattern while the TV plays a rerun of the soap his residents
go ape over. He listens with half an ear for anything juicy he
may have missed the first go-round and lets the monotony of
habit steer him back from the knife-edge of the past and the
uncertainty of tomorrow.

It's ten minutes to the top of the hour and Nash is garbed in
funeral clothes once again, debating whether to leave his car.
He's got more than his fair share of funerals under his belt,
but it's different not having spoken to the deceased since he
was a kid. It's different not knowing if he's welcome. It's
different knowing Teddy's somewhere on the other side of
that door.

Yesterday he was here to say a final goodbye to a
resident after knowing from the start how it was going to
end, but he didn't see this end coming, and if he misses this
last goodbye—that's it. There won't be any more.

He's not keen on repeating past mistakes.

He takes a steadying breath and steps out into
Tennessee's version of autumn bluster.

Inside the building, he stops to absorb the sparse crowd
of the usual type, plus more young, unlined faces than he's
used to in this place. Then he clocks the first of many small
brimless hats seated on the crown of an unfamiliar man's
head and recalls with a start that the Spinozas are Jewish.

He freezes in the doorway. The only Jewish funeral he's
attended was about four or five years ago and technically,
there wasn't a funeral. A few words were said at the grave,

they all took turns shoveling dirt over a plain pine casket, and then he left, unsure whether the brevity was tradition or preference.

Looking around, it doesn't seem he's made a faux pas thus far—everyone is dressed more or less how he is, although perhaps with less black than usual, except he's missing a—

"Kippah?"

A woman beside the door is holding a navy, brimless, crocheted hat out to him with a smile, and on the table beside her is a whole basket of 'em.

"Thank you."

Miraculously, it doesn't immediately slip to the floor when he places it on the crown of his head. He's never really understood how these things stay on, but it seems to be holding well for now. He gives it a pat for security's sake and steps out of the doorway.

It seems most people have already found their seats in the next room with the casket, the folding chairs, and the pulpit—but with him in the lobby are a smattering of familiar faces from around town. On the far wall is a table topped with a tri-fold display of photographs that are more compelling than they ought to be.

He nods at Howard Brunswick as he passes him, but Howie's gaze slides by like he didn't see before he abruptly turns and steps into the chapel.

Howie hired him for his first job at the little deli in Deliverance and used to run with his ma before she drank herself dead, so you'd think Nash'd get a little consideration, but no. Jo thinks it's guilt, Howie bein' the last to see Mama alive 'n' all, but Nash knows too well the delight he took in

Mama's malicious treatment of him. 'Sides, a feigned lack of recognition is about all he expects from anybody outta Deliverance. It's not ten minutes down the road, but he's dead to that place as surely as if this were his memorial service.

Nash approaches the photo display with trepidation, unsure how he'll react to what he sees, but too curious to keep his distance.

Holding the center of the display is a photo of a familiar grinning boy. Narrow-faced and somehow thinner than he remembers, is Teddy. He's holding a spread of Pokémon cards while a pair of adults in the background smile at each other midconversation. They're unfamiliar except in the things they passed on to their son. Teddy's tan, honey-rich skin and curly hair come from his dad, but the russet color, his gaped teeth, and the shape of his eyes are all his mom.

He never knew that.

Between them, smiling wryly at the camera, is Darren Spinoza—a rounder, shorter, and warmer version of his long-deceased brother—both gone now.

Nash takes in the rest. There are several old black-and-whites of a familiar town and two boys who grew into gangly teens. Then of one man in color, well-middled and showing his age in his thinning hair and leathering skin. Even in photos, he has a quiet way about him. Calm. Reassuring. Spotted here and there is a long-haired woman whose crow's feet grow deeper as the man beside her grows rounder and a curly-haired boy sheds his childhood and becomes a man.

Nash wants to linger on these glimpses of who Teddy grew to be, but one photo catches his attention and keeps it.

He recognizes it, not for having seen it before, but for having lived it.

Darren Spinoza is leaned over the front bumper of an old sports car that can't decide what color it should be, pointing at something under the hood. Beside him, holding a flashlight and standing on a weathered step stool, is the back of a boy too pudgy to be Teddy, with dust-colored hair and mud-crusted secondhand jeans.

"He was so proud of that old thing."

He near comes out of his skin at the voice behind him. When he turns, he finds the woman from the photographs—her long, gray-streaked hair twisted around the back of her head and clipped in place. Her dress is neat and simple and black with rose buttons that run the full length to just below her knees.

Julie Spinoza takes in the photo with sad eyes and lines on her face that he doesn't remember.

"What happened to it?"

A soft, ironic smile curls her lips. "Sold it. I talked him around—badgered him, he'd say. He couldn't drive it more than a handful of times a year and we needed the money for tuition." Her smile wilts. "I told him we'd buy another when we had fewer expenses."

Regret. Not knowin' how little time you've got with a good thing until that time runs out. That's a thing he understands.

"I'm sorry for your loss."

Her nose scrunches and a brushstroke of bitterness colors her tone. "Yes, everyone's sorry."

In that moment, she sounds so much like her twelve-year-old nephew that he has to smile, even if it fades fast.

"Some sorrier than others, I'd expect."

She pivots to face him with the ghost of offense on her face, but it's quickly swept away by recognition. "Nash? Nash Owens?"

"Hey there, Mrs. Spinoza."

The smile that had been building a moment prior, turns frigid and her stare moves past him to the middle distance. "I think it's Ms. Spinoza now."

He's heard the same grief and uncertainty countless times over the years, but never from anyone so young. Regardless, he says what he always says.

"I think it's whatever you want it to be, so long as it's what you want."

She regards him silently, grief tucked away for the moment as she considers the statement and considers him. Slowly, she nods. "You may be right." She looks him up and down, more present suddenly. "You're still in town, then?"

"Not Deliverance, no. Me 'n' Jo live here in Buford now. Got a little place on Cherry just before the speed limit ticks up to highway."

"Is Jo..." She looks past him like she expects her to pop out of his shadow.

"Out of town, unfortunately. Saving the world one crisis at a time."

Her eyebrows lift in polite curiosity, which is more invitation than Nash usually needs to brag up his little sister.

"She's a trauma counselor. Specializes in teens and catastrophic events. She must be pretty good 'cause they call from all over, askin' her to come out and talk kids through the tough stuff—losing their home in a flood or, you know, assorted violence. She's in California now. Seems they're always callin' with them damn fires."

A small smile is tickling Mrs. Spinoza's lips. This time, she manages to keep hold of it. "I remember when she'd come over to chew you out for sneaking up to our house without her."

He winces. He wasn't always the most courteous of brothers. "Aw, I'm sure if you hang around long enough she'll have much worse stories to tell about me 'n'— About how I'd ditch her."

His near slip is met with a familiar smile and an appraising look. "All grown up, yet the same as I remember," she says musingly. "We should catch up. Properly, I mean."

He clocks the polite dismissal and responds with the required, "I'd like that," only now realizing how few remain in the lobby. The service must be about to start and here he is, hogging the deceased's wife to himself.

Except, he must have misjudged, because rather than go their separate ways, she loops her arm through his and says, "Let's find that nephew of mine."

CHAPTER TWO

His best friend

He'll be so excited to see you again."

It's all Nash can do to keep his feet moving, cane uselessly trapped between his arm and Mrs. Spinoza as she tugs him into the room with the casket—closed, plain, and pale—the folding chairs, and the pulpit.

His heart races. "Oh, I don't—"

"You can trade numbers properly this time. I tell you, I was furious when we found out what your mother did, changing your number like that. Darren had to hold me back from driving straight through the night to give her a piece of my mind. She never cared for our family, but to drive a wedge between you boys was too far."

Nash's mind reels. Teddy told her *what*? It was never the Spinozas that Mama took issue with—it was him she wanted to hurt—but she never changed their number. It stayed the same 'till the day he sold the house and moved into a crumbling apartment he could only afford thanks to what was left after the bank took their due.

It was his fault Teddy cut off contact, but his aunt doesn't know that. She doesn't know that if Teddy is anything like the kid Nash knew, he won't wanna see him. After twenty years? In these circumstances? He *won't*.

A woman wearing a large hat sits down and Nash's heart skips as he recognizes a head of russet curls spilling out from under a black kippah with a gold star of David in the middle. He's in the front row, his back turned, shoulders too broad to belong to the scrawny hothead he used to be. He's talking to a blond guy their age wearing thick, black-rimmed glasses, too much hair gel, and the same loaner kippah as Nash.

Mrs. Spinoza butts into their conversation without reservation and allows Nash no time to get his head together.

"Guess who I found!"

Teddy turns and Nash freezes like prey. *He has new glasses*, is the first thing he thinks. Metal burgundy frames. Rectangular. Behind the lenses, familiar brown eyes take him in with guarded neutrality, but recognition burns it away quick. Teddy looks at him for the first time in twenty years and every ounce of warmth leaves his expression.

Message received. He should not have come.

Mrs. Spinoza is talking, saying something about where they're staying and when he should stop by. He can't tell if she's oblivious to the murder Teddy is beaming into his skull or if she's deliberately ignoring it, but the moment she pauses for breath, Nash breaks in with an excuse about visiting the restroom before the service starts.

He forgoes the use of his cane and beats a hasty retreat, not slowing until he's alone in the overly perfumed men's room, hip aching and heart racing.

It seems all the moisture that was in his mouth somehow migrated to the back of his neck. He turns the faucet to full and frowns at his flushed face in the mirror. It figures. Jo says he's unflappable (derogatory). She calls him *stony*. So it figures all it takes is one look at Theodore Spinoza all grown up to get him blushing like a schoolgirl. He should've stayed home.

At least the red in his cheeks hides his freckles somewhat, though this side of summer there's really nothin' to do for 'em. Everybody gushes over freckles until they look like his. Like he loaded 'em in a blender, stuck his face in, and hit surge.

To make things worse, his hair is sweat-stuck to the back of his neck and, despite the time spent tidying it and the questionable security of the kippah, it's fallen lank around his face. It's his own fault. He hates going to the barber and is normally content to look a bit scruffier than he prefers until Jo can get around to trimming it for him, but he's regretting that contentment now. The freckles, the hair, and his clothes —gray in the knees, too tight around his wrists—twenty years and the first time Teddy sees him, he looks like a bum at his uncle's funeral. Fucking hell.

He washes his face and stalls until the few voices outside grow distant.

He'll listen to the service through the chapel doors, he decides. And when it's over, he'll slip out before anyone spots him. He won't upset the Spinoza's mourning. He can be discreet and give Teddy the space he needs. It's the least he can do. Besides, if his last experience with a Jewish funeral is right, then it's the burial that's the important part. He hasn't ruined that, at least.

He pats the back of his neck one last time, throws away the paper towel, and then opens the bathroom door nearly into Teddy's blond friend's face.

They freeze and eye each other like rabbits.

"You, uh, need to—" Nash jerks his thumb at the bathroom.

"Oh, no. You're... Nash, right?" His forehead wrinkles like an old map.

"Yeah?" Part of him wonders if he's about to get jumped by a guy with a permanent wince. "Look, I didn't come 'round to start any trouble. I only wanna pay my respects and go."

The wrinkles deepen. "You don't want to talk to Theo?"

Who the fuck is Theo? Teddy didn't—

No.

Really?

Theo?

The name throws him so hard he can't think of a response. *Does* he want to talk to Te— Theo? (God, Theo?) The prospect is overwhelming.

"Listen, just— just— Here." The guy thrusts a folded piece of paper at him. Vaguely, Nash recognizes it as a scrap from one of Henry's brochures. "Go easy on him, okay? He's not in a great place right now."

Easy on Teddy? If anyone is getting the hard end of the stick, it's gonna be Nash. He's the one who didn't say goodbye. He's the one who broke his promise before the Spinozas even made it out of their driveway, let alone

Tennessee.

"I gotta go. Nice to finally meet you!" Teddy's friend looks vaguely panicked, then jogs away and slips through the double doors of the chapel. As they fall closed behind him, Nash gets a glimpse of the rabbi taking the podium.

He unfolds the paper as he listens to the rabbi greet the congregation through the door. Inside is a date, time, and the address of the shoddy chain hotel down the street written in sharp, scribbling handwriting that sends his stomach tumbling.

Twenty years and he still recognizes his best friend's handwriting.

Former best friend, that is.

Nash skips the burial. He feels enough like an interloper lurking outside the chapel, sniffing back tears while Mrs. Spinoza gets escorted away from the podium in the middle of her eulogy, too overwhelmed to continue. He imagines it's Ted— *Theo* that walks her back to her seat, more than grown enough to carry her weight and handle her grief with a gentleness Nash only ever saw from him in fits and bursts.

He returns his kippah to the basket by the door and is outside before the chapel doors open. With the car running, he waits for the procession to start down the pitted highway that leads to Deliverance. He falls in behind the last of them, but he hangs a left into his driveway rather than continue with them out of town.

Inside, he turns the TV to the same channel as last night and picks at quilt fragments while the title sequence to *A*

Rose Without Thorns plays. He distracts himself from the memory of that hateful look on Teddy's face, but doesn't make much progress. When his phone finally rings, he mutes the TV and barely checks the caller ID before he accepts the video call.

"Hey nerd-burger. How're the old folks?"

"Still kickin' mostly," Nash replies by rote. "How's saving today's youth?"

On the tiny screen, Jo sighs and props a full cheek on her fist. She got lucky—her freckles trot in a neat little herd across the bridge of her nose and leave the rest of her face out of it. Her dark eyes flit to something off screen. "Still too much paperwork, not enough laser guns."

She looks worn slap-out like she only does on these long trips. It's not unexpected. Even superheroes ought to get tired after jumping from crisis to crisis and his sister is only human, as evidenced by the dark circles under her eyes fighting her smart smattering of freckles for real estate. Chestnut hair is piled atop her head in a frizzy end-of-day mess, and he recognizes the neckline of her sweater as an old, stained number that she drags out when she needs the extra comfort.

"How much longer?"

"Couple weeks probably, but I'm aimin' for next weekend. These west coasters have turned powerfully wearisome."

She runs her knuckles over her lips, then sets aside a notebook with a scowl. When she looks back at him, her eyes go sharp.

"What's with the funeral duds? Another one bite the dust?"

He frowns, first at her disrespectful tone, then at his shirt, tie, and slacks. With a sigh, he unearths himself from a mound of fabric and pins that will someday, if he's lucky, transform into a quilt, and slumps to his room.

Despite stalling until he's digging through his dresser, he still hasn't thought of a gentle way to break the news, so he goes with blunt.

"Darren Spinoza passed."

He checks her expression as he sets his phone on the dresser and finds a bored look on her face as she turns an ink-laden page.

"He one of your war guys?"

He pauses with his hand on a fresh scrub top in Cherished Hope pink. He doesn't have to be at work for over an hour still, but he can only justify changing so many times in one day. Besides, scrubs are plenty comfortable for sitting around waiting for the clock to tick.

He softly closes the drawer. "No, he was Teddy's uncle. Spinoza, remember?"

The rustle of paper stops. "Spinoz— What the fuck? He *died*? Why didn't you tell me?"

He aims a dry look at his phone and finds her goggling at him. "I just did. Found out yesterday, by chance." He tugs his shirt over his head. "Wasn't even sure I should go."

"Of course you should go. Why wouldn't you?"

"Wasn't sure I'd be welcome."

"Well, were you? What happened? How did he die? Did you see Teddy? What's he like now? Did he finally grow into those ears? And hey, look at me so I can tell when you're hiding shit."

He rolls his eyes. "Hold on."

He changes quickly, hangs his clothes in the center of the closet, and returns to the living room.

"First things first," Jo says in her most authoritative tone, "did he get hot?"

"Wouldn't know. It was closed casket."

"Not— Don't dodge the question, asshole. Should I expect to suffer through your awkward attempts at courting when I get back or is this a dodged bullet kind of situation? Phone up! I can't see your face."

He lifts his phone. "When did you get so shallow, Josephine Hopestill?"

She hisses through her teeth. "Do not invoke my middle name in an attempt to distract me. Are you seeing him again? Yes or no."

"I—"

"Yes or no."

He realizes then that he left Teddy's note in his funeral pants, but he remembers what it said: Friday, 5:00 PM. If he's going, he'll have to find someone to cover his shift last minute. For a Friday night, it'll require a big IOU.

"Maybe."

Jo groans. "Alright, start from the beginning and I'll tell you whether or not you're seeing him again."

It should shame him that the declaration fills him with relief. Historically, he hasn't done so well with these kinds of decisions.

He starts with learning the news from Henry yesterday and ends with being handed the note by Teddy's... friend?

"Do you think they're dating?"

"How should I know? I didn't even get the guy's name."

"What vibe did you get at the burial?"

"I didn't go."

Jo's face contorts with disbelief. "You always go to the burial. Even when the weather's shit."

"Well… this time I didn't."

Her expression goes mild, and when she next speaks, her voice is uncharacteristically gentle. "How are you feeling about—"

"*Don't*, Jo."

She huffs and blessedly drops the therapist veneer. "I'm just saying, he was important to you, and you never got closure. Look how that's changed how you deal with loss. You *always* go to the burial. You've got to be feeling some kind of way."

"I'm *feeling* badgered by my professional meddler of a sister. We used to be close, but now we've both moved on and maybe he wants nothing to do with me. Especially now that— What? What did I say?"

She bites down on her smug smile, but her eyes continue to sparkle in victory. "I wasn't sure if it was Teddy or his uncle that had you all tangled up, but now that you've admitted it's Teddy, I can confidently say you're going to meet him Friday and you're going to call me after and give me all the details. It's beyond time to sort this thing out."

He chews his tongue, then weakly grumbles, "You're insufferable."

She leans back in her chair and twirls a pen between her fingers, smug as a bug and similarly begging to be smacked with a shoe.

She says, "And yet, you suffer me."

That he does.

He spends the next hour listening as Jo narrates her week

and when he hangs up, his world feels right on its axis. Maybe Friday won't fix what broke between him and Teddy, but at least it can't get more broken than it is. And no matter what, he'll still have Jo—for better or for worse.

He doesn't bother unmuting the TV and instead loads an old favorite into the CD player, skips to track three, and lets a peaceful, easy feeling wash over him. With any luck, now that the funeral is behind them and the shock of seeing each other has passed, he and Teddy will find some peace of their own.

CHAPTER THREE

Friday

On Friday, Nash throws all of his residents into disarray by arriving at 7:00 AM for first shift.

"Mr. Owens? My, my, where has the day gone?"

Nash buttons down on a sigh and smiles at Gloria as she lowers herself stiffly into the chair between Marie and Walt, opposite him. Gloria is one of their more ambulatory residents, but he worries it's time for a cane or walker that she's still refusing. Hopefully, his worry is for nothing, and she'll relent without a fall taking the choice from her.

"Good morning, Mrs. Jefferson. The sun only just rose," he assures her. "I traded shifts with Cheyenne. And please, it's just Nash."

"Ah." She peppers her bowl of cantaloupe. "I worried I spent longer in the courtyard than I realized."

He glances to his right and catches the glob of oatmeal that squeezes out the corner of Martin's mouth with a paper towel before it drips from his chin to his pants. To Gloria, he says, "That would be a worrisome lapse of time. How were the birds?"

She closes her eyes as she breathes deep. "Wonderful," she sighs like it's not the too-crispy bacon that she's smelling. "Have you seen the blackbirds in the morning? They're my favorite. So spirited."

"Not in the morning, no. I'm either busy working, or busy sleeping."

"Well, Mr. Owens— Nash," she corrects with a small smile, her dentures bright against dark skin, "some morning soon, before winter, you should make a trip out and watch them with me."

"I'd like that."

Something solid bumps into his leg.

He turns and finds Dale in his wheelchair attempting to run over his foot. He forces a pleasant expression.

"Good morning, Mr. Greene."

Dale responds by wheeling around and making for the door without a word.

Nash motions for another aide to take over helping Martin with his breakfast and excuses himself from Gloria and Marie's company, but they're too busy glaring at the back of Dale's head to notice.

It isn't uncommon for residents to be utterly incompatible. For instance, Gloria is Black, Marie is second-generation Mexican American, and Dale is a racist, misogynistic, homophobic, crotchety old man with an ugly tongue. The home's plan for coexistence has been asking that he keep away from people he can't tolerate, and if he must be around them, then at least be silent. He has, naturally, taken that to an irritating level of compliance, but it's better that Dale be a thorn in Nash's side than outright hostile toward anyone he thinks doesn't deserve to exist in the same space as a white man.

So, as the white male nursing aide on staff, Nash is the one he approaches whenever he has a need or a question or a complaint. If Dale ever finds out he's gay, Nash imagines the tentative peace they've established will crumble like a cake with a stick too much butter.

The moment Nash steps over the threshold from dining room to hallway, Dale sets to wheeling down the hall fast enough that Nash has to lengthen his stride an uncomfortable amount to keep up without his cane. He manages though, same as always, while Dale sets to complaining all about the shoddy service here in the morning, and how he has to eat in silence in his room or in front of the TV like some kind of brain-dead millennial or, God forbid, an iPad kid.

"Martin, Gloria, and Marie seemed to enjoy their breakfast. You could join—"

He harrumphs and ignores the last two names. "That old goat never even knows I'm there. Always off in la-la land."

"Might make a good conversational partner, then."

Dale ignores that too and punches the handicap button beside the restroom. As the door slowly swings inward, he says, "All I'm saying is, it's nice to have you here at the start of the day for once. Finally, halfway decent company."

Nash wishes he could say the same, but he holds his tongue and follows Dale into the bathroom to assist however he needs.

"Yes, tomorrow I'll be here at my normal time."

"Good, good." Darla kicks her feet, clad, as always, in sunshine-yellow Crocs. She turns a severe stare onto Nash that's diluted by the playful light in her eyes. "It's music night, you know. It wouldn't do for you to miss out."

She offered to walk him to the parking lot, but he knew it was only an excuse to gab now that he's off the clock and there's nothin' to pull him away.

He settles his shoulder against the wall and shifts his weight off his bum hip. It's barking after a full shift on his feet, but no worse than usual. He thinks longingly of his cane, not twenty feet away, but makes no effort to cut short their conversation.

"I wouldn't miss music night even if they gave me a whole month off, paid," he says, and he means it.

She laughs and kicks her feet again. "You wouldn't make it an entire month away from this place, music night notwithstanding."

"Aw, you're right. Who'd keep Walt 'n' Spence from barricading themselves in their room and declaring war on the nurses?"

She giggles into her hand like a little girl and peers around to check for eavesdroppers, but there's only the head nurse down the hall, scowling at a tablet, and Martin having a spirited conversation with his reflection in the window down by the bulletin board, which is still covered in paper lotuses from the Diwali festival.

"And I'd miss you, of course," he adds.

She rolls her eyes, smile bright. "Oh, spare me. A fine young man like you can't be wanting for company. I won't believe it."

Nash grits his teeth to maintain the smile that a moment ago came easy. He doesn't have the heart to tell her he spends most of his nights alone, preparing for the next time he gets pulled into a media analysis debate about a wacky soap with a handful of old biddies (Darla included), or else trying to finish a quilt started nearly three years ago by a woman who died near about that long ago.

To say he has no life outside of Cherished Hope Nursing Home and its residents would be an egregious understatement.

"Oh, shoot!" Darla swivels her joystick and she and her power chair spin away. "I was supposed to see Jamie for my three o'clock meds and I completely forgot!"

He stands straight. "I can—"

"No, no," she shoots him a stern look down the bridge of her nose. "You're halfway out the door. Go on and get ready for your date. I'll be just fine."

His stomach swoops.

"Date?" he echoes tentatively. "Who told you—"

"I expect to be the first to hear the details." She wags a finger at him, but her smile ruins the threat and then she's off, halfway down the hall before the word *date* stops ringing in his head.

It's not a date—it's *not*—but he can admit with the butterflies and the nerves and the last-minute haircut, it certainly feels like one. And there was a time, once, when he sorely wanted nothing more than a chance to date Theodore

Spinoza. That was a long time ago, though. Things change. He's changed, and he ought to learn to accept things as they are now, else he'll be in for a world of misery.

Nash arrives at the hotel with a pit of snakes in his belly, but his favorite boots on his feet, his good blue jeans hugging him just right, and his lucky cap covering the premature grays that the barber commented on sprouting from his crown.

"Alright, I'm gonna hang up now."

"Wait!"

He pauses with his hand on the door handle and looks down at his phone to find Jo holding up her hand in a placating gesture.

"What?"

"Just... I dunno. Don't be yourself," she says, all big-eyed and earnest so he knows she's not poking fun, "but don't *don't* be yourself, you know?"

"No, I don't know," he says, deadpan.

"Just talk to him, okay? Don't do that thing where you turtle up and go all quiet."

He frowns.

"Yes, that exactly. Don't do that. Be likable, if you can manage it."

"Right. Goodbye, Josephine. Thanks for the pep talk."

"Don't fuck it u—"

He hangs up. Nothing like a good old-fashioned confidence shakedown from his little sister right before he confronts his life's biggest regret. Fucking, thanks for nothin'

Jo.

The hotel lobby, when he steps inside, looks about how he expects everywhere in Buford Hills to look. Which is to mean, it looks how the funeral parlor would look if someone crammed a coffee bar inside and tried to call it chic. The furniture is dated, and the tile is cracked and stained, which makes the decorations jarring in their modernity. And yeah, there's a coffee bar tucked in the alcove opposite the reception counter.

He doesn't get a chance to greet the receptionist. The moment the doors slide open, his attention is drawn to the sofas and armchairs circled around an electric fireplace and there, looking right at him, is Teddy.

Maybe it's all of Jo's blather burbling around in his head, but it strikes him that, against all odds, Teddy did get hot.

He'd been a scrawny kid—all bones and skin held together by sheer force of will as his body balked at everything from gravel dust to pizza sauce to air that's just a skosh too cold. The man across the room—Teddy, Theo, whatever—he's clean-shaven with a defined jaw and lean, muscular build. Nash has never subscribed to the gym life, but he spends forty-plus hours a week lifting folks in and out of their wheelchairs, out of bed, out of the bath, onto and off of the toilet. He keeps fit enough, but Teddy looks like an athlete.

It's only when Teddy breaks eye contact with a knot jumping in his jaw that Nash notices Mrs. Spinoza sitting across from him, and then, belatedly, his blond friend beside him, watching Nash with a puzzled expression. His gaze drops to his cane as Nash starts toward them and Nash has to master the ridiculous urge to hide it.

Mrs. Spinoza sees him as he stops just outside their pair of sofas and hops to her feet. "Oh, I'm so glad you could make it. We were worried—"

Teddy makes a harsh noise in his throat, but slumps back rather than meet Nash's eyes again.

"Well," Mrs. Spinoza hitches up a strained smile, "I'm glad you're here."

"Uh, me too," Nash fibs.

He wasn't expecting all of them. He thought this was his and Teddy's chance to clear the air and maybe... Well, it all seems foolish now. How are they meant to sort out anything with his aunt and... whoever this guy is staring at them like fish in a tank?

That's one thing at least he can clear up.

He sticks out his hand. "I'm Nash."

"I know." Blond guy blinks at him, then looks at his outstretched hand. "*Oh*, I mean, I'm Luke." He shakes Nash's hand with clammy fingers and pulls away quickly. "We've been friends since we were kids. Me and Theo, I mean."

Theo.

Nash forces a smile and hopes it doesn't look as gnarly as it feels. He'd almost prefer it if they *were* dating. Instead, he's staring down his replacement: neat blond hair, lean build, average height, clear Midwestern accent, and pale unblemished skin. If there's a poster boy for inoffensive and unassuming, Luke is it.

And then there's Nash: a big, awkward, freckled-up, disabled hick.

And Luke has been in the picture since they were kids. That's twenty years, or near enough to it. He and Teddy barely got six.

He wants more than anything to walk out now, go home, and stew in his empty house. It's not like Teddy even wants him here—he can hardly look at him—but Mrs. Spinoza leans toward him all eager, and her husband just died and he's a sucker, so.

He sits beside her, but he doesn't fold up his cane.

"So, Nash," she fills the silence, "we didn't get a chance to talk about you at the— The other day." She pastes on a flimsy smile and waits.

His mind is blank. What is there to say? He can talk about Jo or he can talk about his residents, but he's got nothing to say about himself. He exists. He works. Someday he'll do neither.

Be likable, Jo said.

"I work at Cherished Hope, a nursing home here in Buford Hills." Mrs. Spinoza lights up, but he looks across to Teddy before she can get her next question out and catches him looking back. "What about you? What do you do?"

Teddy's scowl hasn't eased an inch. He unknots his jaw and bites off a single word, "Hockey."

Hockey? He plays *hockey*? The jumped-up little asthmatic Nash followed around for six years grew into a hockey player? Part of him wants to call his bluff, but Mrs. Spinoza shoots Teddy a sharp, disapproving look and then pivots back to Nash.

"And what is it you do? At the nursing home, I mean."

I wipe shit off old people. And Teddy's a hockey player. What's Luke, an underwear model?

He shouldn't have come. He should've thrown out that note and—and— Fuck. And waste his shot. Again. Waste his shot *again*.

He pulls in a steadying breath and flexes stiff fingers. *Be likable.* "I care for the residents. Make sure they're taken care of at minimum, happy if I can swing it."

He knows better than to use his title. Most people only absorb the "nurse" part of "nursing aide" and get the wrong idea entirely. He doesn't deal with medication or any of that kind of thing, and he doesn't want to. Yeah, it's not the most glamorous job on the market, but he's in a position to directly influence the quality of life of people in a stage most prefer to look away from. What he does matters. Maybe not in the grand scheme, and maybe not to the world at large, but it matters to Darla, Gloria, Marie, and Martin. Hell, it even matters to Dale, even though Nash ain't convinced he deserves it.

Mrs. Spinoza smiles naturally this time. "You enjoy it?"

He shrugs. Depends on the day, the hour, the minute. It's less about enjoyment and more about purpose. He doesn't know what he would do without the nursing home, who he would be, what the point of him would be.

There's a lull where he thinks he's supposed to say something to carry them out of this conversation and onto the next, but he can't think of what it should be. Teddy's silence is starting to grate. As kids, the only time he was silent was when he couldn't get enough breath to make the words go.

He wants to ask about that. How does asthma fit with hockey? Does the cold or the exertion set it off first? Or did his asthma go away? Have his allergies gotten better? Can he be outside in the summer without a mask to keep the pollen and dust from triggering an attack? What changed? Or did nothing change? Did he, by sheer force of will, bend the world to his favor?

He'd believe it if he said yes. If anyone could manage it, it'd be Teddy.

"Umm," Luke twiddles his thumbs, "so, do you play any video games? PC or console, I play both."

"Uh, no. Sorry." He doesn't even own a computer. Jo does—a little laptop with more stickers than RAM—but he can't think what he'd need one for. He's not about to spend hundreds of dollars just to play games.

Teddy still won't look at him. *Jump, jump, jump* goes the tick in his jaw. What does he want to say that he thinks he needs to bite back so hard?

"How's your mom?" Mrs. Spinoza asks.

He hesitates. For a wild moment, he considers lying, purely to spare them the awkwardness. He's never been any good at lying, though.

"She… passed. Years ago. It's fine!" he adds when Mrs. Spinoza looks to be on the brink of profuse apology. "Really, we're better off without her."

Her face crumples in concern and he wishes he'd kept his mouth shut.

"May her memory be a blessing." She winces. "And I'm sorry for what I said the other day."

He shakes his head. Shoulda kept quiet. "It's fine."

Another silence descends.

"Was it… health… issues?"

He sucks his teeth. "Depends if you consider alcohol addiction a health issue. Or drunk driving."

"Ah. Well…" She trails off, leaving them all to flounder in the horrible lurch. All of them except Teddy, who seems content to chew his own tongue and glare at the ceiling.

Behind Nash, the doors slip open and admit a couple who greet the receptionist with East Coast accents. He listens with half an ear as they check in, part of him wondering who would bother coming all the way to Buford Hills, Tennessee to stay in their crummy two-star hotel, while the other part digs around for an excuse to get him out of here.

Be likable, Jo said. A simple instruction that he's fumbling badly. Teddy clearly doesn't want to talk to him. Why he even wrote the note if he wasn't planning to say anything is beyond Nash. He's just sitting there glaring at nothing, mouth wired shut like if he loosens the lock he'll start biting.

He'd get it if they weren't twenty years beyond his big fuck up. He'd get it if they weren't grown goddamn adults sitting on the other side of his uncle's funeral with a couple decades of real problems under their belts. He'd get it if they hadn't been twelve when everything went wrong.

He doesn't get it. All at once, Nash's patience with the situation expires. He's never been one for games. Come at him straight with the truth of things or don't bother. What's the use beating around the bush when you can just say what the problem is and set to work trying to fix it?

Teddy wrote the note. It was his handwriting. If he wants to talk, then he needs to talk.

Be likable, Jo said, but the truth is, him and Teddy were too intense in their opposite ways to be anything as middled as *likable*.

Nash leans over his knees so no one can mistake him and says, "Whatever you're chewin' on, spit it out."

Teddy's gaze flicks, not to Nash, but to his aunt who goes stiff like salt lick, and then to Luke whose knuckles are white on his knees.

"Not to them," Nash says lowly, gaze fixed, "to me. Whatever it is, just say it. When have you ever held back from speakin' your mind at me?"

Teddy faces him then, heat in his stare, shoulders bunched, and hands gnarled into fists, and demands, "Why didn't you come to the burial?"

It's not the question he expected. "I… didn't wanna get in the way," he says slowly, truthfully. "You didn't want—"

Teddy leans forward until they're near nose-to-nose and snaps, "He would have wanted you there and you didn't show up. You didn't show up then, and you didn't show up now. Why— You're never where you're supposed to be."

There it is. His original sin come for round two.

Nash lowers his voice but doesn't drop his gaze. "I said goodbye my own way. I couldn't—"

"You could if you wanted. You made your choice, and it wasn't me and it wasn't Uncle Darren."

"What about your choice? Fine, I didn't say goodbye how you wanted, but you chose not to call. You cut me out."

"Because you didn't care enough to—"

"I cared too much to—"

"Bullshit!"

"Theodore James," Mrs. Spinoza hisses, "we are in public."

Nash leans back, breathing hard, but Teddy doesn't give an inch and his eyes don't leave Nash—burning, always burning.

"You gave up on me the minute we found out about the move. I had no reason to think you'd stop pulling away once I was finally gone. Might as well kill it all at once, rather than let you drag it out forever." His jaw turns hard. "Then you gave up on Uncle Darren too."

"I didn't. I wasn't pulling away."

"Bull—" Teddy cuts himself off with a gnash of teeth. The gap that was there, even after his adult teeth came in, is gone now. "You were pulling away all summer. Mourning me like a dead thing, even though I was right there."

Nash ducks forward again. "Because I was losing you."

"You weren't! I would have—"

"You'd've forgotten me. Forgotten the handful of years you spent in some dirty little town bein' followed 'round by a dirty little boy." He swallows thickly. "And I was right."

"I never forgot you, asshole."

"Theo—"

Nash talks over Luke's timid interjection, too well-heated to mind his manners. "Then why didn't you call? And don't give me the lie you gave your aunt."

"I was angry!"

"You're always angry."

It's not a fair statement, he knows it's not. He's seen Teddy soft and smiling. He's seen the peace in him, but it's the peace you find in the minutes between storm walls. There's a motion to it, a cycle, and you learn to embrace it when you stumble into it because it never lasts.

Teddy's jaw works wordlessly, fighting to churn out another zinging accusation past the visible fury eating him from the inside out. He must fail to untangle a coherent comeback because, instead, he juts to his feet and storms out of the circle of sofas, sparing a filthy look for Nash as he goes.

In his absence, Nash becomes aware of his desperately uncomfortable company. Luke's face is tomato-red, and Mrs.

Spinoza's eyes are rimmed pink and shimmering. Guilt lances him. There's an apology on his tongue, but then the sliding door opens behind him and Teddy's voice carries across the lobby.

"Are you coming or not?"

He rises to his feet on instinct, then pauses. Teddy is stood next to the open door with his chin tipped up in challenge, his intentions clear. *This isn't over yet, but this is hardly the place for it.*

"I'm sorry," he murmurs to Mrs. Spinoza. "I'll bring him back calmer, I promise."

She pats his hand. "It's okay. You'll work it out."

He has his doubts about that.

He doesn't know what to say to Luke, so he just nods awkwardly and makes his way to where Teddy is waiting.

As he gets close, Teddy sets off into the gray evening without a word. Long, sure strides made quick by his temper are impossible to match with Nash's limp, but he keeps up, slotting into place beside Teddy with no idea where they're headed at a more ambitious clip than he'd ever bother with on his own.

This is what he remembers. Always pushing limits. Always fighting for the next foothold without caring where the climb would lead or what it would cost to get there—and there *would* be a cost—but it was the climbing that mattered and the effort it took to do it.

It's no longer surprising that Teddy became an athlete. He's been striving for that kind of achievement as long as Nash has known him—mind and force of will dominating the limits of the body.

He figures out where they're going when Teddy turns on

Cherry Street and heads for the outskirts of town.

Nash slows, but Teddy looks at him then with his eyebrows raised in judgment, a healthy flush to his cheeks—alive and burning in all the ways Nash should be but isn't.

Nash picks up his pace.

They race down the street until they pass Jo's sun-faded red sedan parked on the curb. Then Nash turns up the driveway of their little, brown-bricked ranch with Jo's gaudy Halloween jellies stuck all over the front window—purple bats, black cats, and pumpkins, all melting to goo under the quickly fading sun.

He pauses to unlock the door, cane in his armpit, while Teddy stands puffing like a furnace at his back.

Inside, Nash flips on the light and hangs his cane on the coat rack beside Jo's helmet out of habit even though his hip is throbbing and clicking with every step now. Stupid. Work tomorrow is gonna be hell. Even standing with his full weight on his good leg does little to alleviate it.

His quilting project is piled haphazardly around the couch, but the rest of the space is clean enough—he doesn't feel too embarrassed when Teddy brushes past him and begins to snoop. He glances back at Nash, as though to see if he'll protest, but Nash doesn't see why he would. If he didn't want him here, he wouldn't have unlocked the door.

"I'm getting ibuprofen. Need anything?"

"No," Teddy says shortly. He's still breathing hard, but his color is good and there's no telltale wheeze.

Maybe his asthma really is gone. And the allergies must have gotten better; there's no way they could've done what they just did back when they were kids. He'd've had to piggyback Teddy home before they made it halfway.

Teddy picks up the spikey ball of pins then sets it back among the mess on the card table. "This Jo's?"

"No."

Nash limps through the living room to the hall closet for his pain meds and a heating pad, while Teddy stops in front of the glass-doored cabinet that houses their television and Jo's souvenir stash. Each chintzy bit and bobble was allegedly selected with Nash in mind, but he knows how much pride she takes in every snow globe, collector coin, figurine, and vase. Her goal is to collect a trinket from each of the fifty states. He's thought more than once that a plane ticket to Alaska would win him a lifetime standing as brother of the year.

In the kitchen, or what passes for one in their little house, he pours two glasses of water and watches Teddy—the line of his back, the curve of his neck as he takes something from a shelf and gazes down at it.

His posture is familiar even though the way he fills it out is not. He's always had a proud back, and a proud chin to match. Or, no. Proud isn't quite right. Defiant. Not an arrogant claim to what he thinks he's owed, but a belligerent refusal to let the world sweep him into a dark corner to be forgotten. It's funny because Nash has always preferred the corners of things, though the dark, not so much.

"The Eagles?" With a start, Nash realizes the thing Teddy is looking at is a CD case—white with a painted and feathered horse skull in the center. He's holding it in both hands as though it's something fragile and requires the added security. He turns it between long fingers and sounds distant as he says, "Uncle Darren had the same one."

A complex mix of emotions twist his gut. His mouth

feels too small, his heart too big.

"I know."

It took forever to track down the right album. He remembered the cover but not the title or year. Could've been quicker had he braved the internet as Jo urged him to, rather than only popping into the second-hand store around the corner from the group home when he was in town to visit Jo. He found it eventually though, and now, whenever he pleases, he can pop it into the player and reminisce on long mornings spent under slanted sunlight through an open garage door, the smell of engine oil and aftershave, and old school classic rock playing from an old boombox on the workbench in the back. The feeling of belonging and being wanted.

Teddy doesn't respond, but the skin around his eyes has gone tight and his jaw is stiff, so Nash knows he heard him.

Nash steps from linoleum to carpet as Teddy sets aside the case and opens a drawer seemingly at random. He pulls out a photo album Nash hadn't realized was there. He loses track of where Jo stashes things. He'd rather them be out where he can see them and remember to find them; she'd rather they not have to dust everything they own.

He prides himself on only freezing up for a moment upon recognizing it. Calmly, he offers a glass of water to Teddy, but he shakes his head, a deep line between his brows.

Undeterred, Nash sets it on the card table, then lowers himself onto the couch with a grunt he can't fully suppress. He's not making it back out of this thing without help and it's his own stupid fault for getting swept along in Teddy's rip, just like when they were kids.

He plugs in his heating pad, adjusts it against his hip, and waits for the next storm wall.

"Why do you still have these?"

Nash sips his water and thinks. Him and Jo don't have many pictures of their childhood. Most of it wasn't worth memorializing, but for the rest they had no way of doing it. It's not like they had smartphones back then. They didn't even have a digital camera, and like hell their folks would waste money on family portraits or school pictures or yearbooks. Which is why those shitty disposable camera photos from his and Teddy's last day on top of the world are some of the only pictures he has of himself as a kid. Not a single one turned out, but he kept them all.

This is the first Teddy's seen of 'em. The next day, Teddy, his aunt, and his uncle moved to the coast and Nash threw the camera into the back of his closet and forgot about it until Jo unearthed it years later. He wonders if Teddy's stomach is all twisted up in his mouth the way his was when he saw them the first time, all full of longing and regret. Or if to him they're just poor pictures.

"I like 'em," Nash finally says.

"You were a terrible photographer."

"Still am. You should hear Jo bellyache."

It wasn't until she went off to college that he finally bit the bullet and joined the twenty-first century with a camera phone of his own. He and Jo used to videocall every day for a stretch, now it's down to a couple times a week while she's out of town. He never did get the hang of taking pictures, though.

"Aunt Julie said she's in California."

"Yep. Work thing. Should be wrappin' up soon. Been gone a minute."

Teddy nods, nose buried in the photo album as he sinks beside Nash on the couch—the far cushion still claimed by Jo's raggedy blanket. Without looking up, Teddy takes the water from the card table, swallows a mouthful, and returns the glass.

The nearness, the heat radiating off of him, it makes it difficult to focus on anything else. Gone is the frail but larger-than-life boy from his memories. The man beside him is unsettlingly solid. Nash has no idea what to do with him as Teddy continues to flip through the last of their awful, overexposed, badly framed photos—more sycamore leaves and blue August sky than boy.

Teddy pauses and his head tilts as he turns the page and lands on the first photos Jo mailed him from the group home after Mama passed.

Nash frowns at them—teenagers monkeying around outside a convenience store with rainbow slushies in their hands, cheeks pressed together, eyes crossed and tongues out for the camera. He doesn't like remembering those days. It's the loneliest he's ever been. Some would call it bad luck Mama died so soon after his eighteenth birthday and so far off from Jo's, but he wouldn't put it past her to have done it on purpose. She always did go out of her way to make him miserable.

Teddy looks up, and before Nash can look away, their eyes lock. An apology leaps to his tongue, whether for staring or for... everything else, he's not sure.

Teddy looks away first. "What's with the quilt?" He jerks his chin at the mess on the card table. "Thought you were more into cars."

The butterflies in his stomach disintegrate as he recalls the picture of him and Darren Spinoza working on his old sports car. He doesn't have that one. Didn't know it existed 'till just this week.

"I made a promise."

"You keep those now?"

Nash takes a long drink lest he rise to Teddy's bait. He always did love a good fight. "You still mad at me, then?"

Teddy lifts a single shoulder and lets it fall, neck turned so far to keep from looking at him you'd think it was stuck. The muscle in his jaw jumps. "Yeah. I guess."

"After twenty years?"

At that, Teddy turns his head, eyebrows pulled low over his eyes. "No, Nash. You should have gone to the burial."

Again, not what he expected to hear.

"That why you changed your mind about talkin' to me?"

Teddy's stare doesn't waver. "I didn't change my mind."

Nash raises his eyebrows, unconvinced.

With a twist to his mouth, Teddy explains, "We weren't supposed to have an audience. Luke and Aunt Julie made it… awkward."

Ah. That they did. Nash lets it go.

"I was gonna drive over to the cemetery tomorrow. Leave some flowers."

Teddy's mouth tightens into an unhappy pucker. He looks down at the album in his lap. "What time?"

"In the morning. I have to work in the aft—"

"What *time*?"

"Uh, ten?" That should be enough time to get his hip in working order and retrieve his car from the hotel. He'd been thinking he'd roll out the minute his florist opens shop, but his impromptu footrace home killed that tentative plan.

"Pick me up."

Nash nods. He doesn't ask why. It's either because Teddy doesn't trust him to follow through or because he wants a ride back out to Deliverance for his own private grief reasons. Neither of which are things he wants to force him to say aloud.

"You mind a stop at the flower shop on the way?"

"No. Here." Teddy digs his phone out of his pocket and unlocks it. "Put your number in."

Are you going to call this time?

Nash swallows the spiteful question and enters his number while his heart beats wildly. When he's done, he returns Teddy's phone, then silently holds out his own.

He half expects him to refuse, or to enter a random string of garbage, but it all seems legit. Teddy hesitates only when it comes to entering his name. For a moment, his thumbs hover. Then, he types, "Teddy."

Something hot and tight in Nash's chest relaxes seeing it.

This time, if Teddy wants to ice him out, at least he has a line back to him. This time, control isn't entirely out of his hands. And he's still Teddy. He wants to be Teddy. Like he was before.

Teddy doesn't stay long after that, and it's not until Nash is alone and sore in his rapidly darkening house that he realizes what he agreed to. Tomorrow he's going to say goodbye to the man who was the closest he ever got to having a father, and his old childhood crush is going to pay witness.

CHAPTER FOUR

Flowers and stones

The walk to the hotel takes three times as long as it did last night. Nash is stiff and sore before he leaves his porch, there's no Teddy at his side setting a punishing pace to push him through the pain, and because he doesn't suffer enough, it looks like rain. His hip is always extra crotchety when it rains.

Four breaks and he's still sweat-streaked, winded, and limping hard when he arrives and finds Teddy waiting out front with his hands in his pockets and a frown on his face. No way is Nash going to cross the parking lot to collect him, only to turn around and cross it again to get to the car.

He jerks his head at his old Lincoln Town Car, affectionately referred to by Jo as "The Boat," and clicks the key fob to unlock the doors and flash the lights, so Teddy knows where he's headed. Too intent on getting the weight off his hip, he doesn't keep track of Teddy's progress and opens the door as soon as it's within reach.

He drops into his seat with a pained grunt and breathes his first full breath in minutes. His time with the heating pad is officially negated. All the stretching he did this morning got him this far, but no farther. If he keeps pushing, he's gonna find himself bedridden. He's still got two days left in his work week. He can't keep acting foolish. His body can't take it.

The passenger door opens, and he pulls himself together. Before Teddy settles into the car, Nash collapses his cane, tucks it between his seat and the door, and snaps his seatbelt into place.

Teddy pulls the door shut and says, "I could have picked you up if you'd told me."

Nash sticks his key in the ignition rather than look at him. "Flowers?"

Teddy's jaw jumps all the way to the flower shop.

Kim has his arrangement ready when they arrive. She's a short, round Lao woman who perfected the sympathetic smile long before he met her and, he doesn't like to assume, but he thinks he might be her number one customer.

"Good morning, you're just in time!"

There's no chance to return the greeting before Kim disappears through a swinging door to the back, leaving him at the counter, surrounded by plants, with Teddy hovering like a storm cloud. A hard plastic mask covers from the bridge of his nose to his chin as he eyes a Chrysanthemum distrustfully.

Not gone then, but better.

A moment later, Kim reappears with his order: a bouquet of white tulips peppered with forget-me-nots. She told him in confidence once that wildflowers aren't typically sold in flower shops, but since he was always coming in asking for forget-me-nots, she started growing her own. It's why he never shops flowers anywhere else.

"Here you are." She looks to Teddy and her sweet disposition dims. "Anything else?"

Nash raises his eyebrows at Teddy, but he's already stepping up to the counter. In a surprisingly soft tone, he requests a bouquet that plays well with allergies.

"What color? In a vase? No vase? Okay, come here and pick out some ribbon."

After a whirlwind of color and a sneaky credit card transaction while Teddy stares at the wall of ribbons with a glazed look, they exit the shop and get on the road to Deliverance. The silence in the car is near unbearable, but he doesn't know how to break it.

It's not only Teddy's presence and his temperament causing the discomfort. Nash has never handled loss well. No, that's not quite true. When his dad walked out after crippling him, he didn't mourn. When his mom died after years of neglect and unconcealed disdain, he didn't shed a tear. And when his residents pass, he takes his book of promises and sets out fulfilling them. Then, once everything is crossed off the list, he lets them go. It's sad, but it's different when you know how it's going to end from the first meeting.

He didn't handle losing Teddy well.

He didn't handle losing Jo to the state's care well.

He didn't handle her four years of college well either.

He'd like to think he handles it better now when she travels for work, but he can't hide from the fact that his world goes stagnant when she's not around to kick up a current. That's how it's always been. Before Jo, it was Teddy that breathed life into his dusty corner of the world, and without either of them, he sits alone in the dark and waits for the light to return.

But none of that is comparable to the pit in his chest at the thought that Darren Spinoza left the world, and he was none the wiser. Nash had twenty years to figure out how to say goodbye while he was around to hear it, and he didn't. He'll never get another chance.

Their bouquets rest together upon fresh-turned earth. Nash expected there to be flowers from the service yesterday, but there's a neat line of smooth, round stones perched atop the headstone instead. He wonders if that's a Jewish thing but doesn't ask. They stand silent as the wind buffets them like a punishment, or a lashing out. He doesn't feel like lashing out. He feels cold. He feels alone.

"Aren't you going to say something?"

"I've been saying things this whole time," Nash lies. "D'you need me to start over aloud so you can eavesdrop?"

Teddy wrestles with himself for a few seconds. "No," he says. Then, "You're pissy today."

That's rich coming from him.

"My hip hurts. And I'm sad."

The wind continues to tear at them as they stare down at the crisp, clean headstone of Darren Spinoza. At every other burial, he admired the stone—a strong, solid testament to a life lived, but not today. Today it feels like a mockery. There should be a strong solid man standing here, not this pointless fancy rock.

He was the first adult Nash ever learned to trust, and he's gone. He was the first person to invest in Nash as someone worth teaching, and Nash didn't even say goodbye.

A raindrop lands cold and unwanted on the back of his neck as Teddy's shoulders finally come down from around his ears.

"Me too."

Nash digs his fingers further into his jacket. The wet in his eyes could be blamed on the wind, but not the hot lump in his throat. "I know."

"He was the closest thing I had to a dad."

Nash doesn't look at him. He knows what grief he'll see spilling out. "Me too," he says.

"I know." Then, quiet and low, Teddy says, "You should have come to the burial."

His heart is too heavy. He doesn't look away from the stones perched atop the headstone. "I know."

CHAPTER FIVE
Back pain

Cherished Hope's recreation department puts on various activities throughout the week to entertain their residents, but every Saturday night they do a special program, some of which are more successful than others. The worst ones are the themed mixers, where the nursing aides are tasked with all of their usual duties in addition to trying to get everyone to socialize. The best ones involve someone coming in to put on a show, and Elaine and her girls are a favorite.

It takes half an hour to get everyone to the rec room—wheelchairs, walkers, and canes, coupled with a vast range of lucidity and self-sufficiency, make the logistics a hassle—but it's well worth it to see tired faces light up and folks who aren't all there turn a little more grounded, present for the first time in a long while. With the piano under Elaine's fingertips and her daughters on mandolin and fiddle, even the staff spend the day chattering in anticipation of what's as near a proper jam as they can get in here.

Nash misses the first number to fetch a blanket for Darla's lap, but she apologizes for it by handing him her tambourine for the next one. So it's while he's beating a tambourine on his hip, stomping 'round with Loretta on his arm, and hollerin' about that old Joe Clark that he feels someone arrive at his side. He turns to greet them, expecting one of the ambulatory residents to have sought him out with a request.

Nash nearly drops Darla's tambourine when he finds Teddy instead. His nose is pink with cold, rain drops sparkle in his hair, and he's got a visitor's sticker stuck to his jacket identifying him as *Theo*.

Shocked stupid, Nash goes statue-still and heat flushes up his neck and well into his cheeks. He knows it's a magnificent blush when Loretta takes one look at him and bursts into a witch cackle of a laugh.

"Happy Valentine's!" she crows, then plants a wiry kiss smack on his cheek before he can react and bustles off, smacking her lips in time with the rattle of her maraca.

Teddy is smiling—easy and full—the kind that makes his nose wrinkle and sets the lack of a gap between his front teeth at center stage. And Nash realizes it's the first time he's seen him smile in twenty years. The simple curl of his lips sets him ablaze like a sunlit cloud.

Teddy moves in close and pitches his voice over the commotion. "Real tough job you've got here!" He glances down. "Where's your cane?"

Nash's heart leaps, this time in alarm, and he can't help

the way he checks to make sure none of the staff overheard the innocent question. He doesn't use his cane at work. He doesn't park in the handicap spot up by the doors, and he certainly doesn't let anyone how much effort it takes to match even his laziest coworker's simple ability to get from point A to point B. He needs both hands free to do his job. He needs to help residents get around without worrying about where he left his own mobility aid in the process. And most of all, he needs to not give management even the inkling of a sliver of a doubt that he can do the job. He *needs* this job.

The shock and the panic tie his tongue and brain into a useless tangle. "I— What are you—"

A firm, rapid tapping against his elbow steals his attention and he finds Dale looking up at him in silent urgency. Relief crests over him. *This* he knows how to handle. Teddy? Not so much. Not anymore.

"Restroom?" he asks.

Dale nods and spins his chair toward the door.

To Teddy, Nash says regretfully, "I have to go. I don't know how long…"

He doesn't know down to the minute, but he knows he won't be back in this room for at least ten. However, he can't say that without embarrassing Dale. Living with IBS is hell enough without everyone knowing about it.

Teddy shrugs, his eyes bright with interest as he takes in the singing and swaying residents. "I have plenty of company." He smiles at Martin and is rewarded with a gummy smile in return.

Aw hell, where'd he hide his dentures this time?

"I'll see you in a bit," Nash says.

He returns Darla's tambourine and pretends not to notice her curious glow as she eyes Teddy. Instead, he hurries after Dale and catches Kiana, another nursing aide, by the door.

"Hey, can you put out the word to be on the lookout for Martin's dentures?"

"Sure," she says without looking at him. "Who's the guy? Was he your date last night?"

His stomach lurches. He's not out at work, but he's not *not* out at work either. Some have picked up his inclinations, but it's not something he advertises. He glances once at the door Dale left through, but he's well out of hearing range.

"Who told you about that?"

"Quanxi, but she heard it from Cheyenne. She tried to get a betting pool going, but no one would bite."

He grits his teeth. He doesn't have time for this. "Keep an eye out for those dentures."

She scoffs and tears her eyes from Teddy to roll them to the rafters. "This is why she couldn't get any bets. No one can imagine you as anything but this."

He turns away without another word lest she see how close to home she hit.

He returns to find the crowd around the piano has thinned, but not by much. Elaine's daughters are crooning "Kentucky Waltz" in a tight harmony that weaves across itself time and again, a complex dance they make sound simple as sewing a button. A few folks seem to have returned to their rooms, but most of the residents are scattered around, some staring into space while others chat and laugh. He half expects Teddy to be gone, but he finds him absorbed in what appears to be an intense game of checkers against Spencer while Darla and Walt spectate.

He makes for them as Dale returns to the piano, but a distraught Marie intercepts him and asks him to help search for her misplaced rosary.

He mobilizes the other aides who aren't immediately occupied, and they sweep the room, only to find Martin's dentures in the flowerpot that's supposed to be out of reach on the shelf by the window but is currently atop the piano. He smiles awkwardly at Elaine as he retrieves them, then hurries off to give 'em a good wash.

He hears a laugh at his back that he thinks might belong to Teddy. Boisterous and barking, same as it used to be, but fuller now. Adult. Masculine. Nash knows he's blushing again and is thankful there's no one between him and the door to see it.

The rest of the evening passes much the same. Nash is kept busy and Teddy has no trouble making friends in a room full of attention-starved elderly folks, but every now and again the stars align and when Nash has a moment to look, he finds Teddy looking back.

He's regretful and grateful in equal measure to be kept moving. Sad he can't talk with Teddy and bask in this new lightness, but glad his nosy coworkers can't pin him down to siphon answers out of him.

He can't outmaneuver Darla, though. She gets him with a not-unusual request to help her back to her room to prepare for bed. He knows her intentions the moment she near runs him down to get to him before anybody else, but what's he to do but go along with her ploy? She keeps her mouth shut with a secret little smile the whole way back to their wing, but the moment the door closes behind him, she sighs wistfully.

"Ain't it nice how nowadays everybody's free to love who they love?"

He holds out his arm, and she takes it as she gingerly climbs from her chair and perches on the edge of the bed.

"I reckon it is."

"I think it's real nice, Mr. Owens," she says, her eyes all a-twinkle behind her spectacles. She pats his arm. "It's real, real nice."

He's always had Jo's unconditional love, but the idea of acceptance from anyone else is something he abandoned in a stuffy attic bedroom years and years and years ago. It's not something he seeks. He's never noticed its lack, but Darla's hand on his arm, the quiet joy on her face as she looks at him and *sees*...

Suddenly, he can't meet her eyes. Emotion presses down on him with tangible weight.

He pats her hand and pulls away. With his back to her, he opens her dresser and clears his throat. "Please, it's just Nash. Flowers or spots, Ms. Biggins?"

She deliberates, humming. "Flowers," she says, then adds, "You know, if I'm to call you by your given name, don't you think you ought to do the same for me? What's this *Ms. Biggins* nonsense?"

He turns away from the dresser with a floral nightgown and a frown. He sets the gown on the bed beside her. "I wanna be respectful."

"And if I wanna be the same?"

"Then you'll call me what I've asked to be called."

She narrows her eyes, displeased with this response.

He turns his attention to getting the curtains shut over the window just right. "I knew a Mr. Owens growin' up," he says into the paisley folds. "Didn't care for him much then. Don't much care to be likened to him now."

All's quiet 'till he turns around and finds her looking back at him with compassion so thick it clings to his tongue and refuses to go down. He wilts under the smothering gravity of it.

"Darla," he says, "please. I prefer bein' just Nash, that's all. I ain't so tragic as you're thinkin'."

She fingers the weathered cotton of her nightclothes. When she looks up, she's smiling easy again.

"Nash," she says, "ain't it nice nowadays how we can love who we love and be called what we wanna be called?"

He smiles easy in return. "It is, Ms. Biggins. It's real, real nice."

"You'll be in at your regular time tomorrow?" she asks.

He resists the urge to roll his eyes. He switches shifts once and now all his residents'll be calling his schedule into question 'till their dying day.

"Three o'clock," he confirms. "Same as always."

She makes a doubtful face. "The thing about always is, it's far less permanent than you young'uns think. The way that Theo looks at you speaks to all kinds of change 'round this place."

The idea that Teddy's been looking at him in any special way fills him with equal parts thrill and grief, because as much as he'd like to put stock in Darla's intuition, Teddy's leaving. He's got his own life and a home that ain't been Tennessee in a long, long time.

"I'm not going anywhere," he assures her. "I'll see you tomorrow. Three o'clock. Sleep well."

She kicks off her Crocs and sits cross-legged. "Little birdy told me they're doin' fish for supper Monday night. I know it's your day off—"

"Ms. Biggins, would you do me the honor of having supper with me on Monday night? I've a sudden hankering for fried chicken and your incomparable company."

She's smiling too big for her face now. "Personally, I've been having thoughts on lasagna."

"I've a sudden hankering for lasagna and the company of a beautiful woman," he amends.

She laughs, a giggle that she hides behind her hand. "You should know, my gentleman callers always bring me fresh flowers."

"Naturally," he says. "Something bright, I assume?"

"Naturally," she says, and smiles.

Visiting hours end as they always do. He returns from Darla's room and doesn't spot Teddy where he last saw him: dodging Rose's grabby hands while hotly debating with Walt whether NASCAR or baseball is more American. Disappointment clouds him.

"Hey."

He turns with a start and finds Teddy beside him with his folded name sticker in his hands.

"Hey," he returns, breathless.

"I'm getting kicked out, but I had fun." Teddy smiles with his chin tucked low—almost shy if Nash could believe him capable.

"Rose didn't—"

He relaxes into a casual shrug. "Nah, she was fine once I knew to watch for her."

"Oh, good."

Teddy stuffs his hands in his pockets and looks around the room, seeming reluctant to leave. It strikes Nash that he hasn't seen that jump in his jaw once since he arrived. He's been all smiles and laughter in a way that makes the soft core of him ache. If he hadn't been so busy...

"So I'll uh, I should go. I'll see you tomorrow."

"I work—" he starts, but Teddy cuts him off.

"I know. Darla gave me your schedule."

"Oh. Good." He cringes. "I mean— She's— Yeah. Likes knowin' who'll be 'round, you know?"

"She seems to have a soft spot for you," Teddy says with a peculiar smile. "She didn't tell me anyone else's schedule."

He looks away in case he starts blushing again. He likes to think he has a good relationship with each resident in his unit, and a fair few outside it, but he has residents and he has *his* residents. Darla is certainly one of his residents. It's nice that the feeling is mutual.

"So I'll see you tomorrow?" he asks the potted plant— now returned to the shelf by the window.

"Yeah, why not? It's better than listening to Aunt Julie complain about sitting shiva in a town where we hardly know anyone."

After Teddy leaves, Nash's shift continues normally

except for his coworkers' silent attention, but he has no interest in assembling the puzzle for them. He keeps to his residents and keeps busy until his shift winds to an end, same as it ever has.

The next day, he arrives to chaos.

He comes across Cheyenne first, and she grabs him by the arm. "Dude, consider your favor repaid. Holy shit."

"What?"

She abandons him as Quanxi comes around the corner, pink-cheeked and beaming. They continue down the hall without him, huddled together whispering and giggling.

Baffled, he peeks into the rec room and is startled to find half a dozen young, well-built men conspicuously dotted around the room talking in booming voices and waving their arms in big, exaggerated motions.

Ms. Thompson from the north wing hobbles past him and proclaims, "Mr. Owens, it's Christmas! You there! Is that hair real? Let me feel it."

"That's not really appropri—" Nash's protest falls on deaf ears as the man in question bends over and allows her to stroke her fingers through glossy shoulder-length chestnut hair.

"By God, it is. Mr. Owens, feel this."

"It's just Nash, and I don't think—"

All six men turn to look at him like he blew a dog whistle. That's when he finally recognizes one of them as Teddy and, like tumblers falling into place, he realizes this must be his team.

Hockey players.

They came all the way to Tennessee for Teddy?

He breaks out in a cold sweat.

The one with the hair stretches his hand toward him, speaking, but beyond him, Nash spots Rose with her eyes on a prize.

He swoops past Hair and blocks Rose's ass-grab inches before she makes contact.

Flustered, he snaps, "Ms. Hill, we've talked about this."

"Oh, you're no fun," she bites back in her croaky voice.

"It's sexual assault. It's not—"

She scoffs and slinks off, no doubt to find easier prey. "Back in my day, it was a compliment!"

A migraine is coming on. He'll have to find time to document her behavior toward Teddy yesterday as well as this. He hasn't even clocked in yet.

To Hair, he says, "I'm so sorry about—"

"Nash Owens with the clutch save!" Hair grabs him by the forearm and yanks him into a backslapping hug. "Wow, man! I'm so stoked to meet you! C'mon, you gotta meet the rest of the team."

"The— Alright."

They converge on him. *Hockey players.* Amid stooped and chair-bound residents and the mostly female staff, he's accustomed to being the tallest person in the room, unless Barry, the property manager, is around. Opposite Teddy's teammates, he's feeling a mite claustrophobic.

"You can call me Zook." Hair gestures at the name tag stuck to his chest that indeed reads, *ZOOK.* "Everyone does, even the wife sometimes."

"Ay, that's a fine for bedroom talk," a bearlike man says

in Irish brogue.

"You've been calling your girls *Zook*?" one of the others demands.

Zook raises his voice over his team's cross talk. "That's Deli. He's been single so long he's forgotten how pillow talk works."

"Oy!"

He points at a Black man with a shaved head. "This is Jam. If he invites you for a drink, do not accept unless you enjoy waking up hungover in a different state."

Jam grins and winks.

"The pretty boy over there is Peaches. Might wanna keep an eye on him around your sister."

Peaches straightens and flashes perfect white teeth. "A sister, huh?"

Unimpressed, Nash says without undue threat, "Try her. I'll get the morgue ready."

The team explodes into motion, *ohhhh*-ing and slapping at him and Peaches equally. Without his cane for support, he has to shift his weight to his good leg to keep from getting knocked to the ground.

"Alright, you apes! Let him breathe!" Zook orders, but he's grinning. "Last, you've got Benz."

Deli leans in. "Cuz lookin' at 'im too long makes you wanna be sick."

Benz, a wall of meat missing a tooth, shoves him. He sticks his nose in the air, "It's 'cause I'm high class and outta yer league."

For Nash alone, Zook mutters, "His last name is Bentsen." He claps Nash on the back and raises his voice over the bickering. "Team, this is Spin's buddy Nash from back in the day. Don't run him off."

"If he runs, Spin can do better," Peaches grumbles.

Nash taps his bad hip. "Been a minute since I ran anywhere. Guess y'all're stuck with me."

This sparks another minor uproar.

Jam turns and shouts over his shoulder, "You didn't tell us your man could chirp!"

That's when Teddy finally shoulders his way through the wall of hockey players, shorter and leaner than the rest, but you wouldn't know it by the way he carries himself. "I told you he doesn't take shit. What did you think I meant?"

"Shit!" Loretta floats past them with a skip in her step. "Shit, shit, shit!"

Nash refocuses. He's not here to "chirp" his way into Teddy's friend circle. He has a job to do and people counting on him. He can't let this derail him.

He meets Teddy's eyes. "I need to clock in."

"We'll stay out of your way."

Nash is looking over the team, unsure that's possible, when Cheyenne saunters up to him. Her giggles from earlier are gone, replaced by a mask of cool indifference. Out of the corner of his eye, he notices Peaches ruffle his hair and shift into a suave pose out of a magazine. The effect is somewhat ruined by Jam elbowing him and Benz panting in his ear like a dog.

"I clocked you in," Cheyenne informs him as though she doesn't see the hockey team.

"Oh. Thank—"

"Martin is refusing his meds unless you're in the room."

"Alright, I'll—"

"Someone ate the tamales Marie's son dropped off, and

she's dead-convinced it was Dale."

"Again? I can—"

"She also put in a new roommate request."

That brings him up short. He can't quite keep the offense out of his tone as he demands, "What's wrong with Darla?"

"Apparently, she likes to open the window at night and it's too cold for Marie."

That's the kind of thing Jo would label, "irreconcilable differences," and then crank up the thermostat. It's funny the ways their upbringing sticks to them like an old candy wrapper to the sole of a shoe. Neither of them would claim to miss the old attic they used to sleep in, and yet...

"Fine. I'll check with—"

"And speaking of Darla, she's not feeling well and wants you to stop in when you get the chance."

With new gravity, he asks, "What's wrong?"

When someone goes, it's rarely who you expect. As lively as she seems, she's well over ninety. You just never know.

"Nothing serious," Cheyenne says like he's silly for jumping to conclusions. "Her back is sore, probably from too much dancing yesterday."

He frowns and makes a mental note to check on her as soon as he has a minute to spare.

"Anything else?"

"Someone shit in the water fountain in the East wing, so it's tarped off until it gets sanitized." She smiles sarcastically. "Good luck. I'm outta here." Her eyes slide to the side, unmistakably toward Peaches, and then she turns on her heel and strides from the room with swishing hips.

"Hey guys, I gotta grab something from outside."

Peaches hurries after her as his team heckles his back, none fooled about what he intends to find outside.

The team scatters then, dispersing through the room and greeting residents like they've been here hours and already found favorites. Only Teddy remains. He looks almost apologetic.

"They got in this morning and wanted to tag along."

"That's fine," he says, but his mind is whirling with all the tasks on his plate while lurking in the background is the creeping curiosity of *why*? The funeral is over. Teddy and Mrs. Spinoza should head back any day. Why come now? And why come to him when Teddy has so many friends in town that he could hang out with instead?

Then there's the question of what Teddy has said about him. Zook seems to know, simultaneously, more than he should and not enough to grasp the fragility of their situation. You can call it a rekindling, but that won't stop it from snuffing out a second time. All he can do is try to be better than before. So long as he pretends the end isn't imminent, Teddy won't say Nash spent the whole time mourning someone who wasn't gone yet, but he will be gone again, and soon.

Teddy steps back. "Find me when you get the chance."

"I will."

It's an adorable ambition.

Between the usual running around keeping up with more residents than they have staff for and the added chaos of the hockey team, he barely keeps his feet. Before he knows it, it's suppertime and someone has ordered pizza. The residents are bartering grilled chicken and steamed veggies for fat, greasy slices of pepperoni and there are more smiles than he's seen without Elaine around to tickle free in a long time.

Martin is humming a show tune rather than eating. Spencer and Walt are sitting across the table, bullying him about how Teddy lost their game of checkers because he couldn't keep his eyes on the board long enough to notice them filching pieces. Gloria is negotiating with Jam her heirloom family recipes in exchange for Pepsi. And Teddy is sitting with Marie, patiently commenting on each photo she produces of a grandchild or great-grandchild and every time he looks up, he finds Nash and smiles.

Then the intercom chimes and the bubble of peace surrounding him pops.

"Code Blue, room 211. Code Blue, room 211."

Nash is on his feet before the room number registers. He makes eye contact with Kiana, who nods. Then he runs.

There are several codes that could be called to alert staff of the goings on with residents. There are codes for elopements, biohazards, expired residents, fire, and medical emergencies. Code blue is medical emergency and room 211 is Darla.

He arrives out of breath to find the room packed with nurses. A crash cart is rolled up against the bed beside the window, and Darla is barely visible through the commotion. Pale. Her chest falling and rising harshly.

"What's that status, Steph?"

"I'm looking!"

"It's on the first page, highlighted in red t—"

"DNR," Steph says.

The head nurse calls out orders and the nurses hurry to carry them out. One inserts an IV while another fits an oxygen mask over Darla's face. Steph speaks in a low, soothing tone, too quiet for him to make out. It breaks his heart to stand in the hall and watch, but he knows better than to get in the way.

Her back was hurting. Was her nurse the one that dismissed it as overexertion, or was that Cheyenne's guess and not knowing any better? It's not her job to know. She's an aide, like him, but he's been here long enough. He should know heart attack symptoms. He should have come here first. Everything else could have waited. This is where he should have been.

The beeping on the heart monitor trips once, then twice, and then turns into a single sustained, piercing note.

The nurses pause.

"Do not resuscitate does not mean do not treat," the head nurse snaps. "Continue caring for your patient until I call it."

They whirl back into motion, quiet now, except for the monitor that continues its shrill warning for another minute or more, until the activity in the room gradually decreases again.

The head nurse checks her watch. "Time of death: 06:57 PM. Ryan, tell whoever is on the phone with the paramedics. Steph, call the ME."

"This hour on a Sunday? She won't be 'round 'till morning, I bet."

"Call anyway and then get the morgue ready."

Nash backs out of the doorway as nurses file out with grim sets to their mouths. He waits for the last of them to finish up and for the head nurse to nod her permission for him to enter. She's familiar with his habits.

At the side of the bed where the crash cart was, where he

stood yesterday with Darla's hand on his arm, he pulls up a chair, then sits with her cold fingers between his palms. He's spent hours in this very spot, sometimes warming her hands just like this, listening and letting her ramble to her heart's content until the next thing dragged him away.

This time, he does the talking.

They say the last thing to go is your hearing, so he reassures her that he'll carry out the plans he has detailed in his notebook. Everything will be taken care of. That preacher she didn't like won't be the one to preside over her celebration of life, and there won't be a single peace lily in the chapel because, my God, they're ugly things, aren't they? And he swears on his life no one will play "In the Arms of an Angel" because it's bad enough getting walloped with it on TV all the time and nobody needs to feel worse at a funeral.

He rambles through everything he can think of. He tells her about the hockey players she missed and the uproar they caused. And Marie doesn't have to request a new roommate now, and it is so like her to be so thoughtful and accommodating. And she got out of fish night tomorrow and that was so clever even though he was looking forward to their date, and damn, couldn't she have waited for him to get in one last goodbye?

The words dry up after that. He stays anyway and holds her hand with his heart in his throat until the nurses return with the gurney.

Gently, he tucks Darla's hand over her stomach, rubs his palms down his dry cheeks, then nods at the nurses and steps out of the room.

He nearly collides with Teddy.

"Sorry!"

Teddy's hot palm on his waist keeps them from tripping over each other and sends a confused flurry of emotion to batter against his grief.

"Sorry," Teddy repeats. He pulls his hand away and takes a full step back. Then he crosses his arms and drops his chin. "I overheard the nurses. I'm sorry about Darla. She was really sweet."

"She was," Nash says softly.

Behind him, the nurses are moving her onto the gurney. He can hear them speaking in clipped tones, coordinating, the rustling of fabric. Standing and listening quickly turns unbearable.

"I have to get back to work."

Teddy's head jerks up. "Already? You don't get to... I don't know. Process?"

"I have other residents. I'll have to process on my own time."

The nurses must have her on the gurney now. He winces as a plastic buckle snaps together. He turns to walk away.

"How do you do that?"

He pauses but doesn't look back at Teddy. "Do what?"

"Someone just *died*, someone you care about. How do you pick up and move on so fast?"

"I'm not moving on from anything."

Teddy stalks around to glare in his face. "It sure as hell looks like you are."

He's angry. Of course he's angry. But tonight, Nash doesn't have the energy to meet him there.

He checks the clock over the nurses' station. "Visiting hours are over. I have to get back to work."

He arrives home well after midnight, drained and aching in more ways than one. He jiggles the knob until his key turns and then nearly breaks his neck on the pair of ratty sneakers immediately in his path.

The TV mutes on some reality show and Jo pops up on her knees to grin at him over the back of the couch. Then, he gets the treat of watching in real time as she gets a look at him and her smile drops.

"Who?" she asks.

He shuts the door. "Darla."

"Oh. Was she the nice one? With the Crocs?"

"Yeah. Teddy was there. He's mad at me again."

"What? Why?"

Why was he there, or why is he mad? Either way, it's the same answer.

He rubs his face. "I don't know. I'll figure it out tomorrow. Did you eat?"

"I was waitin' for you." She scrambles to her feet and hops from carpet to linoleum to paw at the cupboards while he unlaces his plain white sneakers. Well, they were white when he bought them. He's walking through the soles now and his inserts are on the brink of collapse. He needs badly to arrange a shopping trip in town, but God, he hates shopping trips in town.

"Spaghetti sound good?"

"Yeah, thanks." He shoots her a guilty look that she doesn't see as she puts the pot under the faucet and slaps the water to hot. "Welcome home, by the way."

Jo detests cooking, so he recognizes her immediate jump

into the kitchen as the act of love and support it is. It's a little thing, but it warms him enough to carry him through changing into pajamas while she cooks and chatters about her trip. She keeps up a steady dialogue through the meal and the cleanup after. Then, before he retreats to his room for the night, she hugs him tight and tells him she missed him, and that's enough to carry him through the rest.

CHAPTER SIX

Prove it

Nash brushes imaginary lint from his jeans, recites his apology in his head for the hundredth time, then nods decisively, and steps up to the hotel doors.

They slide open with a rush of air and he's nearly bowled over by Benz and Deli.

"Oh, shit!"

"Sorry, m— Nash! Hey man, are you coming with us?"

He blinks from Benz to Deli and has a *no* on the tip of his tongue when Zook and Teddy appear behind them and he forgets all about responding.

"Oh, shit." Zook elbows Teddy. "You should have told us you invited your boy."

Teddy's posture and expression are all discomfort and surprise.

"He didn't," Nash says. "I sort of— If you guys have plans, I'll just—"

"You should come," Teddy blurts, effectively stalling his retreat. His brow creases. "If you want to, I mean. We're going to the roller rink."

"Or we could do something else," Zook offers.

Deli groans. "Have I cracked? Haven't we just spent a half hour decidin' there's nothing else to do here?"

Through his smile, Zook says, "I'm trying to be considerate, D."

Nearly in sync, Zook, Benz, and Deli glance at his cane and then away.

Ah. Right then.

"I like to skate."

Deli turns a smug look onto Zook, who holds up his palms.

"Last thing I'll say is there's a difference between liking to skate and skating with a bunch of meatheads who've made it their entire personality." He points a stern finger at the others. "Don't dog on him like you do each other."

Zook's stalwart defense is almost offensive. He doesn't need shielding. It's not like he isn't already unpleasantly intimate with the effects of athlete brain rot. But first things first.

To Teddy, he says, "Can I talk to you?"

Teddy's jaw goes tight, but he nods.

Nash follows him inside, past Luke, Peaches, and Jam— of whom only Luke seems to clock the tension between the two of them—down a hallway, and into a tiled alcove with a pair of humming vending machines.

Teddy turns to face him and throws him for a loop by immediately bursting out, "I'm sorry."

"You're sorry?" Nash echoes. "I was an ass."

"No, I was. I talked to Luke—he's been in therapy for as long as I've known him—and he said— Well, he said a lot of stuff but mostly that I was expecting too much from you too fast and people process loss in different ways and one of them is— That part doesn't matter. The point is, I'm sorry."

He looks away, palm on the back of his neck, gaze on his shoes, and it strikes Nash that he's never seen him this contrite before.

"I'm not mad at you, Ted."

Teddy's gaze jumps up to meet his. "You're not?"

"I thought you were mad at me."

"I'm not," he says with feeling. His eyes go all big and bambied. "I got all tangled up about— about Uncle Darren and everything and... and I took it out on you like it's your fault I wasn't—" He drops his chin and swipes his hand roughly up the back of his head. When he looks up, it's with a small, forced smile. "You sure you wanna come? We're gonna be obnoxiously competitive and scare the locals."

The word slurry pools around Nash's brain for a beat before he decides to sort it out later and just respond to the last bit.

"Yeah, why not? You might find some of us don't scare easy."

Teddy's smile shifts, no longer forced, less grin and more something in his eyes that lights up the dark, dusty corner of Nash's heart he stopped paying mind to decades ago.

He says, "I'm counting on it."

Nash ends up driving Teddy and Luke to the roller rink while the rest of the team races them on foot.

"*Christ,*" Nash hisses.

Deli nearly gets clipped by a Corolla as he darts across the street with his arms raised over his head to join the rest in the rink's cracked and crumbling parking lot.

"Did they make it?" Luke asks from the back. He's had his hand over his eyes since Peaches led the charge through the first intersection with no regard for the light that had just turned green.

"Yeah." Nash looks at Teddy from the corner of his eye, then back to the red light in front of them. "You could've gone with 'em."

Teddy doesn't turn from watching his teammates glomp each other in victory. "Nah," he says, but he can't quite remove the wistful look from his face.

The light turns, and they creep through the intersection and into the parking lot. Nash pulls into a handicap spot— the one that doesn't let the driver out into a massive pothole —and parks.

"D'you still have asthma?"

Teddy pauses with his hand on the door. A guarded expression falls over his face. "It's not as bad as when I was a kid. Why?"

Nash shrugs. He cuts the engine. "Just curious. Wasn't sure what with you bein' a professional athlete 'n' all."

Behind him, Luke chokes as Teddy's guard cracks, and then crumbles.

He smiles, something of a wondering look in his eyes. "Nash, I'm not a professional."

"You're not?"

Teddy jabs a finger at the window. "Look at those guys! Look at me!" Deli has Peaches in a headlock while Benz gives him a wet willy and Jam and Zook stomp and holler, laughing. "We're in the rec league. Placed seventh in our district a few days ago. The guys flew down right after they got done losing."

"Oh." Nash tears his eyes off the team as Peaches starts throwing punches and Jam takes out his phone. "So what do you do? As a job, I mean."

"I'm an accountant." His nose crinkles as his smile grows impossibly wider. "You really thought I was in the NHL?"

He shrugs, helplessly caught in the current of Teddy's pleasure. "Figured if anybody could do it, it'd be you."

In the backseat, Luke reminds Nash of his presence by opening the door and mumbling something about "awkward" and "worse than I thought," but Teddy keeps smiling so Nash can't quite bring himself to care.

Nash wobbles as a blur of hockey players rocket past him around the outer rim of the rink. He's a good skater, gets plenty of practice, but today he's off his game. For one, his hip is not happy with him. He's on the tail end of a full work week on his feet sans cane, and besides that, it never did get back to usual operating condition after his and Teddy's little race. He meant to spend his two days off resting it, but, well, he's an idiot, obviously.

The shooting pains and ever-present burn of overexertion aren't the main issue affecting his skating, though. It's the warm, sure hand that wraps around his elbow for the fifth time in as many minutes that's got him shaky on his feet.

"You good?"

He's on the cusp of tripping all over himself from how close Teddy is skating beside him, and if he touches him one more time, on God, he's going to disintegrate. His heart can't take this kind of stress.

"Fine," he says and winces as his voices carries every ounce of that stress.

He looks around the rink again, searching for any of Jo's usual cohort who might be lurking about—waiting to blow the whistle and bring the locusts down on his field—but it's as deserted as you'd expect at noon on a Monday. They had to kick rocks for fifteen minutes before George even opened up to let them in. Then Teddy and the rest rented out inlines while he stuck with roller skates, much to the amusement of the team.

That's the other problem. The bearings on his crummy rentals are all gummed up and the trucks are tight as shit, so they aren't carrying him as far as Teddy's inlines. He has to double-step to avoid tripping on him and then there's his limp to contend with. If Teddy'd give him a little space, it wouldn't be—

The team crashes past them again, and as their slipstream urges him against Teddy, Teddy grabs his elbow a sixth time.

His neck goes warm. Lord, is he gonna blush again in front of all Teddy's friends? Somebody's gotta get him out of here.

Luke, skating languidly in-step on Teddy's other side, says, "They have to have some kind of accessibility aid. I can ask."

"I don't— It's fine," Nash grunts. He doesn't need help. He needs Teddy to quit playing with him. They never babied each other growing up. Why's he choosing now to start?

There's a commotion at the door—raised feminine voices and the familiar clang of skates smacking the door frame. His stomach drops.

"Aw, hell."

"What wrong?"

He doesn't have to answer because at that moment, they round the rink and Jo's voice calls out over the ruckus of what looks like half the derby team piling onto the bench and kicking out of their street shoes.

"What the shit?" Jo hops onto the wall, helmet and pads already in place, thick thighs cased in neon spandex, and wearing an artfully tattered tank top that advertises her status as one of the *Buford Hell Women*. She violently stuffs a socked foot into a skate. "You told me you were going to treat him to dinner, not sneak off to the rink behind my back!"

"Dinner?" Teddy echoes. "Wait. Jo?"

Jo smiles, all teeth and round cheeks. Devil and cherub. "Been a minute, Spinoza. Nice of you to finally come 'round."

Low, so not to carry, Nash says, "Whatever she does, don't hold it against me."

"That's your sister?" Luke asks, all wonder and starlight.

"You're not allowed to talk to her," Nash blurts.

Both Luke and Teddy rubberneck at him as the team rolls past with lots of elbowing and pointing, slower now that there's girls to look at. Nash resigns himself to a long afternoon.

"Why not?" Teddy demands on his friend's behalf.

Nash ignores him and tells Luke, "You'll either combine therapy powers and become unbearable, or she'll kill you." He catches the offended expression on his face and adds, "No offense. As a rule, I don't bet against Jo."

"Damn right!" Jo jumps off the wall and skates around them in a tight circle. Then, effortless, she swings around and skates backwards so they're face-to-face. She looks Nash up and down. "Why're you hobbling around like an old man? Come get me."

She slaps his shoulder as she pivots and takes off down the rink.

She glides past the hockey team on the turn and on the opposite straightway, shouts, "Come on, coward! I'm gonna lap you!"

Teddy's smiling as he asks, "Was she always this obnoxious?"

"You both were," Nash grumbles.

"That says something about you, don't you think?" Luke comments idly while the rest of the derby team clambers onto the rink.

They're all kitted out in their helmets and pads, but not the over-the-top makeup and fishnets they don for bouts. Must've skipped it in their excitement to crash his party.

As he circles past the DJ booth, Nash spots George fiddling with the controls.

"What'd you call them for?" Nash demands.

He puts up his hands and his jowls wobble. "I didn't!"

A palm slaps the back of Nash's head.

"Amber saw you in the parking lot," Jo says as she zips past. She jumps to face him. "Are you gonna skate or not? You're like the useless prep girlfriend in movies, but if she was a hundred years old."

Teddy snorts and unsuccessfully covers it with a cough. It only fuels Jo.

She looks at him with victory in her eyes and delivers a final goad. "Come at me, bro."

"Oh. That's his sister," someone from the hockey team says behind him.

Jo glances up, and that's when he pushes off his back skate and tears after her.

Quicker than she deserves after so long out of state and out of practice, she swings around with a happy crow and the game is on.

She's quick and experienced, but his legs are longer.

She goes into the turn first, leaning into it, and he follows swiftly behind with one shitty skate placed in front of the other in a crouch to keep his center of gravity low. She keeps hers lower and comes out of it better, and now they're caught up to the derby girls.

They part to let her through and then close around him, trapping him in the wall. Luckily, he's been to enough of their practices and bouts to know where their weak points are—that, and he doesn't have to play by the rules.

"Sorry, Bell." He picks Belladonna up by her hips and drops her to the side, where she lands hissing and spitting like an angry cat that fell in a vat of Hot Topic merch. She and Jo have been friends since grade school, but she ain't ever warmed to him and he's long since given up trying to get in her good graces.

Garrett, another of Jo's old friends, steps into a hard bump on his bad side from one of the newer girls and saves him from a nasty spill.

He darts through the gap the move leaves in the wall and calls back, "I owe you one, AJ!"

Garrett, Applejacked on the rink, shouts after him about calling to collect.

He scoots past where Teddy, Luke, and the hockey team are clustered in the center of the rink, watching, and gets in five long strides before he hits the next turn. Jo is already coming out the other side of it and he gets a glimpse of a toothy smile as they pass each other.

He comes out of the turn and barrels after her on the straightaway, knowing if this goes any longer he's gonna run out of steam and be spent for the rest of the day.

She hears him coming and pulls a boost of speed out of reserve that puts her in the turn just before he can grab her. She pulls ahead as she comes out of the turn and—

Teddy darts out of nowhere and sends her crashing into the boards with a yell. She overbalances and falls.

There's no time to stop, so Nash drops to his knees and slides into her.

"God *fucking*— Gah!"

He gets his arm around the back of her neck, pins her bent double, jams his fingers into her ribs, and tickles.

"S-stop. Nash!"

He doesn't let up until she lands an elbow in his sternum and knocks the wind out of him. She twists, and he turns his head just in time to avoid a bloody nose. His jaw takes the hit instead.

"Helmet, Jo!"

"Get off!"

He grabs her ankle before she gets him in the thigh with her skate in her mad scramble to get away, but he has to release her to catch the helmet that flies at his face and gets kicked with the skate anyway.

She scrambles to her feet and spits hair out of her mouth. She looks like she got mauled by a pack of monkeys.

He throws his head back and laughs.

"You fucking cheater!" Jo turns from Teddy to include both of them as she spits, "You guys haven't changed a bit. If you hadn't cheated, I'd've won! *I won.*"

"Sure, Joey," Nash says. "Help a loser to his feet?"

She slaps away his hand. "Don't you have a boyfriend for that? Fuckin' hell, I can't believe I have to deal with this again."

She spares a filthy look for Teddy, then tears off the rink. Garrett and Bella split off from the group of mingling derby girls and hockey players and follow her. "George! I'm putting in a pizza!"

George pops out of the DJ booth. "Amber's not due in for another—"

"I said I was doin' it, didn't I? Christ."

George looks at Nash all wide-eyed.

All he can do is shrug from the ground. "Sore loser. Sorry."

"I! Did not! Lose!"

Snickering, Nash puts his palm on the rink with the intent to push himself to his feet despite the deep ache now pulsing down his right leg.

"Now I know you're not secretly a professional." Teddy is standing over him, hand outstretched. "Tuck those fingers before you lose them."

"Who's gonna take 'em?" They're the only ones on this end of the rink. "You?"

He grabs Teddy's forearm and groans as he pulls him upright. The momentum rolls him forward until his skates bump into Teddy's inlines, entirely too close. His face goes hot, and he moves to pull away, but Teddy holds his ground and his arm.

"I might," he says for Nash's ears only, "if you let me."

He meets Teddy's eyes—far, far too close—and his mind turns all to fog until Teddy finally releases him. He moves back, but not far enough for his heart to calm its nervous fluttering.

"How's the hip? You done?"

Nash grimaces weakly. "I'll heckle you guys from the sidelines."

"I'll sit with you."

"No, you should skate."

A line forms between Teddy's brows. "I didn't invite you so you could sit by yourself."

Nash swallows the obvious next question. Why *did* Teddy invite him? To skate too close? For an excuse to touch him? To— To take his fingers? Or maybe it's all in his head, a wish fulfillment, see what you wanna see kind of thinking.

"I wanna see you skate for real," Nash says. "I bet you're quicker than all those guys."

A sharp smile flicks free. "Jam's pretty fast."

"Faster than you?"

"No."

"Prove it."

It's the magic phrase that has never before failed to goad Teddy into action. He's been setting out to prove himself his entire life, so it's something of a shock when he doesn't immediately jet off to do just that.

Instead, he holds out his hand. "You want a tow first?"

Nash's stomach flips. He only hesitates for a moment before he fits his palm against Teddy's, locks his knees, and suffers the slow trip across the rink. Skating backwards, Teddy pulls him along and watches while Nash's heart batters his ribs. He's sure he can feel it through their joined hands.

When Teddy's inlines clack against the wall, he releases Nash's hand and steps back out of the rink before Nash rolls into him again.

Nash has one skate on the carpet and one on the rink and is racking his brain for something to say to fill the silence when a crash from the kitchen has everyone turning to look.

There's no one at the ordering counter, but it's definitely Jo yelling.

"I'll check on her," Teddy says and speeds off, zipping around tables and chairs like he was born with wheels under his feet.

The kitchen door bursts open and Peaches stumbles out backward with bitty Belladonna shoving him and, behind her, Garrett holding back Jo.

Still, his hip hurts bad enough that he doesn't move until he sees the glint of steel in Jo's hand: a chef's knife.

He curses and hobbles quick as his bum hip will allow through the dining area.

"Josephine Owens, drop the goddamn knife!"

Jo's rant runs aground as she looks first at him and then at her hand. She drops it like it burned her and looks up at Nash, pale, as it hits the ground. "I forgot it was in my hand, I swear. He was comin' onto me 'n' I *told him* to quit it, but—"

He turns on Peaches. "You hit on her while she was holding a knife after I warned you—"

"I *thought* this was the twenty-first century," Peaches exclaims, all red-faced and bristling, "where the woman gets to choose, not her possessive older brother with a hard-on for —"

"You dumbass," Nash snaps, "I wasn't protecting her, I was protecting you! Look around, man. She is the only one I warned you off from and you took it as a fucking challenge. What happened to Cheyenne, huh?"

"She stood me up!" he hisses.

Nash rolls his eyes. Fuckin', typical. He should have guessed.

"She likes games. I'd warn you away but that went over like a fart in a space suit the first time, so."

All the aggression bleeds out of Peaches. "Wait. So you're saying I've still got a shot?"

Nash glances at Teddy, who just shrugs and shakes his head. Hopeless.

"If she didn't hit it and quit it, and she didn't tear your confidence limb from limb for daring to make a pass, yeah. You've got a shot."

He clenches his fist. "Sick. I'll be right back."

"Or don't bother!" Jo calls out.

Peaches flips her off and then shoves out the door.

"Cool it, Jo."

"He cornered me in there and—!"

"You came at him with a knife!"

She sobers. "I swear I forgot I was holding it."

Nash speaks slowly in the hope she cottons on to the gravity of the situation. "I told him if he tried you, I'd get a slab ready in the morgue, and you went at him with a knife."

She blinks. Then her lips pinch in that way they do when she's fighting a smile. "You said that?"

Garrett smirks and even Bella's lips twitch. Teddy ducks his head, but not before Nash catches a telling flash of teeth.

"I— This is serious! He could press charges. That's assault with a deadly weapon and— Stop laughing!"

Garrett at least has the grace to turn away as he giggles.

"Listen," Zook comes up behind him and throws an arm around his shoulders, "Peaches can be a real horn dog, but he's not gonna press charges, okay?"

Jam straddles a chair and says to Zook, "Remember when that model left him on the side of the road and you almost missed the championship game to pick him up?"

Nash shrugs Zook off of him and says, "That's not the same as—"

"Wind chill was in the negatives, wasn't it?" Deli asks.

"Didn't he get frostbite?"

"Yeah, just his toes, though. He can still skate."

"Well, bless his heart, he can still skate," Nash snaps.

Teddy grins at him. "It'll be alright. We'll talk him around if we need to. You want a bag of ice or something?"

That's the other thing. His hip is *killing* him.

He jabs a finger at Jo. "First you run me into the ground and now you're testing my patience. You weren't even invited."

She holds her hands out from her sides. "You came into

my backyard!"

He digs his knuckle into his forehead where a stress headache is determined to bloom. "I need a nap."

One of the guys snorts, which sets off a chain reaction of snickering and choked laughter.

He opens his eyes and stares down the hockey team balefully. "What?"

"They're convinced you're secretly an eighty-year-old man," Teddy says, helpfully.

"God, I wish. Then I'd have one foot out the door."

Jo whacks his shoulder. "Don't be morbid."

"Seriously," Benz starts, "the car, the friends, the—"

"Cane?" Nash interjects.

He turns bashful. "Well, I wasn't gonna say— I didn't wanna be—" He looks at Luke. "What's the word?"

"Ableist," Luke supplies.

"That. Yeah."

Nash narrows his eyes at Luke, who makes a chagrined face and holds his cane out to him.

"Have you been coaching them on—?" He cuts himself off with a shake of his head and accepts his cane, deciding he'd rather not know. It's irritating that people need a whole behind-the-scenes tutorial on how to treat him like a person just because he uses a mobility aid, but he wants to like Teddy's friends, so he puts it out of his mind.

Teddy throws his arm over Nash's shoulders and jostles him. Even on inlines Teddy isn't quite tall enough for it to be comfortable and Nash has to sink toward him.

"So," Teddy says, too close and warm and solid, "ice?"

He's helpless but to agree.

He spends the next hour chewing rubber pizza and watching the hockey players make fools of themselves to impress the derby girls, and vice versa. Then Teddy peels off his inlines to sit with him, and time runs away entirely as they dive into what the other missed over the past twenty years.

Nash gives him the bare bones of what it was like after he left. How tickled Mama was about the whole ordeal and how she held onto that petty distaste for him until the day she wrapped the family car around a telephone pole on her way home from the bar. How he'd just turned eighteen, how Jo was only sixteen, and how the state took her to a group home in the city for the next two years and left him all alone.

He skips what happened after that: dropping out of high school, a string of dead-end jobs, buying a house in anticipation of Jo's return only for her to turn tail and go to university. His friendship with Lori and how it ended with her in a nursing home where her kids visited only a handful of times in the five years before she passed. Then he got his GED. Then his CNA. He doesn't tell Teddy about starting at Cherished Hope and how fucking difficult it was when everyone resented him for trying to do things right.

Teddy tells him about Nonpareil Technical School and science fairs and his high school nemesis and befriending Luke and going north to college together—Minnesota apparently—joining the hockey team on a dare, falling in love with the sport, graduating, joining the county's rec league, and, of course, accounting.

He's an accountant. One of many, at some corporation. Such a mundane outcome for the boy who treated everything from a day at the creek to standing up to an abusive father like a battle to be won.

In all his stories, Teddy doesn't mention ever looking back or wondering what became of Nash, but then again, Nash says nothing about the hole Teddy left behind that he never found the wherewithal to fill.

He doesn't mention Uncle Darren either. Actually, in hindsight, it's suspicious how little he mentioned his aunt and uncle. Did they move to Minnesota with him? Probably not. So they were separated—the elder Spinozas on the East Coast and Teddy in the northern Midwest.

When Uncle Darren died, how long had it been since Teddy had seen him? Nash still hasn't found a tactful way to ask how it happened. It's not like the *how* really matters. He's still gone, and prying won't bring him back.

CHAPTER SEVEN

Miscreants

That night, Jo hops over the armrest and settles on her couch cushion, facing him, with her arms curled around her fleece blanket. "I'm sorry about earlier," she says without preamble in that way that lets him know this has been eating at her all day. "I was way out of pocket."

Nash sets aside his pincushion.

"Pushing you how I did, I mean. The other stuff too—but mostly the skating. I took it too far."

It took five minutes to get from the passenger seat to the couch. Even sitting, his hip throbs. He really should get up and stretch, but standing hurts. Stretching hurts. Sitting hurts too, but he's already doing it, so it's the least of the evils.

"Don't worry about it."

Her features crease with concern. "No, really. I was

showin' off and got you hurt."

He shoots her a wry look. "Oh, were you? I hadn't noticed."

Lightly, she whacks him in the shoulder, then turns contrite doe eyes on him. "But really, I am sorry."

"I knew what I was doin', Joey. You weren't the only one that wanted to do a little showin' off." He levels an arch look at her. "Wouldn't't've killed you to let me have an inch though. You noticed I was in rentals, didn't you?"

The corner of her mouth ticks up in a crooked grin. "You're totally gone on him all over again, aren't you?"

His mood sinks. He picks up his pincushion and turns it delicately between his fingers. "He's leavin'. I gotta be ready for it this time."

Her smile fades. "When?"

He shrugs.

"You don't know?"

"I knew last time and got all in my head about it and messed everything up. It'll be better if it's a surprise."

She scoffs. "That's stupid."

"Doesn't matter. It's all I've got."

"Ask him to stay."

He looks at her the same as he did that time she put raw chicken in the microwave. "Half a dozen people followed him all the way to Bumfuck Nowhere, Tennessee, to support him when he needed it. I can't take him away from that."

Now she's got that sad look on her face that she always gets when they talk about the future, or rather, his lack of one. "You're worth more than you think."

What's that got to do with anything? He shakes his head and says, "I can't be more than one guy."

"Have you thought about—"

"No," he says sharply, "I haven't."

He's not the least bit interested in exploring all the things he should be thinking about. He's not gonna get overwhelmed and shut down again. He's gonna take it a day at a time with the small comfort that he's got Teddy's number in his pocket. It doesn't change the miles or ease the ache, but it's more than he had last time, and that's enough.

"Nash—"

"I'm gonna start a bath so I can function tomorrow."

It's mean, but it shuts her up long enough to get out of the room. He knows round two of this thing with Teddy won't end well, but doesn't that mean he should make the most of it while he can? Then, when Teddy's gone, he'll pick up the pieces and it'll be easier for having done it before.

Tuesday dawns dreary and wet. Which is great because his hip always acts up in the wet and it's not sore enough after yesterday. It's getting bad. Well, it's well-past bad. He always knows he has pushed too far when his good side starts pitching a fit too.

He stays bedridden as long as he can stomach it, helped along by Jo's fretting, but the second she heads out for her afternoon derby practice, he throws off the blanket and sets about preparing for a trip to the grocery store. It needs done, and he hates sending Jo because she always gets weird shit from the freezer aisle and forgets half his list. He'll lay right back down just as soon as it's all put away.

It takes well over an hour to stretch, dress, and walk

outside. When he does, he near clobbers Teddy in the nose with the storm door.

"Oh, fuck." He fumbles his cane in his haste to catch the door. "Shit, sorry."

Teddy stoops to pick up his cane from the porch and hands it to him. "Hi." He looks him up and down with a judgmental slant to his eyebrows. "Jo said you were stuck in bed and needed company."

"Ah, well, I—"

A grin blooms on Teddy's face and Nash's traitorous heart flips.

"Are you sneaking out?"

"No, I'm not *sneaking*. I'm an adult. I can—"

Teddy laughs and steps back to let him out the door. "So where are we going, you miscreant?"

He hesitates, then admits, "Grocery shopping."

Teddy cackles. "You are not beating the secret old man allegations, my friend."

Warm all over, Nash holds out his keys. "Mind driving?"

"The boat?" He eyes the old Lincoln distrustfully but accepts the keys. "I can't promise the parking job will be pretty, but I can get us there."

Teddy dings the door on the cart corral and curses as he tumbles out to inspect the damage. With undisguised frustration, he demands, "Why are your doors five feet long?"

"Why do you still careen around like a kindergartner?" Nash returns mildly. He's not worried about the door. He's not gonna tell Teddy, but he's dinged that door more times than he can count. They *are* ridiculously long.

He opens his door more carefully and sets his boots on damp asphalt. After a moment to brace himself, he readies his cane, grits his teeth, and pushes himself upright. If there's one thing he doesn't like about his car, it's how low it is. Bad days would go a lot easier if he had something higher off the ground.

Teddy rounds the back of the car and pauses as he gets a look at his face. "They have those little motor carts, right? You want me to grab you one?"

His first instinct is to say no, he'll get it himself, but Teddy didn't park in the handicap spot despite the tag hanging from his rearview mirror, and the trek across the parking lot will be long, damp, and uphill.

"I'll grab one," Teddy says. "Be right back!"

Nash shuts his door and sags against it as Teddy jogs off. You're not supposed to take the electric buggies out of the store, especially in the wet, but he's hurting bad enough he's willing to face any flak he and Teddy might get for breaking the rules.

The automatic doors roll open to reveal Teddy with his knee on the seat of an electric buggy and his hand shading his eyes. When he spots Nash, he points like a sailor spotting land and slowly rolls down the parking lot.

Nash bites back a smile and shakes his head.

"Your vessel, Captain!"

"Oh, am I the captain?" he asks dryly as Teddy hops off the buggy and it beeps its displeasure.

"Who else? Want me to carry your cane?"

Nash grits his teeth as he sits and only breathes when he's settled.

"Nah, folds up, see?" He collapses it down until it's folded into four equal parts, then snaps the lock bar into place to keep it square. The crocheted sleeve stretches all weird and tugs down to reveal old, faded stickers.

Teddy's lips twitch. "You do the decorating?"

"Jo thinks she's funny."

"And this thing?" He plucks at the sleeve. "Looks like it's seen better days."

He's not wrong. It's faded, dingy, and misshaped from being folded and unfolded and walked around in the elements for years. "A friend made it for me."

"A resident?"

"No."

Teddy lifts his eyebrows. "You have friends that aren't old people?"

"Well... no."

Teddy laughs. "So you're friends with old people outside of work too? Do I get to meet this one?"

Nash pulls an apologetic face. "She died while Jo was in college. Parkinsons."

Teddy's good humor dies with a cringe. "Oh. Sorry."

"It's okay. Been a long time. She's the one that convinced me to get my CNA, actually."

"What was her name?"

"Lori to friends. Lorelei to enemies."

Teddy snorts. "Sounds like a riot."

"She was great."

She was the only thing that kept him sane while Jo was in the group home and then in college.

Teddy rocks back on his heels and jerks his chin at the store. "Shall we?"

It's the first time Nash can remember shopping being fun. Teddy sticks with him instead of running off to chase his every whim and chat with familiar faces the way Jo does. So he doesn't have to keep standing to reach the shelves over his head or to see down in the produce bins, and Teddy keeps up a constant stream of chatter.

It's light. It's easy. It's dangerous.

Apparently, Teddy's still allergic to everything under the sun, and between allergies and keeping kosher, he's on a pretty strict diet, which makes living out of a hotel room an exercise in misery. It's not like he can order in a pizza without repercussions, and the team is great, but only Zook thinks of his dietary needs when they go out. It'd all be a moot point if they were observing shiva correctly—he and Aunt Julie would be drowning in deli platters, according to Teddy—but Uncle Darren wanted to be buried in his hometown, even though that meant forgoing a Jewish cemetery and removing Aunt Julie from her community for the first mourning period. She's been sitting shiva, but Teddy technically exists in a gray area since he's a nephew rather than a son and he's been exploiting that loophole to spend as much time with Nash as he can.

It's while he's talking about how he scarfed down a pack of cold deli-sliced turkey when he got back from the roller rink yesterday that Nash begins to plot. He doesn't get far before he's found out and the interrogation begins.

The third time he points at a vegetable and asks, "Can you eat that?" Teddy crosses his arms and demands to know what he thinks he's doing.

"I'm gonna make you supper."

"Why?" he demands. "Because you feel bad for me?"

Nash barely refrains from rolling his eyes. How could he forget Teddy's aversion to even the semblance of pity?

"No, because you've been helping me out and—and well, what else are we gonna do?"

His eyebrows crush together. "That's all?"

For a moment, Nash can't figure out what he's fishing for. He dodged the pity accusation, so what's the prob—

"You're just settling a debt?"

Oh.

He licks his lips, wondering how honest he should be. Teddy is leaving. Does that mean he should hold back or go full steam ahead while he's got the chance? He doesn't have time to figure it out, so he aims for something in the middle.

"And... and I want to. It would be nice, wouldn't it?"

A dangerous frisson sparks between them despite the care in his words. This is what he needs to avoid if he wants to make it out the other side in one piece, but he can't bring himself to take it back or downplay his meaning. Because he wants this. God help him, even after all these years and the heartbreak of their first falling apart, he still wants this.

"My flight back leaves—"

"Tomato!" Nash blurts.

"Uh, what?"

"I almost forgot. I need a tomato. You're allergic, right? I'll grab—"

"Sit down. I can pick up a tomato without keeling over." Teddy uses a produce bag to handpick the perfect tomato, frowning as he does so. "I didn't tell you I'm allergic to tomatoes."

"Yes, you did." It was one of the first things he learned about Teddy's health issues. "I didn't understand how someone could be allergic to pizza, remember? And you asked if I wanted to hear about all the stuff that's wrong with you or play Pokémon."

Teddy sets the bag in the cart and frowns at him. "I meant today." He watches Nash thoughtfully. "You remember that?"

"Of course."

He remembers it all.

"What about, uh… What was his name? Chad? Chip?"

"Chuck," Nash supplies without looking up from the chicken sizzling in the frying pan. "He wasn't so bad without you around stirrin' up trouble."

"Hey, he stirred just as much as I did."

Nash snorts. "That's not even a little true."

"He had it out for me!"

Nash turns away from the stove to stare incredulously at Teddy where he's perched atop his formerly clean countertop. He points his spatula. "You found the biggest guy in the prison yard and set out to prove yourself. I saw through you from the start."

Teddy doesn't even have the grace to look embarrassed. "How come you always backed me up, then?"

"I wasn't backing you up; I was making sure you didn't go squish and lose me a best friend."

"Aww, I was your best friend?"

"Can it. We both know you didn't have better prospects either."

Teddy laughs. "Fair." He tips up his chin. "So who replaced me?"

Nash pulls a face and returns to poking at the chopped chicken. "Chuck."

"*Chuck*? Are you messing with me?"

"I— He really wasn't bad. We weren't close, but I'd fix up his truck sometimes and he was someone to talk to at school, so..." He shrugs.

"You don't talk anymore? I was getting the vibe you don't have any friends our age."

"Well, there's the derby team."

"Those wild animals don't count."

He snorts but doesn't argue. They've always been Jo's crew, and him no more than a tag-along. "He enlisted after graduation and... Well, I had my own stuff going on. He came back a few years after and was real quiet. Wasn't long before he left again. Last I heard, he was at that military base in North Carolina, but that was years ago. Could be anywhere."

"He's a military dog and you're defending him?"

Nash shoots him a sour look. "Don't do that. He didn't have money for college and his parents didn't have good enough credit to cosign for loans, and all the scholarships are for super athletes or marginalized kids. If he'd stuck around, he'd be living paycheck-to-paycheck like the rest of us. Besides, you know how they prey on poor kids."

He says it, but when Teddy stares blankly back, he thinks maybe Teddy *doesn't* know. He went to that fancy technical school—on a scholarship, but still. Put a name like that on your transcripts and you could go anywhere you please so long as you keep your grades up. A school like that wouldn't have to put up with army recruiters lurking in the parking lot, targeting the kids with worn-through sneakers, biking home or walking because their folks can't afford a second or third car. If he hadn't been singularly focused on being around for Jo, they might've gotten him too. Lord knows he didn't have a speck of ambition to draw him anywhere else.

"You live paycheck-to-paycheck?"

Embarrassment heats his skin. "I— No, not with Jo's job. If you don't got a doctorate, healthcare pays shit. And sometimes even then."

"How come you haven't gone for that, then?"

"Get a doctorate and nobody's gonna hire me as an aide. I'd be over-qualified. I'd have to try for the resident doctor's position, and ours only sees residents a few minutes at a time, once a week, unless something concerning's going on."

Teddy swings his feet, chin tipped up, thoughtful. "And spending time with them is the entire point?"

"Exactly."

He doesn't mean to sound surprised as he says it, but... Understanding isn't something he expects from anyone except maybe Jo, and even with her, there are gaps stemming from fundamental differences in who they are as people. She's baffled by the widespread appeal of romantic relationships, something he has always quietly longed for, but he can always count on her to back him up about refusing to climb the occupational ladder. Meanwhile, his coworkers look at him keeping promises in a little black book and call him strange and obsessive. But not Teddy. Teddy looks at his choices and sees through to the core of truth.

"The chicken sounds angry."

With a start, Nash scrapes the chicken around the pan and they pull away charred. "I said blackened chicken tacos, right?"

Teddy laughs, and the sound inspires a pang of grief that Nash quickly tucks away. He's not going to get stuck in his head this time. He's not.

CHAPTER EIGHT
Me and my two words

Supper is quick and quiet. Teddy inhales the tacos so fast Nash isn't sure he tasted them until he asks for seconds. Then Jo calls and tells him derby practice turned into a sleepover at Bella's and she'll see him tomorrow after work—which is too convenient after *she* invited Teddy over to be believable as a spontaneous change of plan. Still, he doesn't press her; he doesn't look his gift horse in the mouth, and when Teddy shouts his hello and goodbye into the phone, he pretends he doesn't hear her smug undertone as she tells him not to have too much fun.

He thought after cleaning up, Teddy might make his excuses and go, spoiling Jo's manipulations, but instead he moves to the living room and starts poking around the mess of fabric on the card table, trying to make sense of it.

"Is this what you do with your free time now? Quilting?"

Nash hangs the dish towel over the oven handle to dry. "Not usually. Getting the lines straight is giving me fits."

"Expanding your horizons?"

He hesitates at the back of the couch. "Sort of."

Teddy cranes his head back to look at him. "You're being cagey again." He looks Nash up and down. "Gonna hover all night?"

Lord, is he planning to stay all night? It's a thrilling thought, but one he can't afford to entertain. Not for more than a second, anyway.

Nash points at the couch. "If I sit on that thing, I'm gonna be stuck there 'till somebody helps me out of it." He couldn't use his cane and cook at the same time and his hip is nowhere close to forgiving him for yesterday. Once he's down, he'll be staying down. Another reason he can't let himself hope Teddy will hang around much longer. He'll get bored now that all Nash is good for is sitting around.

A devilish grin creeps across Teddy's mouth, and Nash hastily quells the fluttering in his stomach.

"At my mercy, huh?" He scoots to the center cushion and pats the one he vacated—Nash's usual spot. "Come on. I promise not to abandon you here."

Well now, if that don't kick right at the core of things.

He rounds the couch and Teddy doesn't hesitate to pull the card table in close and sidle up beside him for easier access.

"So why don't you want to talk about your quilt? I don't think it's lame if that's what you're worried about."

Nash smooths out a section that's sewn together to resemble a fish. It could have used another go with the iron.

"It's not really my quilt."

Teddy frowns. "But you're sewing it, right? It's not *Jo's*."

Nash snorts. No, she doesn't have the patience for this kind of thing—months and months of precision and repetition. In her words, a shitty quilt will keep her just as warm as one meticulously pieced together, but it will never top her cheap shit fleece blanket that she didn't spend more than thirty seconds and fifteen dollars picking out at the store.

"I had a resident pass a few years ago, and she left her quilting supplies to me. All her fabrics, her patterns, her sewing machine, all of it."

"That was kind."

Kind? *Kind*?

"You have no idea—" Nash pivots to ensure Teddy fully catches his gravity as he explains. "These folks guard their crafts like dragons. It was humbling, to say the least. She hadn't been able to do any serious work for some time, arthritis got too bad, but she talked to me about it a lot. She made her granddaughter a new quilt every five years for Christmas, and she'd been hoping to get one more out. Had the pattern put together and everything, just couldn't get her hands to do the work."

Teddy slowly sits back and takes in the unfinished project with a familiar gleam.

"This is it? Her last quilt? And you're trying to finish it before Christmas?"

"Trying," Nash says. "Put it off too long, I think. You wouldn't believe how much ironing there is."

Teddy grins. "Well, I've spent my entire adult life avoiding ironing, but I'm game to see how far we can get tonight if you are."

"It's tedious," Nash warns.

"It's a puzzle." With careful fingers, he slips the worn sheet of graph paper Maureen sketched her vision onto from under a heap of scraps and loose thread. He holds up a sewn panel beside it to see where it fits in the whole. "I like puzzles."

"It's not half as exciting as hockey, so I get it if it's not up your alley."

Teddy lowers the paper and looks at him. "You keep forgetting I'm an accountant. Tedious puzzles *are* my alley. It's even got math." He flicks at the measurements carefully inked along the edge in shaky script. And then he looks at Nash like he sees straight through his "cagey" demeanor and "stony" disposition and says, "You don't need to worry about entertaining me. I promise I'm just as lame as you remember."

And maybe that's the problem, because he doesn't remember Teddy as the nerdy loser the both of 'em were. He remembers a storm wind—wild and tempestuous—sweeping out the bad, imbuing life in dry, cracked earth, and then blowing out the same way he came in. All at once.

After a night spent tossing and turning, with Teddy top of mind, and in too much pain for a deep sleep, Nash spends the next morning lying in bed cycling between thinking and trying desperately not to. Without Jo around to pester him, he doesn't slump out of bed until noon, and even that feels early.

On top of his hip pain, his neck and back are stiff after hunching over the card table until the wee hours of the morning, but the quilt is visibly coming together and seeing it soothes the queasy knot in his stomach that watches the calendar days tick by.

Somehow, he forgot it was their similarities that initially drew him and Teddy together. When they were kids, it was times tables, strategy games, and the invisible "other" label stitched to their foreheads that their classmates could somehow read. Now that they're older, it seems they've each been cultivating something of a perfectionist streak and a fixed focus that tunnels them into project work until they lose time entirely.

Which is why they worked on the quilt until Teddy received a concerned phone call from Mrs. Spinoza just shy of one in the morning. Then Teddy pried him out of the couch, Nash dropped him off at the hotel, and then, back home, laid in bed while his mind went round and round — half sick with heartache over what he lost out on all these years, and half over what he's on the cusp of losing a second time.

He doesn't expect to see Teddy again before his shift starts this afternoon, but there's a part of him that waits for a knock while he stretches, while he hobbles around the kitchen preparing an afternoon breakfast, and even while he soaks in the bath.

But the knock doesn't come.

"Mr. Greene needs help with his socks."

"Oh, Nash! Mrs. Jefferson was looking for you. Something about her glasses being loose?"

"Mrs. Hernandez's brother dropped off a meal this morning. Make sure she gets it for supper, would you?"

"Hey, Owens."

Nash stops halfway past the nurses' station and faces the dark-haired woman that called out to him, hoping his irritation doesn't show. It's not her fault he's sore and exhausted, and his demanding job isn't doing him any favors.

She lowers a chart and looks at him over the top of her reading glasses. "Mrs. Vanders said to send you home."

He blinks at her. Mrs. Vanders is the administrator for all of Cherished Hope. He's had maybe a handful of one-on-one interactions with her since she got hired on a few years ago, but he doesn't recall ever having a conversation with this nurse. What's her name... Jessie? Jackie?

"Excuse me?" he asks.

"You're barely keeping your feet—her words, not mine. She called in someone from the agency to relieve you and they arrived ten minutes ago, so you can leave."

He stares. "I'm gonna talk to her." If she wants him gone, she'll have to tell him to his face.

Jennifer? Janice? Jenine? rolls her eyes. "You do that."

It takes nearly a quarter hour to track down Mrs. Vanders. By then he's sweaty and in pain and full regretting his choice to hunt her down rather than continue working 'till she found him herself.

She's exiting the kitchen, exchanging a few final words with the Food Service Director about a lettuce recall, and when she turns, she finds him waiting for her.

Mrs. Vanders is a tall, stately woman with a preference for pearls. They've gotten on since she arrived, but mostly they keep out of each other's way. After spending a decade butting heads with Mr. Pellegrino over every which thing, that's the way Nash prefers it. If he doesn't have a reason to see her, it means she has no concerns with his work, and if she doesn't have to see him, it means he has no concerns with hers.

So her surprise at this confrontation is understandable.

"Mr. Owens. I'd've thought you'd be home about now."

"Just Nash, please."

She dips her chin. "Nash, then. Is somethin' the matter?"

"That's what I wanted to ask you, ma'am. Has my performance been lacking?"

The corners of her mouth turn down. "I hear nothing but praise from our—"

"Then why—" He buttons down on his agitation and tries again. "Why did you call someone from the agency to replace me?"

This isn't his first time being targeted by management. His first few years were fraught with ploys to make him look incapable or to bully him into quitting, but he outlasted them all. He even got the worst of 'em blacklisted when they were found guilty of elder abuse. It's been a long time since he felt he had to watch over his shoulder, but his old instincts are still sharp.

Perhaps too sharp.

Mrs. Vanders' expression turns gentle. "The day I have to replace you will be a difficult one. I can't think of anyone more dedicated to Cherished Hope, and that's why I feel it's my responsibility to step in when I see you giving too much."

She gestures at the way he's got nearly all his weight on his poor overburdened good leg, which by now hurts near as much as the bad one. "It's clear you're in pain. I wouldn't ask a resident to keep on the way you have been if they were hurting."

"I'm not a resident. I'm staff."

She nods. "Then it's even more important that you take time to recover yourself lest you work yourself into a state where you can no longer serve. We rely on you. That means you ought to take care of yourself."

He hates that she's right. If he keeps pushing the way he has been, he'll run himself into the ground and be useless to everyone. He has only once pushed himself so far beyond his limit that he needed to file for short-term disability, and he hates repeating mistakes.

Still, it grates.

"I'd appreciate if you would come to me directly in the future."

"Of course. I apologize. I didn't realize it'd be a problem."

She doesn't ask outright, but the question is clear on her face. Since she seems to be sincere about helping him, and he really is in pain and would love to be off his feet, he throws her a bone.

"I... haven't always... had the best relations with my coworkers."

"I see," she says gravely.

It's clear she doesn't.

"After you've called the state three or four times and lost people their jobs, you get a bit of a reputation." His has only just mellowed from "hardass narc" to "that weird workaholic." Actually, after last week, he's probably now "that weird workaholic the hockey players keep coming for".

"I see," she repeats and means it this time. "In the future, I'll come to you directly. I apologize for any distress."

"Thank you."

She smiles. "You're very welcome. Now. The parking lot is a long way off from the kitchen. Would you allow me to fetch a chair for you?"

His pride balks. It's *embarrassing* how hard his pride balks. He works with people at all levels of mobility and his first instinct on being provided a mobility aid when he sorely needs one is to flinch? He's not worm-brained enough not to realize that when he is of a certain age, he'll need a chair of his own, but he's not there yet. He's still—

He's in immense pain and if he doesn't get sensible quick, he'll be in that chair shopping for a new career far sooner than he'd like. And she's right. The parking lot is an awful long way from the kitchen.

"That'd be— Yes, thank you."

So it's with the administrator at his back that he arrives on the main floor in a loaner wheelchair and is greeted by a gabbing pack of residents and, naturally, the hockey team. It does his pride no favors, but he tamps that part of himself down and smiles sheepishly as he assures everyone that he only needs rest and he'll be back on his feet.

And when Teddy bounds forward announcing that he'll drive him home so no one needs to worry—he tries to bury the part of him that balks at that too.

Nash doesn't move or speak as Teddy parks crooked in the

driveway. He only just sat down and now he needs to stand again? The prospect is exhausting. All he wants is to get horizontal without moving a millimeter more than is unavoidable. But Teddy is here...

This morning he wanted him here. He was *sad* that he wasn't, but now he thinks he'd prefer to lie in bed and be ugly without the audience. He doesn't want to entertain a guest. He doesn't want a witness to this breaking down. He wants Teddy to give him his keys and leave and not look back as Nash slowly and painfully makes his way inside and to bed.

He doesn't know how to tell him that, though. He can't think of a kind way to phrase it, and besides, no matter his intentions, sometimes talking to Teddy is like talking to a lit powder keg. Talk as sweet as you want, but understand when the fuse runs out it's gonna go off.

Nash elects to start small and says, "You don't need to stay."

"Sunday," Teddy replies.

He stops. Wracks his brain for context. Finds none.

"What?"

Teddy removes the key from the ignition and holds the ring out. He's looking into Nash's eyes and his expression is wooden when he says, "I leave on Sunday."

Nash stares, short of breath like he was dealt a blow. He doesn't reach for the keys. "You... Why would you tell me that?"

"Why are you avoiding it?" The wood is turning black. Smoldering. "Do you think I didn't notice how you bit your own tongue off to stop me from telling you yesterday? I'm not stupid, Nash."

Sunday.

That's no time at all. Three working days and he'll be saying goodbye. Three days distracted by his abused body and then Teddy'll be gone all over again.

Sunday.

"I wasn't supposed to know." His voice sounds hollow, echoing in his ears. His chest hurts.

Teddy doesn't look surprised, only irritated. "Why the hell not?"

"Because you don't want—"

"Oh, rich." Teddy folds the keys into his fist and kicks the door open. "It's my fault, naturally. Whenever you get all weird, it's my fault."

Teddy slams the door and in a few angry bounds reaches the front porch, where he fights with the lock before the door swings open. Then he turns on his heel, storm door slamming, and marches back to the car to wrench Nash's door open.

"Do you need help?"

What he needs is for Teddy to slow down.

Nash clutches his cane tight in his lap. "I need you to listen to me."

"Listen to you?" His lips peel back around a smile. "Does that mean we're talking now?"

Confused, Nash can only stare. "We've been talking."

"No, *I've* been talking." Teddy looms in the doorway, every line of his body held taut. "*You've* been keeping me at arm's length. If I want to know something, I have to badger and pry and fight to get you to tell me, and if I don't know to do that, I don't get to know anything. All I've ever wanted is for you to let me in, but you *won't*."

Nash's mind churns through it all like a windmill through clay. It's coming too fast and out of nowhere.

"Teddy, I—"

"Don't call me that," Teddy spits.

Nash's teeth clack together. He blinks through the hurt and tries again, tongue trapped against something sour. "Theo—"

Teddy roughly shakes his head. "No, you're not supposed to— No."

Nash pushes out a frustrated breath. "Then what the hell am I supposed to call you?"

"You should— Teddy. Always Teddy, but don't— You're not saying it right and I just— I can't deal with—" Teddy cuts off abruptly and half-turns away, forcing a hand through his hair, but his fingers catch in the curls and he has to yank to get free. He breathes out in a careful, controlled way, then faces him again.

"I'm leaving *Sunday*, Nash, and I feel like I don't even— Like I don't know anything." He stares down at him with raw intensity. "Do you even care? Are you just tolerating me? Waiting for me to be gone so you can go back to—" He flaps his arm at the door and the dark, empty house beyond it. "You've always been like this, but I forgot— I *forgot* how fucking hard it is to keep bumbling around, hoping for the best with no idea what you're thinking or what you even want.

"Do you know how bad it sucks that I'm leaving on Sunday and you didn't even want to *know*? When we're together, it's like— Sometimes the way you look at me— But then I go back to the hotel and I sit in the quiet with Luke and Aunt Julie, and all I can think about is how you don't even know how much longer we've got. You haven't even *asked*. You're acting like it's not happening. Like if you avoid it, then it won't... Or maybe you just don't care. Maybe you haven't asked and you don't want to know because you don't care."

Stiffly, Nash says, "You got mad last time because all I did was think about when you were leaving, and now you're mad again because I tried the opposite. Maybe it's you that —"

"So you *are* ignoring it!"

"Yes! Because you said—!"

"Why is it always extremes with you?" Teddy bursts with something like a laugh in his tone. His lips are curled but there ain't a lick of humor in his eyes. "You either try too hard or not at all. Do you even care? Yes or no, do you care that I'm leaving?"

"Of course I care."

"Don't say it like it's obvious and I'm stupid for not noticing. I've never been able to figure you out. You're so damn quiet, Nash. I feel like for every hundred words I say, I get two from you."

Nash scowls. "Well, if you'd quit talkin' over me maybe you'd get one or two more."

Jaw clenched, Teddy crowds into the doorway. "If you care, act like it. You let me go without a fight last time and now you're—"

"We were kids. What was I supposed to—"

"I'm not talking about last time!" He demands, "Ask me to stay."

Nash flinches. He flexes his fingers around his cane and says to his lap, "I can't."

Teddy puts his hands on either side of the door and leans inside. "Ask me to stay, Nash."

He looks up and meets Teddy's burning stare with a set jaw. "I *can't*."

Teddy breathes in through his nose and then out again. His eyes never stray from Nash's face. "Why not?"

"Because you might say yes."

Teddy's expression flickers with hurt. His hands slip down the car and then drop to his sides. He turns away.

Nash calls after him, "I can't take you away from your family, Ted."

Teddy's head tips back as he inhales. He stands for a moment with his back turned, hands on his head, and when he speaks his voice trembles with emotions barely held in check. "My *family*? My family is down to two and we—*fuck*." He drops his arms and turns so Nash can see the hurt pooling in his eyes. "We don't even live in the same *state*. What fucking family are you talking about?"

"Your team. Luke. They followed you here because they care about you. I can't compete with that."

His mouth drops open. "It's not— There's no competition! I'm not comparing—"

"The only thing to do 'round here is the skating rink, remember? No hockey. No— no university. What're you gonna do when you get bored with quilting and all you've got is me and my two words to fill the silence?"

Teddy opens his mouth, then closes it, expression scrunched with whatever conflicting thoughts are crashing around in his head. He approaches the car and crouches so they're eye level. Almost pleading, he says, "Then come with me. There's so much out there and you're—you're so much bigger than this place, Nash."

The words hit him in the tender heart of memory. Despite his best efforts, his gaze falls to his lap and to his fingers, tangled in faded, fraying yarn. A sticker peeks from under the sleeve, a pickle with text reading, "*I'm sort of a big dill*," except the L's have been crossed out and replaced with a "ck."

Nash swallows. "Your uncle said that to me once." Soft but firm, he looks up and says, "I thought he was wrong too."

Complicated emotions flicker across Teddy's face like brief glimpses beyond the window glass as lightning flashes. His gaze drops as he stands and scrubs his knuckles across his lips. Twice he inhales and opens his mouth only to lose the words before voicing them.

Nash sits silent and aching and waits for him to admit what they both already know. It's for the best. No good can come from entertaining these fantasies. He knows because they've done this before. It hurts, but it's a necessary hurt. Defensive bruises rather than a bloody gaping hole that won't ever heal right.

Teddy sniffs hard and passes a hand over dry eyes. When he meets Nash's eyes again he seems to have reached the same realization, but in typical Teddy fashion, he refuses to accept that some things just aren't meant to be.

"Look," Teddy says, "I'm sorry. I didn't— I'm not handling this very well. I swear I'm done yelling. Can we go inside and talk? Please?"

Nash can't think of anything more agonizing than drawing out this conversation for even another minute. He whispers, "I don't think so."

Teddy wants him to uproot and move across the country

to some northern city with snow and— and— He doesn't even know the name of the place. And what about Jo? Is he meant to leave her here? Or is she expected to abandon her childhood friends and her team and move with him? Tennessee is lacking in a lot of ways, but this is his home. It always has been, no matter what the Spinozas think. This place is a part of him, same way he's a part of it. What would his life be like without rolling green ancient hills gracing every horizon? Without fiddles and mandolins and good hardy folk to keep him grounded and humble and to send him home when he begins to break?

And what about him and Teddy? What if they're a poor match? What if they do everything right and they fail? Maybe it wasn't bad circumstances twenty years ago. Maybe they're too opposite where they should be aligned, and the same where they should be balanced. What if he bares his heart with all of its old scars and it ends up broken all over again?

Teddy dims. "You don't even want to try?"

"I didn't get sent home for a holiday, Ted. I'm tired. My body hurts. Can we just…" *Let it go?* "…put a pin in it?"

"You're doing it again," Teddy says, looking impossibly sad as he does. "You're giving up before we've even lost."

Before they lost? They lost twenty years ago. All they're doing is retracing their footsteps to the same old cliff's edge. Only difference is this time Nash isn't going to make believe there's a pool at the bottom to catch them should they be foolish enough to jump.

"I'm in pain," he says without inflection. "I need to rest."

"Right." Teddy scrubs a hand roughly down his face. "Sure. Do you need help getting inside?"

The thought of Teddy touching him even for the most practical and platonic of reasons makes his heart squeeze and his throat burn.

"I'll be fine."

"'Course," Teddy murmurs. He holds out the keys, but when Nash closes his hand around them, Teddy doesn't let go. "Are you free in the morning?"

His stomach swoops. "I'm not," he says, and he isn't. Tomorrow is Darla's funeral, and he has promises to keep.

Because that's something he does now.

CHAPTER NINE
Promises

It's lucky I packed funeral clothes," Teddy jokes as they step into the funeral home.

Nash doesn't respond. He has had little to say since Teddy arrived at his door early this morning looking like he'd hardly slept, claiming he didn't want to miss the funeral, and telling him to, "*Just pretend like I'm not here until it's time to leave.*"

Fucking, impossible, first of all.

It's not that it's too awkward after yesterday's inevitable butting of heads. He's too irritated for awkward. The problem is the *gleam*. Maybe it's the way Teddy is carrying himself or the way he looks at him, but Nash sees him, and he knows a gauntlet has been taken up. Teddy is in the throes of meeting a challenge and Nash would be a fool not to recognize himself at the center of it.

All the more damning is the fact that Jo returned home this morning scant minutes before Teddy's arrival, looking equally wrung out. Sure, nobody sleeps at sleepovers, but you don't come home from 'em a day late at seven in the morning either. If his suspicions are true and Teddy recruited her to his cause, that means Luke and possibly the entire hockey team are involved as well.

He's never been pursued before and he's finding it makes him feel a bit like a cornered animal—hypervigilant and suspicious of Teddy's every mundane action and banal comment.

As if today needs any complications.

It's for all of those reasons, plus his various aches and pains that weren't never gonna get soothed away by a single day of rest, plus the weird glob of acid in the pit of his stomach every time he thinks about Sunday—that he's mad at Teddy for being here. Nash has no patience to spare, and Darla's funeral isn't the place for the game he thinks he's playing. It's disrespectful—to Darla and to him.

"Thank the heavens, you're here."

With a sinking in his gut, Nash turns as Henry rushes to meet him at the door.

"What's wrong?"

Henry worries his hands and leans close as his gaze flits around the room. "Dan canceled. Flu laid up him and his wife both. Going 'round early this year."

"Dan?" Dread sweeps over him. "You mean Pastor Mullins?"

Henry nods and wipes his brow with a ragged tissue. "I've called 'round and Mike's the only one that answered.

That's Reverend Daniels to you."

Nash closes his eyes for a long beat. "Darla was very specific—"

"She don't want him, I know, I know, but what else is there to do?" He looks at him, pleading for understanding. "If the family don't reschedule, you and I hold very little power to change anything."

"Can't you officiate?"

"No, son," he says with gravity. "Near put me out of business last time. Frightfully mortifying mess it was, 'n' the wife made me swear to never take the podium again. I can try callin' 'round again, but I left messages so I don't know what good—"

"Aunt Julie can do it."

As one, he and Henry turn and stare at Teddy.

"Mister… Spinoza, yes?" Henry asks through a wince. "Perchance is this the same aunt who became inconsolable, and you yourself had to help down from the podium?"

Teddy's expression turns steely. "She's a great public speaker when it's not her dead husband she has to talk about."

Henry cringes. "I'm sure— I apologize. It's only that an important event like this, left to someone inexperienced at the last minute—"

"She's not inexperienced," Teddy says, indignant. "She's been a public relations coordinator for twenty years. Let me call her and see if she can convince you."

"She'd need to be here 'n' speakin' ready in about twenty minutes." He looks to Nash. "Can you vouch for her?"

Sweat pinpricks along Nash's spine as Henry and Teddy, phone in hand, look at him. This is the first he's heard of Mrs.

Spinoza's career and, like Henry, his only experience with her competency was Uncle Darren's funeral last week. Yesterday, he would have taken Teddy at his word and backed him up without hesitation, but what if this is part of whatever he spent all night plotting? What if he's trying to force something that has no business working out, for the sake of winning whatever it is he thinks he's competing for?

Then again, their only other option is to call the mealy-mouthed preacher that Darla expressly did not want officiating her funeral.

"Call her."

Teddy slips outside with his phone and Henry shakes his head. "I hope you know what you're doin', son. There ain't no do-overs, you know."

He's all too aware that he has one shot at ensuring everything goes without a hitch. It's his very last goodbye, so it has to be everything she asked for.

Mrs. Spinoza arrives fifteen minutes later with a print-out under her nose, muttering along as she reads. She's wearing the same rose-buttoned dress from last week, soft pink lipstick, and her hair is swept up into a fancy twist.

Henry gives her the bones of the service structure, and all seems to be well as she nods and folds away her print-out.

She smiles when Nash joins their circle and kisses his cheek. "I was worried we wouldn't get another chance to see each other before Sunday." She points at him sternly as the piano plays in the other room. "Saturday. Brunch. And afterward you and I are going shopping."

He winces. He knew his pants were showing their wear. "Yes, ma'am."

"Good boy. Will you be joining the service?"

"Of course."

When she smiles, there's a tinge of sadness to it. "Perfect. I'll see you in there. Mind my nephew for me."

She squares her shoulders like she does this every day and makes for the chapel, smiling tenderly and shaking hands as she goes.

It's only then that Nash considers she might be in on Teddy's game too.

During the ceremony, Mrs. Spinoza strikes a perfect balance of sorrow and levity, which Darla would have appreciated. Nash successfully prevents Darla's adult niece from plugging her Tupperware scheme and convinces her grandson to go up and say a few words during the open eulogy period. It's as he's checking that one off the list that Teddy peers over to see what he's doing.

Nash slaps his notebook shut and clamps his hands around it as he turns his attention to the softly spoken story about Darla and an indoor water balloon fight.

Against his ear, Teddy whispers, "What is that?"

Nash screws his lips shut and pointedly faces forward for the remainder of the service.

Mrs. Spinoza closes out with a familiar bit of scripture, which he'd guess is what she was practicing when she arrived. She gets it close and with enough confidence that anyone who caught the few changed words would likely attribute it to a different version rather than a Jewish woman doing her best to carry a Presbyterian funeral service.

He leaves Teddy to congratulate his aunt and mingles with the crowd, keeping his eyes peeled for the argumentative cousins he's tasked with keeping civil or else separate, the sister that will need a shoulder and a tissue, and the mean niece (not the Tupperware one) that he needs to find an opportunity to speak to and slip in the phrase, "coup de grâce," as a little beyond-the-grave retaliatory justice. Darla promised a reaction.

He's disengaging himself from one cousin after successfully steering him across the room from the other when Teddy catches up with him.

"Aunt Julie left. Jo said you always go to the burial, so I told her she'd see you Saturday for brunch."

"When did Jo tell you that?" he asks flatly. There's a frail gray-haired woman standing alone with a photo album. His money is on sister.

Teddy hesitates. "Uh, she… Tell me what?"

Nash shoots him an unimpressed look. "I'm not an idiot."

Teddy's shoulders sag. "When did you figure it out?"

"Figure out that you're plotting and you dragged Jo into it? Or that the pair of you pulled an all-nighter and thought I wouldn't notice? Both were first thing this morning."

"I'm— It's not *plotting*. And Jo hardly had to be dragged."

"I don't care," he snaps. "You've got no business doing it here. This is important."

"I know—" Teddy catches his wrist as Nash tries to turn away. He steps too close and lowers his voice until it's for Nash alone. "I'm here *because* it's important. That's the entire point." He searches Nash's eyes for a second, and then two more before he releases his wrist. "Are you going to tell me what the notebook is for?"

Nash wills himself not to grasp the burning skin on his wrist or to let the racing of his heart show. He swallows past the lump in his throat and says, "Quit the game and I'll show you."

"There's no game, Nash." Teddy steps forward, entirely too close now, but hell if Nash can convince himself to move away. "All I'm trying to do is show you I'm serious, and you can count on me."

"That's all?" Nash croaks. "You're not... I dunno, trying to trick me into—"

"No! Why would I— I'm not trying to *trick you*, asshole."

Nash watches him, measuring his sincerity, but the thing about Teddy is, he has always worn his heart plastered across his face. If there's one thing he can always count on, it's being able to tell what Teddy's feeling just by looking.

Nash hesitates only a moment longer, then hands Teddy the notebook. "Only read the pages with check marks."

Teddy skims his thumb over the paper edges and fans through it without stopping anywhere particular. "What's so secret about the other ones?"

"They're still alive."

Teddy wrenches his neck to look at him. Then he returns to the notebook with reverent fingers. "Oh," he breathes, "these are your promises."

Nash doesn't remember if he mentioned them, or if Teddy knows because Jo spilled the beans last night. The past week is starting to blur from stress. He needs to stop letting himself get swept away. If he doesn't keep his feet, he's going to find himself in a free fall over that cliff whether he jumps or not. Three days. He needs to keep his heart and his head for three more days.

Teddy skims over a few pages, then jumps to the ribbon-marked page: Darla. "This is why you always go to the burial."

No. Well, sometimes. He rarely has promises related to the burial, though. The burial is the part that's for him. Promises kept. The work finished. Time to let go.

But Teddy doesn't need to know that.

Teddy runs his finger down the list. Roughly half the items remain unchecked. "What do you need help with?"

"Nothing."

Teddy looks up with a scowl. "Give me something. You can trust me."

Can he? When they were kids, Nash kept so much held back. He tiptoed around Teddy's temper in a way that, at the time, was second nature. He kept his irritation about all the fights scrunched up in a little ball behind his sternum so he wouldn't have to tell him he thought he was acting childish. And he never, never told him how he felt or how mixed up he was about it.

But even then, he trusted him. They were best friends. They were partners. There was no one in the world he trusted to have his back the way he did Teddy.

"We've got one shot at this," he warns. "No do-overs."

Teddy meets his eyes. "Tell me what you need."

The promises that come into play during the funeral service are the easiest to arrange because Henry helps with the details like flowers and music. It's the people things that get tricky.

He and Teddy make it through the social hour without any slip-ups. While Nash chats with Marie, Walt, Spencer, and a few other residents who came to pay their respects, Teddy distracts one of the cousins with incomprehensible hockey talk. Then, when Nash fears he won't be able to disengage from his residents gracefully, Teddy pulls Spence into the hockey talk. Naturally, Walt follows and before he knows it, Nash is free to slip away.

He finds a softly sobbing woman clad in a pair of sunshine-yellow Crocs by the window and tells her gentle stories until her tears dry. Then he scrubs her glasses with the cloth he keeps in his pocket for that exact purpose and sees her to her car where her son's anxiety eases at the sound of her laughter.

Then everyone is piling into their vehicles and Nash gives a scowling lady the fright of her life by calling Hummer limos the *coup de grâce* of vehicular design as he helps her into her car.

The hearse leads the procession down the pitted highway to Red Oak Cemetery just outside of Deliverance, the same cemetery where they laid Darren Spinoza to rest last week.

Teddy gets real quiet.

The burial is solemn, but the sky is bright and a pair of ducks on the pond honk happily through the entire scripture reading led by Darla's brother-in-law.

He thinks she would have approved.

The family is slow to finish their goodbyes, but he doesn't crowd them. When near-all have gone, he lays his bouquet of forget-me-nots and tulips at the base of the headstone. Instead of his usual white tulips, they're sunshine-yellow—the brightest ones Kim had.

If caring for his residents at Cherished Hope is like changing their oil and airing up their tires before they leave on their big trip, then upholding his promises is him waving goodbye from the foot of the driveway just in case they check the rearview and see him there, sending them off. Which makes the burial the part where he steps back inside the house and stands silent and aching, in the way freshly emptied things are, and accepts that they've gone.

It takes longer than normal for that acceptance to find him, damp grass soaking his knees, but when it does, Teddy is waiting for him by the car. He's reclined against the door, staring off into the distance where Nash knows he'll find a familiar mountain, just down a familiar road.

He clears his throat and tucks his chin.

Teddy refocuses on him. "Ready?"

"Yeah. Unless you wanted to…"

Teddy glances across the green lawn to the headstone topped with a line of round, smooth stones. He shakes his head and faces south instead. If you know to look, you can spot the old wooden sign that boasts *Welcome to Deliverance*.

"I haven't been back since I was a kid."

Nash fixes his lips together and frowns. "I don't go there."

Surprise flicks across Teddy's face, followed by curiosity. "Really? You live ten minutes away."

Deliverance is steeped in memory—bad ones and ones that could have been good, if it weren't for the bad ones.

You look just like your mama.

Whatever happened to that little Spinoza boy? You two was thick as thieves for a time.

I remember your daddy. Such a shame he left the way he did. He seemed a good man.

Buford Hills was his fresh start—his slate wiped clean. So, no. He doesn't go back. He's got no reason to. Everybody who mattered in that place left a long time before he did, and not one ever came back.

"C'mon, we've got just enough time to fix dinner before I've got to get to work."

CHAPTER TEN
Sycamore leaf

Nash throws open the front door with a glower firmly fixed on his pillow-imprinted face. Teddy looks far too awake to be on his stoop, grocery sack on his arm whilst behind him the sun struggles to crest the mountains that hug his little valley. Nash takes a moment to appreciate a view he doesn't often see—morning mist clinging stubbornly to ancient green —then he sighs and looks at Teddy.

"We really doin' this again?"

"Good morning to you too." Teddy cranes up onto his tiptoes to look over Nash's shoulder with an expectant jaunt to his eyebrows. When Nash fails to invite him in, he ducks under his arm in a breeze of spearmint and cool autumn morning.

"You know," Teddy says conversationally as he unpacks

his sack onto the counter, "once upon a time, it was you waking me up at the butt crack of dawn."

Nash closes the door. "I work second shift. I don't get to bed 'till two most nights."

Teddy opens the fridge and pokes around the condiments. "Well, it must be your lucky day. I would have been here an hour ago if the grocery store had been open. It's nuts that this town is totally shut down for a whole twelve hours overnight. What do the people who live here even do until eight in the morning?"

"We sleep, Theodore."

Teddy perks up and grins at him over his shoulder. "I like it when you call me that in your raspy morning voice."

Nash scrubs his hands over his face and pads for his bedroom. "I'm not awake enough for this."

"You should brush your teeth. It'll wake you up and take care of your morning breath. It's pretty rank, just saying."

Nash closes his door and throws himself facedown onto the mattress. If there's a God, he'll let him suffocate.

Shouting and a burning smell drag him from sleep's embrace sometime later. He's awake in an instant, on his feet, and throwing open his door so fast his vision swims.

Jo and Teddy are elbowing each other in front of the stove, their voices intermingled in a jumble about eggs and Gordon Ramsey, but nothing seems emergent.

"What's on fire?" he demands.

They whip around to goggle at him like toddlers caught sneaking cookies. Then Teddy jumps like he's been scalded and pops the arm on the toaster. Four blackened slices of toast emerge, smoking faintly.

Jo guffaws. "You imbecile."

"What setting do you guys keep your toaster on?" he whines. He pinches a slice, but drops it immediately and shakes out his fingers. "Charcoal?"

"Hey, girl's gotta have her waffles. You're supposed to check that stuff before you just put bread in and hope for the best."

"Oh, well, fuck me for assuming toasters get used for toast."

"I'll leave that to my brother. Now let me save the eggs."

"I don't care what Gordon Ramsay says! They're better *cooked*."

"Oooh, big man can't handle being inferior to a famous chef."

"I— That's not— It's not an inferiority issue! I just like my eggs crispy."

As a single malicious entity intent on ruining his day, they turn on Nash as he delicately lowers himself onto the couch.

"Tell him he's nuts."

"Tell her to get out and let me cook!"

Nash drops Jo's blanket over his face. "Unless somethin' needs extinguished, I'm not here."

He fuzzes out as their argument continues and their voices turn to wash.

It's comforting in a weird way. He grew up quiet. Jo did too, at first, but she was little enough when Daddy took off that it didn't take root in her the same way it did him. Mama was no parade, but she wasn't a suffocating cloud of imminent violence. She was quiet, though. Quiet in the same way rot is quiet. You don't realize the danger until you peel back the wallpaper and find evidence of decay all the way through to the supports.

So it's comforting, the bickering. No longer do they have to fear retribution for living their lives out loud. No longer do they live shrouded in silence, waiting for the covers to be ripped away to reveal clenched fists and hateful words.

He must drift off again because next he knows, the couch is sinking under him and the warm weight of Jo's blanket has been lifted away. Cool, fragrant air greets him as he blinks the sleep away to find Teddy seated on one side and Jo on the other mashing some charred eggs into a slice of cinnamon-sugared toast.

Teddy hands him a plate without looking. His attention is on Jo as she folds the toast and takes a large bite.

She wrinkles her nose and crumbs spew onto her plate as she says, "This is the driest sandwich I've ever been subjected to."

"It's eggs and toast," Teddy snaps. "No one told you to turn it into a sandwich."

She swallows with effort. "Everyone knows *bread* plus *protein* equals *sandwich*."

"It's eggs and toast!"

Nash snorts a laugh.

"Ah-ha!" Jo crows. "Not a zombie. You owe me five bucks."

"No bet. With all that snoring, no one could mistake him for a zombie."

Nash lowers his plate and asks, "How come it always ends up with you two ganging up on me?"

"Easy target," they say in unison and then high-five over top of him.

Jo hops up with her plate and heads for the kitchen. "I told Garry I'd run errands with him, so I'll be gone most of the day. Try not to miss me."

"Won't need to try," Teddy says, and gets whacked on the back of the head for his troubles, which loses him a few bits of overcooked egg to the carpet.

Nash forks up a mouthful of eggs and pauses midchew. "Hey Joey, mind bringin' me a glass of water?"

"*Oh come on. They're not that dry!*"

Jo cackles and sweeps off to her room, leaving Nash to suffer the eggs without a drop of moisture to help them down while Teddy sulks.

Teddy lingers all day like he's got nowhere better to be. Which, Nash supposes, he probably doesn't. Together, they clean up the kitchen and then settle in front of the card table to continue puzzling together the quilt until Nash's alarm pierces the quiet to tell him he needs to get to work.

Teddy stands and stretches. "You mind dropping me off at the hotel on your way? I'll collect the guys and we'll be over in time for dinner."

Nash ducks into his room and doesn't bother with the door. Jo minds more when he closes the door midconversation than she does glimpsing him in his underwear. He pulls off his shirt.

"You know y'all don't have to keep comin', right? I'm sure it's lost its charm."

"Are you kidding?"

Teddy appears in the doorway while he's sniffing the armpit of yesterday's scrub. He smirks, "Classy," and makes himself comfortable against the doorjamb, not shy at all about letting his gaze roam. "Spencer owes me a rematch, Jam promised Marie a dance, and Zook told Gloria he'd watch *Fat Albert* with her. We're committed whether you like it or not."

He clenches his shirt in his hands and says down to the wrinkles, "You know, I never really thanked you guys for—"

"Oh, fuck off. No one needs thanked. We come because— What is that?"

Nash checks over his shoulder. "What?"

"No, on your— Is that a tattoo?"

Nash slaps a hand over his left pectoral. "No."

Teddy laughs. "You're a terrible liar. When did you— I thought you were old man through and through." He approaches, grinning widely. The one that crinkles his nose and makes Nash feel all warm and fluttery from his toes to his ears. "What is it? When did you get it? Why?"

"I—" He leans away but doesn't step back as Teddy draws near. "Jo and her friends got really into poke tattoos in college."

"You let them experiment on you? Dude."

"I…" He trails off. *Let* isn't the right word. He didn't volunteer to go first so much as insist. If anyone was going to end up with an infection or fucked up blotch of permanent ink, it was going to be the guy going nowhere, not the industrious college girls with the whole world at their feet.

"Well, let me see it. I already know it's there, so there's no point covering it up like it's indecent."

Resigned, Nash drops his hand and watches Teddy's reaction broadcast across his face, hoping he'll get lucky and he won't connect the dots.

He's never been all that lucky.

Teddy sucks a breath through his teeth. He lifts his hand as though to touch but catches himself and hovers instead. "A sycamore leaf?" He meets Nash's eyes and demands, "Why?"

It makes sense that he recognizes it. It was only last week that he saw the photos.

Teddy squares his shoulders in the face of Nash's silence and tips up his chin with a gleam in his eyes. "Stop hiding and tell me the truth. Why did you get that tattoo, Nash?"

"It's a reminder," he admits woodenly.

Teddy doesn't lose an ounce of intensity, but his voice goes soft as he asks, "Of what?"

Nash's chest rises under the weight of Teddy's hovering fingers. He averts his eyes and says, "That avoiding goodbye doesn't stop the leaving, just leaves open a door for regret."

A single point of heat presses against the fingertip-sized tattoo over his heart. His fingers twitch, desperate to touch in return, but that way lies the cliff. Nash keeps his hands fisted in yesterday's shirt.

In a rough whisper, Teddy says, "I'm sick of regret."

Nash closes his eyes. "Teddy, I can't do this."

There's a long beat of horrible silence. Only Teddy's breathing breaks it. Nash doesn't think he's capable of drawing a full breath with Teddy this close.

"Why not?" Teddy finally asks. "Nash, I—"

"I can't—" he interrupts before Teddy says something he can't take back, and Nash will never be able to forget. "You broke my heart last time and you're leavin' again. I can't keep doin' this. I can't."

Surely, he can feel Nash's heart crashing around like a caged, frightened thing.

"So come with me."

"D'you realize what you're askin'? You want me to drop my whole life in the trash and start over when I've spent the past twenty years building something of a life, and trust that you'll be worth it?"

Teddy pulls back and only then does Nash risk opening his eyes. His chin is tipped up, his jaw tight, but Teddy doesn't lash out like Nash expects. Instead, he says, "You can trust me. I'm not any different."

Nash presses his lips flat and shakes his head, chest aching. "That's what I'm afraid of. I want a quiet life. I'm not... I'm not lookin' for an outlet the way I was when we were kids." He forces himself to look Teddy in the eyes so there's no mistake when he says, "I'm ready for a little more calm and a lot less storm."

There's a strange expression on Teddy's face as he pulls away entirely, leaving a cold print over Nash's heart. It's an expression he's never seen on him before. He only sees it for a moment longer before Teddy buries his fingers in his hair and turns his back. He scrubs his hand through his hair vigorously.

Without facing him, he says, "I changed my mind. I'll walk back."

And easy as that, Nash lets him go.

Teddy doesn't show up that night, but his team does. Nash expects bridled antagonism at best, or a fist to the mouth at worst. Instead, he's met with more curiosity than anything.

When Zook gets him alone to ask him what's going on with Teddy, he tells him the truth. They're having a fundamental disagreement, and Teddy is struggling to come to terms with the reality of it.

Zook must spread the word because no one approaches him after that.

CHAPTER ELEVEN
Code E

He expects brunch on Saturday to be more of the same—no Teddy, just concerned loved ones fended off with vague explanations. So Nash is surprised when he arrives and Teddy is seated opposite Mrs. Spinoza with Luke at his side.

Jo steps around him when his feet drag, and she and Luke make a big show of acting like they haven't seen each other since the skating rink.

"You can drop the act," Teddy says tonelessly. "He figured it out."

"What?" Jo barks. She squints at Nash. "When?"

"Like, immediately," Teddy says.

"Scheming already?" Mrs. Spinoza asks with a smile. "Some things never change."

Teddy flinches, but Mrs. Spinoza is too busy waving Nash over to the seat beside her to notice.

The restaurant is one he's been to with Jo and the derby girls when they grow tired of the local barbecue place they typically haunt, but it's more upscale than their usual preference so he hasn't been here more than a few times. The windows are tinted and low lights create an intimate atmosphere that he might enjoy if Teddy wasn't sitting across from him.

Or rather, he *would* enjoy it if it was just him and Teddy alone in a universe where Teddy never left and they came together in their own time how he always hoped they would. Or something like that.

"Miss Josephine," Mrs. Spinoza says as the waitress leaves with their orders, "Nash tells me you're a hot commodity. It sounds like your career is thriving."

Jo's uncomfortable expression evaporates. "Oh, jobwise. Yeah! It's going really well."

"Do you like the traveling?"

"It's the only thing that keeps me sane."

"Where have you been?" Luke asks.

Nash settles back in his seat while Jo warms to the subject, hands waving as she goes on about disappointing beans and bridges of the wrong color. Now that she's started, they'll be stuck on the topic for a while. Which suits him fine. He'd rather not be in the spotlight.

Across from him, Teddy is slumped over the table, fiddling with the straw in his iced tea. He hasn't looked at anyone since Nash arrived, even though Luke keeps sending him sideways looks full of worry. If Mrs. Spinoza has noticed something is off with her nephew, she has elected to ignore it.

Their food arrives and the waitress retreats.

Mrs. Spinoza clasps her hands. "I have some news. I've decided to move back to Deliverance."

There's a pause where Teddy sits up straight and everyone looks at him without actually turning to look. Then Luke and Jo offer their congratulations and Mrs. Spinoza glows.

"I met up with some old friends that also moved away and then back, and we've been looking at apartments. Since Darren is gone and Theo is in Minnesota, there's really no reason for me to stay all the way out on the coast. It's cheaper and there's an opening at a consulting firm here in Buford Hills that I applied for. They've asked me to interview."

Nash nearly comes out of his skin as she closes her hand over his on the table. He tears his eyes off of Teddy and finds her smiling warmly.

"I was hoping we could keep close. Breakfast together sometimes, or something like that. I could stop by the nursing home and visit. Maybe get some knitting tips from the ladies there." She smiles hopefully.

"Uhh..."

Luke is watching Teddy with outright concern now. Meanwhile, Teddy is statue-still, face blank like a stalled computer.

"The umm... The bird watching is good in the mornings," Nash says. "We could—"

Teddy lurches to his feet, upsetting the table as he goes. Half of Nash's hush puppies roll to the floor.

"Theo—"

He plants his palms on the table. "I'm trying to get Nash to move with *me*. Stop digging his roots deeper!"

Mrs. Spinoza's cheeks flush pink. "Theodore James—"

He continues over her, relentless. "When I asked if you'd move to Minnesota with me and you said it wasn't a good time, were you already planning this? Were you just... just putting me off until you worked out your own plans?" His volume climbs as he demands, "What is it about this place that you all like so much better than—" He cuts himself short with a gasp of air and a clack of teeth. His eyes glint under the low light as he flaps his arms as though in surrender, then storms out of the restaurant.

Nash watches him until the door swings shut on his back. When he turns back to the table, everyone is watching him.

"What?"

Luke levels a disappointed look at him, then stands. "I'll check on him."

The rest of the meal is subdued. Luke returns after nearly a quarter hour and shakes his head when Mrs. Spinoza asks if Teddy is coming back. He flags the waitress for a box.

It's not until Nash is returning from paying the bill under the guise of a trip to the bathroom that Luke catches him alone.

"I told you he's not in a good place right now. Just stay away from him if you don't care."

Baffled, Nash fails to respond before Luke ducks his head, show of loyalty delivered, and returns to the table.

It's Teddy that's been coming to *him*. And Nash has never been any good at stopping him from doing what he wants, no matter how much damage follows in his wake.

"Code E. All available staff report to the dining room for instructions. Code E."

Quickly, Nash finishes tying off the handkerchief in Marie's hair. "Better?"

"Si, gracias." She continues to fan herself, but at a languid pace.

"You call me back if it slips and I'll fix it, alright?"

"I will. Thank you, Mr. Nash."

"You're very welcome."

He steps out of Marie's room and nearly headlong into Quanxi. She hardly looks at him as she continues a rapid pace toward the heart of Cherished Hope.

He hurries to keep up.

"Who is it?"

"Not sure," she says. "I was just with Loretta, so my usual escape artist is accounted for."

"I saw Martin maybe five minutes ago, and he's not much for venturing anyway."

"Someone from another area, then. We're lucky we don't have many elopement risks."

That they are. There have been long stretches when that wasn't the case and he sorely wished someone would invent cloning already so he could be in half a dozen places at once. Or, you know, that the business side would see the benefit of hiring more staff, but the cloning thing's got better chances.

In the dining room, they only have to wait about a minute before Barry calls everyone's attention. He's a tall, willowy man, so it's no trouble to spot him in the crowd of nurses, aides, custodial, and kitchen staff.

"We're looking for Thomas Santiago. He's Hispanic, around 5'7", and has dementia. He was last seen at the nurse's station in the south wing about twenty minutes ago. Be thorough. Check closets, bathrooms, and closed doors, including ones that should be locked. Grounds and maintenance are already checking outside. If you find him, go to the nearest nursing station. Let's bring Mr. Santiago home safe."

They disperse. The first place Nash checks is the stairwell that leads down to the laundry and boiler room and finds the doors at the bottom locked, as they should be. He hikes back up the stairs and takes the long way to his wing, checking doors, and under beds as he goes. When he returns, Marie is waiting for him in the hall, handkerchief in her hands.

He helps her tie her hair up off her neck again, then continues to search in between helping his residents with their usual late night issues: too hot, too cold, so-and-so is being too loud on the other side of the wall, the nurse woke me up for my medication and now I can't sleep can you please talk to me about the latest episode of *A Rose Without Thorns*? And, naturally, trips to the bathroom.

It strikes him that if Darla were here, she'd be wanting all the details on the search and she'd be off in her power chair, monitoring the halls, helping out of the goodness of her heart —and because she always was a leech for drama. They're already prepping the other side of Marie's room for a new resident. He knows the practicalities of it. They've had an empty bed in their unit since Geraldine passed two weeks ago and now there's two. It don't make it any easier though. It's too soon.

He's just returning with Martin from the restroom with the intercom pings.

"Code E is resolved. Nash Owens, please come to the lobby. Code E is resolved. Nash to the lobby."

Perplexed, he gets Martin back to bed, makes sure he gets the covers tucked up against his neck how he likes, then hustles to the lobby. It's a good ways away, so he's lathered up a light sweat when he steps onto the tile and stops dead.

Luke and Mrs. Spinoza are standing with one of the maintenance folks and a nurse.

His sweat turns cold. Teddy is nowhere in sight. It's closer to midnight than supper time. There's no good reason for them to be here.

The maintenance worker, Rhonda, he thinks, steps forward. "They were in the parkin' lot." Her forehead wrinkles. "They said it's an emergency."

His heart squeezes silent. "What happened?"

"We can't find him." There are tears in Mrs. Spinoza's eyes and her nose is an angry red. "It's my fault. I shouldn't have— Please. You know where he would go."

He doesn't. If it was twenty years ago, he might, but Teddy's an adult now. He doesn't have a closet he can tuck into with his bulky cobbled together desktop computer. He doesn't have a *house*.

"When did you see him last?"

"Brunch," Luke says stiffly. "He said he was going back to the room, but when we got there, he was gone."

After brunch, they went shopping. He suggested Walmart, but Mrs. Spinoza insisted on driving nearly an hour to the mall in town. By the time they got back to Buford Hills, he had just enough time to drop them at the hotel, dart home for his scrubs, and truck it back to Cherished Hope. In all that time, he hasn't looked at his phone once. He itches to run to his locker and see if Teddy has reached out at all.

Luke holds out a piece of paper. "He left this."

Nash accepts the neat white square stamped with the hotel's letterhead. Upon it is familiar chicken scratch.

Tell Nash same place as last time. Don't chicken out.

"I don't know why he thinks I'd be too scared to tell you." Luke looks distressed at the idea. Or maybe he's just distressed in general.

Nash shakes his head. "That part was for me."

"Do you know where he is?" Mrs. Spinoza asks. "I can't lose him too. I can't."

"I— Yeah. Yeah, I know where he is."

How that asshole climbed a mountain though, he's not sure, and now Nash is on the hook to do the same. It's pitch-black outside and getting colder by the minute.

Dammit, Teddy.

"I need to call my sister."

Nash agrees to far more compensation than the favor is worth before Belladonna lets him leave with the ATV. She swindled him good and was transparent in her anticipation of collecting. Every time he's asked Jo what her problem with him is, he gets brushed off with a cagey, *"Don't worry about her, she's harmless."* But after tonight, it's feeling decidedly harmful—to both his wallet and his pride.

He takes the time to fill the tank (he's not gonna get stranded halfway up the mountain like an idiot), dress himself appropriately (he's not gonna get hypothermia on the mountain like an idiot), and collect everything he thinks Teddy might need after climbing a mountain and sitting up there for hours alone in the cold and dark like an idiot.

Only then does he tear off down the highway with naught but a wobbly headlight to show him the way.

The drive to Deliverance is all potholes and clenched teeth until he turns onto a familiar road. The gravel is somehow smoother than the pavement and he kicks up a cloud of dust over Red Oak Cemetery as he opens the throttle. He doesn't slow as he passes the house he grew up in. He's seen it in the light, so he knows he'll only see boarded-up windows, a sagging barn, and overgrown weeds crawling over the rotted fence and dirt driveway.

He tears up the hill.

The Spinoza's old house looks the same as he remembers: gray from sitting too close to the road and the porch light aglow, illuminating the last place he ever saw Darren Spinoza. There's even a gray sedan in the drive, although it's a Buick rather than a Toyota.

He keeps going until he comes upon the little dirt track that splits off the road and curls around the base of the mountain. It's no worse than the gravel, but when he comes to the weed-choked trail he used to walk anytime he could get away—back before his old man busted his hip for him— he slows dramatically lest the roots, rocks, and the slick bed of pine needles spill him down the side of the mountain and strand him and Teddy both.

He crests the last incline and rolls around the bend onto a wide, flat overlook. The headlight cuts through the black night and there, huddled at the base of a tall sycamore tree still clinging to a full head of brown leaves, is a Teddy-shaped shadow.

Nash cuts the engine but leaves the headlight gleaming. The shadow stands and as much as he wants to stalk over and shake some sense into him, he grabs a blanket first. He's only wearing a hoodie, idiot.

Teddy's face is pale, his honey-gold skin washed in moonlight, but he doesn't seem hurt and his eyes are clear. Nash resists the urge to shove the blanket into his chest and keep shoving until Teddy topples over. He's not like that. He won't be like that. He's Nash, just Nash. He is not and will never be a Mr. Owens. He won't.

He holds out the blanket and when Teddy takes it, Nash stuffs his fists in his armpits and snaps, "What the hell d'you think you're doin' up here?"

Teddy wraps the blanket around shivering shoulders and just looks at him, all dark eyes and down-turned lips.

The worry-born fury wrapped around Nash's heart takes a solid whack, but he refuses to let it go so easily. "Why didn't you at least bring a coat? Hold on, I have a hat and gloves."

Teddy trails behind him as he returns to the ATV. Softly, not like himself at all, Teddy says, "I didn't think you were coming."

He turns around, incredulous. "They didn't find your note until late and I don't keep my phone on me at work. They were knocking for an hour before maintenance found 'em and let 'em in. I got here quick as I could."

"Oh."

He resists the urge to tuck the hat over Teddy's head himself, to make sure it's snug over his ears, and then to crush him in a hug and tell him he's glad he's okay even though he's the dumbest jackass he's ever met.

He stews while Teddy garbs up. His heart is pounding but he can't tell if it's from fear or anger anymore. His palms are itching with the need to grab him. To touch. To reassure himself nothing terrible has happened.

"So what is it?" Nash demands. "What'd you think this was gonna do for us? You think the middle of the night on top of a mountain'd be when I'm most open to tossing my hands up and doin' whatever you want? I have a life now, Ted. A pretty good one, I think. If you want me to throw it away you've gotta—"

"That's the second time you've equated being with me to throwing your life away," Teddy interjects without heat. He looks exhausted. Plum wore out. Or maybe just sad.

"That's what you'd have me do! Hop on this plane, Nash. Run away with me, Nash. You can stow away in the moving truck, Nash. Nothin's *changed*. Your plans are still half-assed and childish, and I still *can't go*."

The small fury he stoked the whole way from Buford Hills flickers and then gutters out at the sight of the sorry look on Teddy's face. His chest aches.

Softly, he repeats, "Ted, I can't go."

Teddy drops his chin for one beat and then two. When he lifts his head, his jaw is set.

"Why not? There are nursing homes and old people in Minnesota. There are shitty little ranches and roller rinks and — There are birds in the morning and places to get brunch and— Or is it me?" A muscle jumps in his jaw, but his eyes are wide and dark. No fire tonight, just Teddy. "If it's me… I can take it, you know? The past few days were supposed to be about showing you, showing both of us how good it could be if we were all together again, but if the problem— If it's me you don't like, you can say it."

"What d'you mean 'all'?" Nash asks slowly. "If we were all together again—who is all?"

Teddy frowns. "You, me, and Jo. Just... just like we used to be."

His voice threatens to rise again. "You want me to ask Jo to move across the country too?"

Teddy shoots him a queer look. "Jo's on board," he says. "She said she gave up trying to get you out of here forever ago and wished me luck." He grimaces. "Probably should've taken her more seriously."

"Jo wants to move?"

Teddy's expression turns incredulous. "Do you two talk at all? She wants to live in a city, Nash. Somewhere she can step outside at nine PM and find some lights on. But she won't go without you. She said Liberty was the perfect compromise—close to St. Cloud but with plenty of small-town charm to keep you from tearing your hair out and going full recluse."

Nash's lungs burn. He wants to deny Jo would ever want to leave him, but if that were true she wouldn't run every time she gets half a chance, would she? He's always known, somewhere deep in the back of his mind, that he does nothing but hold her back from living the life she wants. She hasn't needed him in a long, long time, but she's kind enough to let him continue playing the role of big brother.

"Liberty," he parrots. "Is that where you live?"

"That's where Jo's been looking at houses."

"What?"

"I have an apartment in St. Cloud."

"What?"

Teddy flaps his arms. "I don't know what you're whatting!"

"You're moving? You got Jo looking at houses for you?"

"For *us*, Nash. For the three of us."

"What? Why?"

"I don't know," Teddy snaps. "Maybe I'm just a dumbass with anger issues like you think I am, but there isn't a day I haven't regretted how things ended between us. And now—" His voice cracks, but he holds Nash's gaze even as his eyes turn glassy. "Now I have to regret not keeping Uncle Darren close for the rest of my life. I can't fix that. There's no— There's no do-overs. So fucking sue me for trying to fix things with you. I know it's twenty years too late, but it's not dead-and-gone too late, so just... Could you think about it, please?"

"I'm sorry about Uncl—"

Teddy shakes his head roughly. "That's not what this is about. I don't want— I shouldn't have said anything." He rolls his eyes skyward and takes a steadying breath. When he blows it out, his voice and gaze are steady once more. "My point is, I want us to have the fair shot we never had."

"I've never even been out of the state before and you're asking me to move north right before winter at the drop of a hat. You're asking me to give up my residents and my—my *florist*. What if it doesn't work out? What if I can't hack real winter or the town or the new job? What if you and me... There's so much that can go wrong and you're shaming me for refusing to jump just because you said so."

"I'm not shaming—"

"I'm not gonna argue definitions, Teddy."

Teddy gravitates closer and all Nash's arguments turn to static. He wants to grab him by the wrist and just... just hold him there. Keep him from coming any closer, keep him from running off and doing something else stupid. Keep him... Keep him here. Keep him from leaving again.

He curls his fingers into his coat. He's already one person's leash. There's no reason to tie down another.

"Nash," Teddy says, too close, too intent, too Teddy, "you know I don't expect anything from you today, right? I'm not asking you to get on a plane tomorrow."

"You're not?"

"No!" He laughs a little, soft and damp. "No, that would be— That would— All I'm asking is for you to think about it. I know you've got stuff to tie up. I'm not asking you to break any promises. Just, maybe don't make any new ones. Give me a chance to make good on the promise I should have kept back then. I'll call every day."

Nash swallows, pulse fluttering. "For how long? We're talkin' lives, Ted. It'll be years."

"Does it matter? Five? Another twenty? I want you back in my life, Nash."

"You'd wait that long for me?"

"I mean, yeah." Teddy looks at him like it's all so apparent. "I already have, haven't I? And how long are your residents usually good for? Another five years? Ten max, right?"

Nash blanches. "That's— I'm not speculating—"

"No, I know." Teddy hides his face in the blanket but only for a moment. "I'm not asking you to. What I mean is," he turns earnest eyes up to him, knit hat low on his forehead, blanket clutched at his neck, "I promised to call every day until we turned eighteen, so depending on how it all works out, it might be less than that, but—but who cares, right? I've missed you." He searches Nash's face and whatever he finds there encourages him to say, "I've never felt close to anyone like I feel with you."

Nash drops his chin and peddles his usual excuse for why it all felt so big back then. "We were kids. Teenagers."

"You mean you haven't felt it this week?" Teddy shifts like he means to move closer but changes his mind last second. "I swear, sometimes you look at me and it's like…"

Nash meets his eyes and a frisson passes between them. Suddenly, he's overtly aware of the black night swaddled around them, the only people left at the top of the world, the stars, bright through dancing leaves, and Teddy, the heat of him all along his front, dark eyes looking at him like he's the only spot of light left in the universe. He can't remember why he's fighting so hard against the gravity that pulls him toward Teddy whenever he's near.

"Like that," Teddy says in a hush. He searches his eyes. "Nash, can I kiss you? Just… just once."

Nash's pent-up breath leaks out of him. "God, I hope it's not just once."

A smile tries and fails to lift Teddy's lips. He shifts closer until their knees knock, eyes locked on Nash's like he doesn't dare look away. Tentatively, Teddy links his fingers around Nash's wrist. His fingers are surprisingly warm. Nash doesn't pull away and he doesn't touch him back.

"I can kiss you?"

Nash's heart is beating so hard his voice quakes as he responds, "Yeah. Yes."

It's fitting, he thinks, that it's here. The very spot where he planned their first kiss to be, but then chickened out.

Teddy slips his fingers along Nash's neck and into the hair at the base of his skull, a trail of sparks, setting his skin on edge.

"Don't run on me," Teddy whispers, and then presses their mouths together. It's a simple kiss. A chaste meeting of lips, press of mouth to mouth, a brush of noses.

To Nash, it's lightning, cracking through him, waking him up.

They part and somehow his fingers are curled deep in Teddy's hoodie, the blanket is in the grass, and Teddy is looking up at him, shining.

"More than one, huh? How many did you have in mind?"

Nash's mouth is dry, his stomach in a knot, and for some reason he feels like crying. His fingers are still tangled in Teddy's sweater, and he doesn't remember how to make them let go. Teddy is pressed against him, body heat saturating his skin, breath tickling his throat, closer than he's ever been, and Nash can't let him go. He won't let him go.

Guttural, he says, "One for every day you were supposed to call but didn't," and then he kisses him again.

Fingertips dig into his jaw, his cheek, the base of his skull, and he holds tight to Teddy's hoodie and doesn't let go.

Again, Teddy breaks the kiss. Nash keeps his eyes screwed shut and Teddy keeps his palms spread flat, one on his jaw and the other around the back of his neck.

"Does this mean you're thinking about it?"

"Nothin' to think about. You want me to go. Jo wants me

to go. And I..."

He's never handled being left behind well.

He opens his eyes and pulls Teddy forward half a step so they trip over each other's feet. It doesn't seem possible to get any closer, but all he wants is closer. He ducks forward until their foreheads press together. "You gotta scope out that town for me. Find me the nursing home with the most interesting residents. They gotta have good taste in TV programs."

"I'll put together a grading rubric," Teddy says, all rapid tongue and dark eyes, "and I'll find you a flower shop—one that sells forget-me-nots and tulips—and if there aren't any, I'll grow them mysel—"

Nash kisses him, no longer sweet and chaste, but a binding, searing promise made between grasping hands and hurt hearts. Teddy presses into him and Nash has him between his hands and for a moment, he can't breathe, because even though he has him and he's holding him and they're kissing under the moon—he wants, and he wants, and he wants.

It's several minutes before Nash remembers Mrs. Spinoza and Luke, waiting anxiously for word on Teddy. And so it's him that breaks away to send a text assuring her that he's got Teddy and he's safe.

"You were serious, right?" Teddy asks. His hands are in the pocket of his hoodie and his shoulders are curled in, reminiscent of the Teddy of their childhood, save his kiss-swollen lips.

Nash belatedly remembers to hit send and tucks away his phone. "About?"

Teddy licks his lips. "No more promises. We're really

doing this?"

Nerves tangle in his gut, but he nods. "So long as you hold up your end, I'll come."

Teddy creeps closer. "And my end was to call every day?"

"And find me a nursing home."

"Right, with good people."

"Interesting people," Nash corrects as Teddy takes his hands from his pocket and places them almost experimentally on Nash's hips. "And a flower shop."

"With forget-me-nots." Teddy leans in and his hands slip from Nash's hips around his waist. Seemingly satisfied with this new position, he cranes his neck to look at him.

"Are you okay? This was... I know this was hard for you."

Nash can't meet his eyes. "I'm terrified, Ted. This is all I know. This place... The people. It's all I know."

"I'll take care of everything, I swear. And we have time. We'll take it slow. As slow as you want. You don't have to go anywhere until you're ready."

"Okay." Part of him fears he'll never be ready, but for Teddy, for Jo, he says again, "Okay."

"Are you going to see me off at the airport?" Teddy asks.

Nash buries his face against Teddy's neck because he's never been allowed this close before, and because Teddy's leaving, and because he can't stand to see him disappointed.

"No."

He doesn't even see Jo off at the airport.

"Why not?"

He presses his forehead into Teddy's shoulder and admits, "I hate goodbyes."

Teddy smooths his hands up Nash's coat and presses them against his spine. "Is this our goodbye, then?"

It's one of them. There will be another when they load up the ATV. And another as Nash gets Teddy safely down the mountain. A third as they pass Uncle Darren in Red Oak Cemetery, and one more when they get to the hotel and Teddy goes inside and Nash drives away.

As long as he's the one driving in the end—

As long as it doesn't end with him watching helplessly—

Just as long as he doesn't get left, he can take it, but Nash is damn tired of bein' left all alone. He's due a change, even if it takes some leavin' on his part to get it.

THE EPISTOLARY PERIOD

Teddy
Nov 15th, 11:21 AM

Text me when your flight lands

Landed

Good

Teddy
Nov 16th, 9:57 AM

Ugh. Work sucks

Can't relate

You're unbearable

Teddy
Nov 19th, 2:05 PM

The coffee here is terrible

So don't drink it?

Preposterous

Ough my tummy

I don't know what you want
me to say

Teddy
Nov 23rd 10:46 AM

*Picture Message: a plate of
fluffy, moist, scrambled eggs*

Eggs.

get fucked

Teddy
Nov 26th 8:30 PM

*Picture Message: a blurry and
opaque selfie of Nash, Spencer,
and Walt*

The guys wanted me to send
you this

Can I make a request?

Shoot

Wipe the fingerprint off of your front lens.

...I thought I messed up
something in the settings.

Better?

*Picture Message: a selfie of
Nash frowning, the pink of his
scrubs just visible atop his*

shoulders

Old man allegations stay winning...

Picture ID: A postcard showing the green and blue slopes of the The Great Smokey Mountains –Tennessee.

The reverse side has a handwritten note addressed to Teddy Spinoza, that reads:

"Hey Ted, dropping off the quilt and thought I'd send you something too. Hope you're enjoying Hanukkah...unless it's one of the remembering ones and "enjoying" isn't the right word... This got dumb. The Post Office lady is staring. Okay. Sorry. Bye. - Nash"

December 11th

Nash,

Got your postcard! It had a near miss with the trash (thought it was an ad) but I caught it in time. Finished that quilt, huh? Got any pics? Not gonna lie I got attached to the thing. Maybe we could do a new one someday. One we can keep I mean. Sorry if that's lame.

I talked to Aunt Julie yesterday and she said you two did your bird watching and breakfast. Thanks for making time for her. I worry that... I dunno. I just worry. I'm glad you're there to pick up my slack even if it's not forever. She shut me down really hard when I suggested I should be the one to move to you guys. Guess I complained too much about rural living back in the day. She doesn't want me to resent her which I get, I guess.

Sometimes I think though, maybe she doesn't want me around. I know that sounds dumb but without Uncle Darren to remind us to cool off we can get into it pretty bad. And it's like... are we even related now? Uncle Darren was my dad's brother, so with him gone what are me and her? Maybe that's why she doesn't want me there. It's not like she asked to have a kid you know?

Did I tell you I hadn't seen Uncle Darren in over a year when he had his stroke? Biggest regret of my life and I worry me and Aunt Julie are gonna go the same way.

Sorry this got depressing. I'll include a picture of a puppy or something to make up for it. Text me a pic of the finished quilt when you get this!

    Yours,
    Teddy

PS. couldn't figure out how to make the printer do color sorry

Enclosed: a printed grayscale photo of a golden retriever puppy, ears perked and tongue lolling.

Teddy
Dec 16th 11:56 AM

Picture Message: A quilt of blues and whites. In the center is a fishbowl containing three goldfish. Some seams wobble and pucker.

Are we pen pals now?

Hey that's legit! Bet the next one turns out even better. I'll see if I can come up with a design. It's just geometry right?

And yes

We are

December 16th

Dear Teddy,

I've never had a pen pal before or been much good with words but I guess we can give it a shot. If this sucks you don't have to write back. I get it.

Sorry about Uncle Darren. I know it's not the same, but I know what you mean about the regret thing. If I'd known the last time I'd ever see him was... well the point is, I'm sorry.

Your aunt (and she is your aunt by the way) came to Jo's derby practice the other day. I think she's gonna turn into a mega fan. She's looking for things to keep busy I think. Bird watching wasn't it. She seemed restless, I guess. But she made Jo show her the tournament schedule coming up in a couple months. We'll keep her close. I promise. And for the record she loves you. I dunno about all the other stuff you're worried about but I know she loves you and family is something you choose for yourself, blood or not.

Spencer took a turn last week and hasn't really gotten back to his old self. Walt's worried. I'm worried. Those two have been glued at the hip since they arrived within a few weeks of each other. If Spence goes I don't think Walt'll be far behind. I hope they don't give him a new roommate. It's like Fort Knox in there. Probably booby trapped. Their PTSD plays nice together, but not so nice with anybody else.

Hey look at that. We both wrote about depressing shit. Something about letters I guess...

    Best,
    Nash

Enclosed: a dried sprig of forget-me-nots and a rough sketch of a sleeping dog

Teddy
Dec 19th 12:12 AM

Can I call?

> Give me 10. About to drive home

Ok

> Ok I'm home

Teddy is calling...

"Hey."

"Hey, sorry. I know it's late and you just got off work."

"It's alright. You mind if I put you on speaker and cook?"

"No, yeah, of course not. This is probably kind of stupid, anyway."

"I don't doubt it."

Teddy snorts. He takes an audible breath. "So... I don't really know how to ease into this, so I'm just going to blurt it out." He hesitates. "Jo's not around, is she?"

"Passed out. Can hear her snorin' from here. Everything okay?"

"Yeah, sort of. I just... I was talking to Luke, and he said I should tell you if it's on my mind and it's been on my mind, so here goes... I really like you."

"I—"

"I'm not done."

"Oh, sorry."

"It's fine. It's— I... I really like you, but I don't know how you feel about me. Don't say anything yet. I have to—" He blows out a breath. "After Uncle Darren passed, I was kind of in a, a bit of a spiral, I guess. He had his stroke, and I couldn't get there in time even though it was hours before he— And then my flight got canceled and the only reason I didn't miss his fucking funeral was because Aunt Julie called the director and begged him to push it back a day— Which, by the way, is a huge no-no in Judaism. The rabbi was so fucking judgy about it. One, because we flew him back to where he grew up *like he wanted* instead of getting him in the ground immediately, and then we delayed another day for me to get there. We're on God's shit list for sure.

"Umm, but anyway. Then you were there, right? And I was already... I wasn't handing everything very well. I was angry because I wasn't where I should have been. And I was angry because you weren't either and he loved you, and I wasn't there, and you weren't there, and it was all my fault because I was a dumb angry kid and—and you didn't go to the burial even though he would have wanted you there and that was my fault too because I can't ever let anything go. I have to— I have to break things and—"

"Teddy—"

"I'm almost done, I swear. I'm sorry. You said— When I first asked if you would move, you said no, and you said it was because I'm the same as I was when we were growing up."

"I didn't—"

"You *did* though. You said you wanted more calm and less storm, and I think we both know that when we were kids, I was all storm. And like I said, I really like you. I mean, it's stupid how much I still

— My point is, I'm not all storm anymore. I know you haven't really seen it because of everything that's been going on and I was kind of—of bouncing between extremes, and I can't promise I'm completely reformed or whatever, but I think I'm better? I think, you know, when things are normal, I think I'm more calm than storm. Luke hasn't given up on me yet and he's a bundle of raw nerves all the time, so—"

"Teddy, I like you too."

An exhale crackles across the line. Then, softly, Teddy says, "Oh."

"Sorry, I wasn't sure when else I'd be able to get a word in, but I like you and I like— I've always liked the storm."

"But you said—"

"I was being an asshole. I was all freaked out about... how fast things were changing, so I... I said that to make you leave. I'm sorry. I didn't know— I would've apologized sooner if I'd known it was messin' you up. I didn't mean it."

"Oh." Springs creak. "So... so you like the storm?"

"Yeah. It, uh, it wakes me up."

"Oh. And you like... me?"

"Ted, I haven't been able to get you out of my head for twenty years. Now that I've got a few kisses rattlin' 'round up here, that ain't likely gonna stop."

"Oh. You liked it then?"

Nash makes a breathless sound. Almost a laugh. "I been meaning to ask you something, actually."

"Kissing pointers? I'm not sure you need them."

"Thanks for that, but umm, no. It's just... Well, Jo's been tellin' everyone you're my boyfriend, but she's been callin' you that since grade school, so I wasn't sure..."

"Nash, we're looking at houses together."

"No, yeah, I know, but we never officially said— And that's years off still, so anything could— I just wanted to hear it from you. We're exclusive, right? We're—"

"I've been telling literally everyone that we're dating. Please don't make me walk that back."

"So we're exclusive?"

"Yes. All the love and respect for the poly people living their dreams, but I'm no good at sharing."

"Only child syndrome."

"Hey! But yeah. Does that sound good to you? Is that what you want?"

"Yeah. Yeah, it's all... Look, I don't know how to say it without sounding like a Hallmark movie—"

"I don't care. Just say it."

"It's cheesy."

"I think you owe me some cheese for lying to me."

"You're lactose intolerant."

"We all make sacrifices, sweetie."

Nash snorts. "Alright, well, I... I've never been too good at wanting things. I think because of how I grew up with my old man 'n' all— Well, I'd sooner swim along in Jo's wake than dream up wants of my own, but you fly in the face of all that. You always have. Even when I thought wanting you would be the death of me, I wanted you anyway."

There's a long pause before Teddy says, "You're not allowed to claim you're bad at words anymore."

Nash laughs softly. "Well, it took me about six weeks to come up with those. Maybe I'm not bad, just slow."

"I can work with slow." He pauses, then asks, "How come you thought I'd be the death of you?"

"I didn't think *you* would; I thought me wanting you would. I thought... Well, it wasn't 'till Jo was in college and tellin' me stories about what her classmates were gettin' up to that I realized the world isn't half as hateful as I thought."

"It can still be pretty hateful to people like us."

"Not like I thought, though. Daddy trashed my hip for bein' talked to out of turn. I thought for sure he'd've killed me for how I felt about you, and I thought everyone would think him right for it."

"That's my fault about your hip. I should've kept my mouth shut."

"How could you have known? All you knew were good, kind folk. You couldn't have known what he'd do to me for you callin' out his bullshit."

"I still think—"

"I don't think anything of it beyond the day-to-day and you shouldn't either."

"But if I hadn't—"

Nash's tone goes sharp. "Teddy, I'm serious. Don't be lookin' at me like somethin' you broke. You're the last person I should have to worry about thinking me damaged."

"I— No, you're right. Sorry."

There's a fraught pause, but when Nash responds, it's gentle.

"It's alright."

There's another pause, then Teddy fills the silence.

"How's your dinner coming along?"

"Pitiful. Forgot to cook it."

Teddy laughs. "Well, I'll let you go so you can—"

"You don't have to," Nash says quickly. "I mean, it's late, you have work in the morning, but if you want—"

"Tomorrow is *Sunday* and I work office hours. If you don't mind the distraction—"

"How 'bout we turn on the cameras so you can keep me on task."

"Deal."

Teddy's face fills the screen and softens into a smile. "Hey."

"Hey, yourself. You usually go around half-naked?"

Teddy pats his bare chest, then ducks away. "Sorry, I was pacing. Hold on."

He reappears, looking tousled but now wearing a deep blue thermal with the top buttons undone over his clavicle.

"Better?"

Nash makes a considering sound in his throat as he takes him in. "Can't say it is, no."

Teddy laughs, eyes bright, smile daring. He lowers his voice. "Are you saying you want me to take it off?"

"I... Well—"

Teddy cackles. "Look at you blush! If I was there in person, I'd be all over you right now."

"Don't tease," Nash says weakly.

Teddy softens. "I really want to kiss you again."

"Yeah. I mean, me too."

"I like talking to you and seeing your face. You're a terrible texter."

"I know. You and Jo can form a complaint committee."

"Bold of you to assume we haven't."

"If you had, I'd already have a filing cabinet full of 'em."

"Aw, I don't think I have that many complaints."

"Jo's got enough for a small army. She tried to smother me in my sleep yesterday because my nose was whistling."

Teddy laughs. "She was well within her right to commit fratricide for that."

"So I've heard," Nash says dryly.

Teddy just smiles. He asks, "Can we do this again tomorrow?"

"You quittin' me already? Pan ain't even hot yet."

"No, no. I just wanted to ask while I was thinking about it."

"You said you'd call every day. So far, 'every day' is much spottier than I thought."

"I didn't want to be annoying."

"Darlin', you annoyed me without pause for six years and I still walked up that hill every day to see you. If you want to call me, call."

"What if I want to call but I don't have clothes on?"

"Uh... Well, maybe text first. Give me a chance to... to get in a similar state."

Eyes hot on him, Teddy declares, "I'm going to visit soon."

"I thought you used up all your PTO."

"I'll come for a weekend."

"I work weekends."

He tips back his head and groans. "Maybe that would be enough! Maybe... I just want to— It's so frustrating that I can finally say all this stuff, but I still can't touch you."

"Well. You know, I been thinkin'. I never take PTO except for funerals, so I kinda have a stack. Maybe I could come to you."

Teddy's back is ramrod straight. "Really? Would you want to? It's the dead of winter and I'd have to work."

"Well, if we time it for the weekend... You office types get New Years off, don't you? It's on a Thursday this year. You'd only have to request off Friday."

"You looked into this," Teddy accuses.

Nash hesitates, then admits, "Already took the time off too. You haven't made plans that weekend, have you?"

"If I did, I'll cancel. Did you buy a ticket?"

"I got one in my cart. Didn't want to pull the trigger 'till—"

"Let me buy it."

"I can afford—"

"No, I want— Let me treat you, please? It's your first time coming out here and I want it— I don't want you to have any regrets."

Nash sighs. "Ted, I'm not gonna—"

"Please? It's winter in Minnesota. The odds are already against me."

"Alright. Okay, fine. I'll text you the link."

"Don't bother. I'm already looking. Would you hate me if I booked you first class?"

"Would I have to sit with a bunch of stuffy money types?"

"Yeah, never mind. I got a little excited. Stepping back in my lane now."

"Should I bring anything?"

"Just your handsome face. I'll take care of everything, I promise."

Teddy
Dec 30th 6:04 AM

I don't have a passport

Nash

First of all you're adorable

Second I feel like in my heart of hearts
you should know better as a 32yo man
even if you've never traveled before

Looked it up. Don't need for
domestic flights. Thanks for
not being a dick about my first
time on a plane.

Third I can't wait to kiss you

Any time babe (˘ ³˘)❤

I don't have to let you kiss me

Picture Message: shocked-pikachu.jpg

Alright okay I'm sorry

Mmm

I'M SORRY

Nash?

NASH???

Teddy
Dec 30th 4:12 PM

I feel like I'm forgetting something

Whatever it is I'll buy you a new one

No it feels important

I mean what all is there? Toothbrush charger underwear you're set

I have all of those

I don't know

It's probably fine

THE CAR KEYS ARE IN MY POCKET

JO IS MAD

LMAOOOOOOO

Best case scenario tbh

The flight attendant won't let me off the plane

Do NOT get off that plane Nashery Owens

We will overnight her the keys

DO NOT GET OFF THE PLANE

Nash???

please tell me you're still on the plane

                                        I'm still on the plane.

Don't scare me like that fukc

                              It's gonna cost $300 for her to
                                                get home

This means she doesn't have to pick you
up monday

Small win?

I'm gonna tell her that

                                              No don't

Too late

oh

oh she's MAD mad

                                                Teddy.

I've made a grave error

                              The flight attendant is telling
                                me to turn off my phone...
                                             Good luck

Teddy
Dec 30th 6:09 PM

Landed

Not sure what to do next

Disembark. Follow the crowd. I'll find you.

Ok

There are so many people here
and it's massive... Where are
you?

Teddy is calling...

Teddy
Jan 1st 11:33 AM

Where did you go? I left for 20 min...

Next door

Your neighbor sounded
distressed. It was her cat
apparently. Now we're having
tea somehow...

Warm tea I mean

I don't understand the weird draw you
have to old people.

On my way over.

Bring sugar. She's low.

You're unbelievable

Teddy
Jan 2nd 12:50 PM

Orange juice eggs bread spinach chicken
something sweet

Why did you send me this?
Aren't you in the bathroom?

Sorry didn't mean to send. Was making
the list

Well you forgot condoms

Trust me I don't need to write that one
down

Condoms

Ha

Shut up

Teddy
Jan 3rd 7:48 PM

*Picture Message: Back view of Nash
standing in a sea of people in a posh,
minimalistic open room with a domed*

ceiling. He's wearing a ball cap, jeans, boots, and gray flannel, has a duffel bag on his shoulder, and is holding his phone to his ear.

Picture Message: Selfie of Nash and Teddy, cheeks nearly touching, Teddy beaming, and Nash blurred. It's dark and snow is falling around them. Their ears are red with cold.

Picture Message: Nash, in his flannel and ball cap, is grimacing at the camera with his hands in his armpits standing beside a squashy, knee-high snowman that's listing to one side. Overhead is an outdoor light affixed to an apartment building.

Picture Message: Hat gone, ears and nose pink with cold, Nash is sitting on a brown couch frowning over a mug of hot chocolate while Teddy smashes a kiss against his cheek.

Picture Message: A selfie of Nash and Teddy nestled together in a heap of blankets on a brown couch. Nash is smiling softly. Teddy is half out of frame and looking at Nash.

Picture Message: Nash is sprawled face down on a stripped bed. A thick comforter can be seen on the floor, but only a dark sheet covers his backside while freckled limbs and torso splay out from under it.

*Picture Message: Nash bundled up in a
too-small coat, knit hat, and mittens
pushing a shopping cart through a slushy
parking lot. He doesn't look happy.*

*Picture Message: Nash and Teddy kissing
in the front seat of a sedan. Visible out the
back window is a sign reading "Drop Off."*

You took a lot more pictures
than I did

Send them to me

*Picture Message: A blurry
photo with no discernible
subject. Snowflakes are falling
through the yellow glow of the
parking lot lamps. The back
end of a beige Honda Accord is
visible in the right corner.*

*Picture Message: a close-up of
a lopsided snowman with no
nose and gravel eyes.*

*Picture Message: Teddy sitting
cross-legged in bed with a
computer in his lap, glasses on
his nose as he frowns at the
screen, his complexion washed
blue. His hair is a wild mess,
and he's shirtless.*

*Picture Message: a blurred
close-up of Teddy, laughing.*

So you're still a terrible photographer

Thank christ I've got you

Bout to take off I'll text you
when we land

<3

Teddy
Jan 3rd 10:15 PM

Got my bag about to head
home. It's crazy how much
warmer it is here.

No frost to scrape huh?

None

Miss you already

Teddy is calling...

Teddy
Jan 7th, 11:56 PM

Check out this listing! Four bedroom two
bath farm house. Spacious kitchen. Large
patio. Perfect for entertai...

Check out this listing! Two bedroom
bungalow located ten minutes outside St.
Cloud. Hurry this offer won't la...

Check out this listing! Two bedroom one
bath. This charming starter features a
walk-in closet, his & her sinks, an...

You're killing me

You don't like them?

I know the farmhouse is kind of pricey but
I thought you'd like the location. It's a bit
more rural you know?

If you and Jo wanna share links
and shop around that's fine. I
really don't mind but it feels
shitty for me. Since I'm waiting
for people to die n all.

Oh

Ok yeah sorry

I'm not mad. I trust you guys to
pick something I'll like.

Sure drop that responsibility on me (●_●;)

Maybe looking won't feel so
wrong after a year or two...

How many residents have you made
promises to again?

Five

Gotcha

Teddy
Feb 10th 12:26 AM

I'm home. Call?

Teddy is calling...

Teddy
Mar 5th 12:19 AM

Home. Call?

Teddy is calling...

Teddy
Mar 25th 12:40 AM

Home

Teddy is calling...

Teddy
Mar 29th 6:37 PM

What are you doing?

I miss you

Calling Teddy...

Teddy
Apr 16th 6:24 AM

Picture Message: a small indoor plot of forget-me-nots in bloom.

Teddy
May 13th 9:11 AM

Text me when you can talk.
Don't call.

??? In a meeting give me 20

Nvm left early. What's going on are you
okay??

I'm fine. Jo just had an epic
breakdown. That 8 week long
work thing was for a school
shooting apparently. She didn't
say anything. I didn't know
until she started crying about
me throwing out stale
Cheetos.

Shit. Where is she now?

With me. Asleep. I feel like I'm
not saying the right things. I
don't know what to do.

I don't think there are right things for this
kind of shit. Just keep doing what you're
doing. Be there.

Yeah ok. I wish there was an
easy button.

Or a reset button.

Felt

Maybe you should host a girls night. Get
Aunt Julie involved. She'll eat it up.

Now you're trying to torture me

I would never •🐻•

Will you talk to Luke? Maybe he has some advice...idk

Yes. I'll let you know ASAP

Thanks

And Teddy?

You make me happy. You know that right?

I'm figuring it out

You make me happy too

<3

<333

It's not a competition

That's what losers always say <33333333333

Teddy
Jun 10th 9:11 AM

Having a fucking week

Call?

Can't. Stuck at the shop (¬_¬")

Shop? Car troubles?

Yeah.

Some idiot drifted into my lane and to
avoid him I slammed into this fuck off
huge pothole.

Blew my tire. Bent the rim.

Now they're telling me the passenger axle
got fucked up too and needs replaced.

Should've let him hit me so his insurance
could pay for it.

That sucks.

Yeah

And on Monday the apartment above me
started leaking into my bathroom and
there's still a big hole in the ceiling I'm
waiting for the drywall guy to patch

I can hear everything up there now

I thought they were loud before

I'm just tired

Watch for the third

???

Bad things happen in threes.
You've had two. After the third
you'll be good for a bit.

I didn't realize you were superstitious.

It's just how things usually
shake out.

Well I bought the wrong coffee last night
so I must be out the other side.

No it'll be equal to the first
two.

Great.

Looking forward to it.

Teddy
Jun 11th 2:46 PM

You did this to me

I had Shavuot plans Nash

I was going to eat so much cheesecake
and do unholy things to the toilet you
don't even know

What?

I'm in the hospital

Calling Teddy...

Teddy
Jun 11th 5:34 PM

> Flight's gonna get in at almost
> midnight so we'll see you
> tomorrow

> Bright and early

> As early as visiting hours will
> let us I mean

You seriously don't have to come. I'm fine.
Not my first allergic reaction.

Wait

We?? Is Jo coming?

I really don't want this to turn into a
whole thing

> Not Jo. Julie.

You told my aunt? Nash. Come on.

> She misses you. It's as good a
> reason as any for a visit.

> Besides I can replace your axle
> while I'm in town. Save you on
> labor.

You know how to do that?

> Yeah it's easy. Could have it
> done before you're released if

you want.

No no I need to supervise

You don't trust me?

I trust you. I want to watch.

Oh ok I can show you how if
you want.

I have zero interest in learning car
mechanics

Oh ok

OH

;)

You're so fucking precious I could die

Well you're in the hospital.
They could probably bring you
back.

Opportunity is ripe!

Teddy
Jun 12th 10:34 PM

*Picture message: a pair of denim-clad legs
sticking out from under a beige Honda
Accord—one sticking out straight while
the other is bent at the knee.*

*Picture message: Nash, ball cap
backwards, mallet in vinyl-gloved hand,
frowning at the rusted metal where the
tire should be.*

Just so you know what's going in my spank
bank

                              80% flattered 20% objectified

A respectable ratio. I offer no apology.

Teddy
Jun 13th 9:59 AM

                              We're at a booth in the back

Order me an iced tea. I'll be there in 5

                                              Sweet?

Unsweetened

                                        Yuck. Fine.

<33333

Teddy
Jun 13th 9:04 PM

                                              Home

Teddy is calling...

Teddy
Jul 20th 9:04 PM

How was practice?

Exhausting

Ready to drop

Eat first

Yes mother

Want company?

Won't be any good. I'm going to inhale a
sandwich and pass out

I don't mind

Just wanna see you

Teddy is calling...

Teddy
Jul 29th 7:51 PM

This storm is wild

I swear the building is swaying

Don't like that. Can you stay
with Luke or someone?

I'm sure it's fine. Just really windy. Lots of
lightning. I'll send you a video.

Can you just ask?

Are you serious? It's just a storm.

I work tomorrow

It'd be different if I wasn't 900 miles away Teddy.

Please?

Ok fine I'll ask Luke

Thank you

Teddy
Jul 29th 8:28 PM

Video Message: The video opens on an iron-barred one-story balcony. It's dark but for the parking lamps. The slap of rain on cars and concrete is loud. The rain turns white as the wind drives it sideways. Lightning momentarily blanks the screen and Luke is heard muttering, "Jesus."

Wow that's incredible

I know right?

Also Luke has brownies so I forgive you for being a worry wart

He bakes when he's stressed

And he's always stressed so

He's a good friend to have

I'm so relieved.

You should be.

Teddy
Aug 14th 3:28 PM

Walt went last night

Funeral Tuesday

Let me see if I can get away last minute

I thought Spence was the one not doing well?

Yeah. Took us by surprise.

Oh. I'm sorry. May his memory be a blessing.

It's alright. I think Spence is gonna fade fast without him though. We're getting things ready just in case. It happens like this sometimes... Nothin for it but to keep em comfortable.

I guess.

Teddy
Aug 14th 4:42 PM

PTO approved. I'll see you tomorrow
night.

> Ok. Spence went. Might do
> two Tuesday. Checking with
> families. Stay tuned.

May his memory be a blessing

Good luck

Teddy
Aug 15th 4:15 PM

> Turns out Spencer's family's a
> real nasty bunch. None of em
> are coming. Walt's family liked
> the double funeral idea though
> so that's what we're doing.

What the hell? None of them?

> Bunch of homophobes. His
> daughter said some real ugly
> things to our social worker.
> Had her in tears.

Wait

Walt and Spence were together?

No Walt was straight. Spence
was dishonorably discharged
for being gay in the 70s and
Walt's been in that chair since
he got back from Nam. He had
big opinions about how the
military treats its people. They
linked up day one at cherished
hope and have been best
friends since.

Kind of a relief that they went
so close. I was worried.

It's kind of poetic.

Sometimes life works out.

It does

Teddy
Aug 15th 5:03 PM

I don't want to be insensitive...

Give it a week Ted

Yeah ok

Teddy
Aug 15th 11:28 PM

Landed. Only brought a carry-on so I'll see
you in a few.

Gonna learn how to iron on
your funeral duds?

...didn't think about that...

I'm sure you'll pick it up quick

(;˘•_•˘)

You don't want to do it for me?

No.

Stop texting and get out here.
Jo's been whining for twenty
minutes.

Ugh

Jo's there?

I'll take my time.

Might grab a snack.

I miss you

Running

:)

★❤✿ TEDDYBEAR✿ ❤★
Aug 17th 9:42 PM

Next time we should get a hotel room

> Jo told me she's going to

Even better

What if we booked the room right next to hers lmao

> Gross. No.

It was a joke!

About to take off. I'll text you from MN

> Fly safe

★❤✿ TEDDYBEAR✿ ❤★
Aug 17th 10:15 PM

> I miss you already

> Two days wasn't long enough

> You forgot your jersey

Landed. I didn't forget it. Let's plan a long trip for after hockey season. I don't care which state. These little ones are kind of fucking me up.

Let's do it here. I'll take a week off and you can come to one of Jo's bouts.

Are you okay?

That sounds good

Yeah I'm just tired. And sad. I want to be together.

Me too

Text me when you're home?

I will.

Home

Calling ★❤✿*TEDDYBEAR*✿ ❤★...

★❤✿ TEDDYBEAR✿ ❤★
Aug 21st 10:11 AM

Gloria Marie and Martin

?

Technically Martin hasn't asked for anything but I still want to see it through. He doesn't have any family left and he doesn't really have coherent days anymore. I worry he'll just... get swept away when the time comes.

Oh

Thanks for telling me.

For the record I hope they all live full
happy lives

Me too

★❤♣ TEDDYBEAR♣ ❤★
Oct 3rd 10:19 PM

*Picture Message: Teddy and Zook wearing
matching white-and-blue jerseys, arms
around each other's shoulders and
smiling. Zook is missing a tooth.*

Ouch

He's a little loopy on pain meds.

Keeps asking the nurse if the tooth fairy
will still come if he lets the dentist put it
back lol

What's his wife think?

They are so horny for each other it's
disgusting

Jealous?

Yes

The second I get you here we're going to
fill the fine jar to the brim with PDA

I'm not really into PDA

Dammit Nash let me have this

What else do they fine for?

Pet names. Being affectionate. That kind
of thing

Well honey it sounds like we've
got options

I want to grope you in the locker room
though (˘•_•˘)

...I'll think about it

Lmk if there's anything I can do to
persuade you   (人^ᴗ^)

★❤✿ TEDDYBEAR✿ ❤★
Oct 31st 1:26 AM

Don't answer if you're trying to
sleep but I think a resident is
transferring to a different
nursing home because he
found out I'm gay. Not sure
how I feel about it.

What the fuck? Good riddance I guess.

Who was it? How did he find out? Have
you been making eyes at other guys ⌐_⌐

Dale

I sort of told him

Who the hell is dale

And how do you sort of tell someone
you're gay?

I'm not making eyes at anyone

Not that I think you should hide it or
whatever

I'm just curious and you're being
frustratingly vague

Per the norm so shame on me I guess

Nash?

Sorry I was getting ready for
bed. Didn't think you'd be
awake. Don't you have a game
tonight? I'm laying down now
so I can talk

Nash

Please details

Yes game day Sunday but that's not
important rn

Sarah B. Elisa

Are you in trouble?

>Dale has been our problem
resident since he got here. I
don't think I've talked about
him much because. Well. I
don't like him. But he thinks
we're best friends or
something because we're both
white guys surrounded by
women and minorities. Or he
thought that until last night
when I got tired of pretending
and told him I'm gay.

Holy shit

I repeat

Good riddance

>You type too fast

Built for speed sorry not sorry

Maybe you should get good

>I don't think I'm in trouble

That's good

>But no one has told me
anything. I only know because I
overheard the nurses
complaining that he threw a fit
when they couldn't get his
records sent to the new place

the second he asked.

Oh.

Do you think anyone will be mad?

I mean

If he tells your boss or your boss's boss or
whoever do you think you'll get in trouble
or fired or anything?

I think anyone with eyes and
sense who's seen me and you
together already knows I'm
gay. If they didn't fire me then
they won't now.

I think you're overestimating how easy to
read you are

Have I mentioned before that it's difficult?

Bc it is

Not complaining just saying maybe we
shouldn't assume they know and are cool
with it...

I think you're underestimating
how different I am when
you're around.

Cute if true

Jo likens it to a sad moldy
pumpkin turning into a

                              princess if that helps

Lmao I love Jo

                              I'm telling her

DO NOT

NASH NO

You're the worst

Top ten anime betrayal

                    She said keep it in your pants
                         she's trying to sleep

I thought you were in bed?

Tell her I listened to that song she told me
about and it sucks

                    I am. She's just across the hall.

                                          Ok

                    She said I have to divorce you

                                          :(

Don't you dare.

Tell her I have a better lawyer and would
get her in the divorce so watch out.

                         And leave me alone?

I would never

You have a lawyer?

I'd sell her to the circus and then me and
you could get undivorced

Kinda?

Zook is a lawyer

He'd do it pro bono

He sort of loves you

Like I mean he thinks you're good for me
or whatever

And that you're cool

In a dorky secretly 80 kind of way I mean

Hey Ted?

Yeah?

Have I mentioned texting you
is like strapping my brain to
propeller and cranking the
motor?

I'm going to assume you mean that in a
good way

Like oh wow talking to my beloved
boyfriend really gets my motor revving.

Remind me to call next time.

Wow hurtful.

Well I mean

It would've been

But now I know you turn into a pretty
pretty princess when I'm around (^.^ʃ♡ʅ

I'm going to sleep now.

WAIT

What

I miss you. Call me when you wake up?

I will. Now sleep so you'll be
awake for it.

Putting my ringer on full volume so I don't
miss it

Cute

Goodnight (ˇ ³ˇ)

Night <3

★ ❤✿ TEDDYBEAR✿ ❤★
Oct 31st 9:37 PM

*Picture message: A close-up selfie of
Teddy, frowning at the camera, hair wild,
damp, and held at bay by a white
sweatband. There is a bloody cut across
the bridge of his nose, which is bent at a
strange angle.*

Calling ★ ♥ ✿*TEDDYBEAR* ✿ ♥★ ...

Calling ★ ♥ ✿*TEDDYBEAR* ✿ ♥★ ...

Answer the fucking phone
Teddy

Calling ★ ♥ ✿*TEDDYBEAR* ✿ ♥★ ...

Can't. No phones in the locker room

Then leave.

Calling ★ ♥ ✿*TEDDYBEAR* ✿ ♥★ ...

"If I'd known you'd freak out I wouldn't have—"

"What the hell happened? Turn on your camera and let me see it."

Teddy huffs, irritated, but a moment later his face fills the screen. He's standing in a bland hallway and purple bruises are blooming around his eyes.

"I'm fine."

"Your nose is broken. How does that even happen? You were wearing your helmet, weren't you?"

"Well, yeah... until I took it off."

"Why would you do that?"

"So I could punch the other guy better."

There's a fraught pause. Then Nash says, "This happened because you were fighting."

"In my defense, this guy is a total pigeon. Every time we play him, he fouls everything and this time he slew foot Peaches and didn't even get a penalty for it. Somebody needed to get him off the ice."

"What's slew foot?"

"It's a dirty move where you knock someone's feet out so they fall on their back, which hurts and is dangerous when you're on ice with a bunch of burly dudes with knives on their feet. Deli had to check one of their guys into the boards to keep him from goring Peach."

"So, you were defending your teammate?"

"*Yes*. From an *asshole* who sucks at hockey and makes up for it by doing us dirty whenever he gets half an opportunity."

"Okay." Nash sucks in a deep breath and blows it out. "Okay. So it wasn't the puck?"

"No, no, nothing that bad."

"How's your head?"

"Fine. My face hurts, but my head feels fine."

"Okay, that's good." Nash scrubs his hand through his hair, flashing the gray at the roots. "I'm sorry. I didn't mean to freak out."

"I probably shouldn't have sent it without context."

"Not being able to answer the phone didn't help either," Nash points out.

"Yeah, yeah, I hear you. I'll think it through next time. You were chill about Zook's tooth thing, so I didn't even think about it. I thought you'd think it was funny."

"I'm not dating Zook. And if you had a concussion, I'm nine hundred miles away. I don't like feeling helpless."

Teddy's expression softens. "A few more months and then I get an entire week to annoy you until you send me packing."

"Darlin', there's nothin' you can do in a week that would annoy me enough to want you gone."

"*Fine!*"

Teddy turns toward the voice out of frame. "Fuck off, Peach. What are you even doing out here?"

"Coach is looking for you," Peaches says, out of view. "Couldn't tell if he wanted to give you an earful or an award. We were all looking for an opportunity to stick Turner."

"You alright? You had a hard fall."

"Oh, you know me. I'm just Peachy."

"Ugh, fuck off."

"Tell lover boy I say *hiiii!*"

A door closes, and Teddy faces the phone with pink-tipped ears. "Peaches says hi."

"I heard, lover boy."

"Can I call you later?"

"Yeah. Make sure you ice your nose and get it set."

He touches it tenderly. "I was thinking I might leave it. I kinda like it."

"You gotta breathe through that for the rest of your life. Set it."

"Yeah, alright, fine. I'll talk to you soon."

"I'll be waiting."

★❤♣ TEDDYBEAR♣ ❤★

Nov 14th 10:26 PM

We lost

We're out of the championships

I'm sorry.

Call?

No I'm on my way to the gym to hit stuff.

After?

Maybe tomorrow

I'm going to be a shithead if I talk to anyone tonight

I'm used to it

Not in a joking mood Nash

Ok sorry.

Call when you're up for it. Even
if it's late.

Sure

★♥♣ TEDDYBEAR♣ ♥★
Nov 15th 12:02 AM

★♥♣TEDDYBEAR♣ ♥★ is calling...

"Hey."

"Hey," Teddy says, glumly. "I just wanted to say I'm sorry about earlier."

"It's okay."

"It's not. I was being a dick. I missed an easy pass that could have turned the game around and I'm up my ass about it."

"Did the gym help?"

"Not really, but I knew I wouldn't be able to sleep without apologizing first. And you deserve more than a half-assed text."

"Are you going to sleep now?"

"I'd just glare at the ceiling for hours. Was gonna try a movie. See if that takes my mind off it."

"What movie?"

Teddy sighs. "I don't know, Nash. I haven't gotten that far."

"Pick one I can watch too. We'll watch together."

"I'm not— I won't be good company."

"I'm not asking you to be. Put me on video and let's watch a movie. You're not supposed to talk during movies anyway."

Teddy sighs again, but a moment later the video flicks to life, revealing a plain white ceiling. His voice is echoey and distant as he says, "Let me look through what I have on DVD."

"Are you— Nevermind."

"What?"

"I was just... Are you hiding on purpose?"

"I'm not *hiding*," Teddy snaps. "I'm picking out a movie like you wanted."

"Okay. Sorry I asked."

"This isn't working. I only wanted to call and apologize, but I'm making everything worse."

"Nothing's worse. You don't have to be a peppy, happy boy every time we talk."

"I'm so angry with myself and I can hear what a shithead I'm being to you and it's making me angrier."

"Then let's stop talking. Pick a movie and I'll keep quiet."

"I don't get what the point of this call is if we're not going to talk."

There's a shuffling of plastic cases off screen.

"Wow, you're really not going to talk to me." Teddy continues in a grumble, "I hate it when you stonewall me. You're too good at it."

More shuffling. Plastic against plastic.

An irritated sigh precedes Teddy appearing on the screen with a scowl etched in tired lines across his face. He blinks and his expression softens, nearly into a smile.

"Don't smile like that when you see me. You're going to give me a complex." His shoulders unbunch and he sinks until his chin rests low on the table beside the couch. He suddenly looks exhausted.

"I wish you were here. I could go for a hug. And maybe if you were in the audience, I wouldn't have sucked so bad."

He turns his cheek against the wood, and the view on the screen becomes all russet curls.

"Do you ever resent me for not moving to you? Sometimes I do."

"No," Nash says.

"Never? Sometimes I think I'm the most selfish bastard on the planet. You're there. Aunt Julie's there. Uncle Darren... I stayed for what? Hockey? A sport I'm not even good at? What's the point? Why am I doing this to us if all I do is lose?"

"You didn't stay for hockey."

"What did I stay for then? I thought it was hockey."

"You stayed for Luke and Jam and Deli and Benz and Peaches—"

Teddy snorts. "I definitely didn't stay for Peaches."

"You love those guys and they love you. I'm moving because you deserve to keep the family you've found, even if you never score another touchdown."

Teddy picks up his head to glare into the camera. "I know you know touchdowns are football."

"You got me. I just wanted to see you smile."

Teddy ducks his head as the aforementioned smile curls his lips.

"What movie did you pick for us?" Nash asks.

Teddy holds up a case.

"Good. What snack are you making?"

"I've got a bag of those frozen sweet potato fries. I was gonna eat the whole thing and call it dinner."

"Okay, I was thinking popcorn."

"You're so classic. Hey, Nash?"

"Mmm?"

"Thanks for being a stubborn bastard."

"Can I get that in writing?"

"Absolutely not."

"Hey, Ted?"

"Yeah?"

"Happy anniversary."

Surprise flicks across his features. Then he closes his eyes and drops his forehead to the table with a thud.

"Fuck."

★❤✿ TEDDYBEAR✿ ❤★
Jan 12th 11:50 PM

Apparently me taking a week
off is equivocal to the
apocalypse.

That's sad man

When we live together I'm going to
work/life balance the hell out of you.

You already have. I've taken
more PTO in the past year than
I have in a decade.

It was mostly funerals before.

If you're trying to make me pity you you're
winning (˘-_-˘)

How do you do those so fast?

What? The faces? (⩿)

Yeah they're cute. I don't even
know where to find half that
stuff on my keyboard.

Oh me neither lol there's a website

kawaiiface.net

Click to copy and then

(-_-。)人(。-_-。) profit

Are you serious? This whole
time I thought you were so

smart and creative but you're
just clicking buttons...

Are you going to say it or kawaii it? (^o^)

Fine hold on

This is how you make me feel
(=Д=)彡╶┴──┴ but also
(/)w(\) and
(人´∀`)♬ and (not right now
bc I'm (¬_¬") but soon I'll want
to (*￣3)(ε￣ *)

youre so fucking precious

three weeks is too long

it's killing me how bad I miss you

Calling ★❤✿*TEDDYBEAR*✿ ❤★ ...

★❤✿ TEDDYBEAR✿ ❤★
Jan 25th 1:14 PM

Chicken fried steak or chicken
and dumplings?

Got a recipe for either that doesn't mix
meat and milk?

Oh fuck. Hold on.

A familiar lament of those who try to feed
the dietary nightmare that is Theodore
Spinoza.

You don't have to worry about it

Really

I'm pretty good at fending for myself

> Shut up I'm not gonna invite
> you here and not feed you. It's
> not that hard. What about pot
> roast?

With potatoes?

> As I recall you're allergic. I was
> thinking carrots and sprouts
> unless you've got an objection
> to either. If pressed I could do
> yams.

Carrots and sprouts sound good.

> Cheesecake for dessert?

I'm lactose intolerant sweatie

> Yup. So yes to cheesecake?

You realize what this will do to our sexy
times right?

> I've got a figure. Cheesecake?

Yes please

I can't wait

For reasons more than cheesecake

Obviously

Obviously

You're the light of my life

Mmm

I desire you carnally

More than cheesecake?

Let's be reasonable

(¬_¬)

★❤✿ TEDDYBEAR✿ ❤★
Jan 30th 6:26 PM

The guys keep changing your contact in
my phone. If I didn't have my recents I'd
never find you

What did they change it to?

uwu babyboy uwu

Haha did you leave it?

No

(˘-_-˘) I'm not your baby boy?

FINE

Picture Message: A screenshot of the

*above conversation. The recipient is
named, "I love this asshole."*

Say it to my face on Saturday.

Yeah?

Yeah. First thing. I mean it.

Ok

★❤✿ TEDDYBEAR✿ ❤★
Feb 5th 4:12 PM

Touchdown

I'll meet you at baggage claim

Will you judge me if I run across the
terminal and leap into your arms?

I'll be disappointed if you don't

CHAPTER TWELVE
Welcome home cheater

Nash's cane hits polished tile with a clatter an instant before Teddy slams into him at a full run. He barely keeps from toppling as Teddy wraps his legs around his waist and seals their mouths, swallowing his surprised oath. Before he can reciprocate the kiss, Teddy moves on, pressing lips against cheek, jaw, nose, and eyebrow.

"Ted—"

The first murmured *I love you* lances Nash's heart with shocking vibrancy. His ears are ringing by the second, and by the third he's forgotten all about the crowded baggage claim and his burning arms as they support Teddy's solid weight.

He cinches his arms tight, cranes to find Teddy's lips,

and says in a rushed whisper, "I love you too."

Teddy's palms bracket his face as they sink into each other, brief kisses interrupted by murmurs of longing and relief, noses pressed to cheeks and fingers holding tight.

Someone coughs.

Nash is the one to pull away. Teddy chases, but he finds only cheek as Nash turns his head.

"Your bag," he says, breathless. "We'll be stuck here longer if we miss it."

Teddy groans but stops trying to kiss him.

"I hate when you get rational."

"You'd hate being stuck at the airport all day more."

Untangling is a careful dance, but one they manage without experiencing an uncomfortable meeting with the floor. Nash's arms are grateful, but his flesh and soul mourn the loss.

"That's what's so frustrating about it." Teddy stoops to collect Nash's cane. "I can't complain when it's for my benefit."

Teddy presses the handle into Nash's left hand, laces his fingers with the right, and the anxious thrum under Nash's skin eases.

He looks past sideways stares and a trio of glaring middle-aged women to the conveyor belt where a line of unfamiliar bags lap around a large pillar, then disappear through the flap on the other side.

Teddy tucks against Nash's side as though he too feels the unbearable distance.

"Did Jo come?"

"I, uh, asked her not to."

It earned him a disgusted look and silence—save for the

rapid tapping against her phone as she arranged other plans
—but she must have seen his wisdom because she didn't
pitch a fit.

"Smart. Thoughtful. Know any secluded spots we could
park?"

"She's staying with Garrett for the week. We've got the
house to ourselves."

Teddy presses a kiss to the underside of his wrist and
murmurs, "The house that's a whole hour away?"

Warm all over, Nash says, "Oh. I'll, uh—I'll find us a
spot."

"Excuse me?"

A wave of unease washes over Nash as he turns to find a
pair of college-aged girls cautiously approaching them. He
vaguely recognizes them from earlier while he was waiting.
They were sitting together chatting over coffee and he
thought them friends, but he revises that assumption upon
seeing their linked hands.

The dark-skinned one says, "We just wanted to say hi
and, umm, thanks."

"For what?"

Teddy knocks Nash with his elbow and smiles at the
girls. "He'll catch up. Have a good one, okay?"

"Thanks, we will."

The blonde blurts, "Y'all're really sweet." Then she tugs
her partner away and they exit the baggage claim, giggling
and bumping against each other, fingers laced.

Teddy looks up at him and snorts. "You are so red."

"What was that?"

"The magic of gay PDA. Nothing puts baby gays at ease
like older gays macking on each other in public with wild

abandon."

"You're tryin' to talk me into letting you grope me in front of the hockey team, aren't you?"

Teddy tucks back against his side and smiles up at him. "Is it working?"

His little heart is working overtime trying to adjust to having Teddy so near and so affectionate after so long apart. It's been *months* since they last touched. Teddy could ask him to strip naked here and now and he wouldn't hesitate.

"Little bit."

Teddy laughs and the glaring women fade into irrelevance as everyone else in the crowded baggage claim chatters, laughs, and carries on watching the bags go 'round the pillar—as though everything is right and nothing is unusual about the two men pressed together as if to separate would be intolerable.

In the front yard, a large white fluttering something catches Nash's eye from a block back—a bedsheet strung up between the elms.

"What is that?" Teddy asks.

"Jo's sense of humor," he says with dread.

He pulls into the driveway and the wind turns to reveal, *"Welcome Home Cheater"* sprayed across the face of the sheet in jarring red.

Teddy chokes on a laugh. "Wait, which one of us is the cheater?"

"Definitely you."

He parks, cuts the engine, and when he looks up, he

catches Teddy smiling quiet, like a satisfied cat.

"You *like* being the cheater?"

Teddy leans over the center console and kisses him sweetly. Against his lips, he says, "I like being welcomed home."

And well, if that ain't an arrow to the heart.

In unspoken agreement, they abandon the luggage in the trunk and stumble, kissing, onto the stoop.

Nash wrestles the door open and stops.

"What—"

Teddy laughs. "Jo again?"

The lights are off, but a dozen pillar candles dot the room with tiny flickering electric flames. Rose petals trail down the hall and cheap paper streamers dangle at intervals from the ceiling. Most notable, however, are the cordoned off zones. Masking tape creates an X over Jo's usual spot on the couch with a sign slapped in the center that reads in all capitals, "DON'T FUCK HERE."

"What gave it away?"

A similar No Fucking Zone has been established on the kitchen table—the tape encompassing both chairs—and a third is taped, bewilderingly, to the fridge.

"Look up," Teddy says, and kisses the underside of his chin when he does so. "Mistletoe. You know, Jo's not a bad wingman when she's not being an insufferable cockblock."

"She felt bad after last time."

"We all felt bad after last time," he says darkly, then kicks out of his sneakers.

Nash stoops to unlace his boots. "We planned better this time. It'll be just me and you most of the week."

"Most?"

A private smile curls Nash's lips at Teddy's tone of dismay. "Yes, most." He stands and peels his feet free. "Don't you wanna see your aunt?"

"I'll see her next month for Purim!"

"Well, you're also going to see her tomorrow for dinner."

"Dinner as in lunch or dinner as in supper?"

"Dinner as in dinner."

"Ah, come on. With the church people?"

"Be grateful I talked her down from breakfast. But, umm, no. I thought we'd do it here. Might be nice to cook for everyone." He looks around the room. "We'll have to clean up first."

Teddy sways toward him. "Two questions: who is 'everyone,' and"—his fingers find the hem of Nash's sweater and creep under it until cool fingers meet warm skin —"should we open a window to air out the place now or later?"

"Uhh, just Jo and Julie," he says, distracted as Teddy's thumb caresses the soft skin above his waistband. "Later. Don't wanna scar the neighbors."

Teddy kisses him, a soft meeting that ends too soon. "What do you suppose they think about that sign out front?"

He doesn't look away from Teddy's lips. "I really don't care."

Their next kiss is made shallow by Teddy's smile. He hooks a finger in Nash's waistband and shuffles him away from the door, following the flower petals.

They're still kissing as they step over the threshold of his bedroom, so he doesn't notice the changes until Teddy stumbles over a case of water bottles and nearly bites him as he falls.

"Are you o... okay?"

Along with the water, displayed atop the dresser is an eight-pack of sport drinks and a variety of energy bars, trail mix, and fruit snacks.

From the floor, Teddy crows, "Did she make us a fuck nest?"

Nash winces. "There are peanuts in that trail mix. I'm gonna—"

"Leave it." Teddy springs to his feet and crowds him toward the bed. "I've waited so long for this; the peanuts can get in line."

Reluctantly, Nash falls back. Under him, the bed crinkles. Plastic.

He goes stiff. "Am I laying in a pile of condoms?"

"Flavored ones," Teddy confirms, aglow as he climbs onto his lap.

"This is getting weird."

"No, no, no, stop thinking about it. It's just you and me."

"I—" He shifts and the condoms crinkle. "Nope. Can't. Let me up."

"Dammit, Jo."

Teddy throws himself to the side dramatically and the moment he's free, Nash hurries off the bed.

There's a startlingly large rainbow of plastic on the bed. He scrapes them into a pile as his face heats and prickly tendrils of embarrassment crawl over him.

"We can't even— These are latex."

"Does this smell like sabotage to you?" Teddy demands of the ceiling. "It *reeks* to me. We should have known the second we walked in the door. Hell, we should have known when we saw the sheet on the front fucking lawn."

"But why would she…"

He goes silent, arms full of condoms, as his eyes catch once more on the trail mix—centered amid the snacks and boasting twenty percent more nuts than the leading brand.

"Oh. Yeah, this is revenge."

"What did I even do to her? Recently, I mean. I've been nice, right?"

"No, it's— It was me." Nash screws his face into an apologetic grimace and faces Teddy. "I might have gone a little overboard getting everything ready for you."

Teddy props himself on his elbows. "What does that mean? What even needs to be *gotten ready*?"

"I… Well, I might have gone through the cupboards and thrown out anything you can't have. She took the peanut butter a bit personal."

Teddy goggles at him. "*Why*? Nash, why would you do that?"

"I didn't want— You were just in the hospital, and I didn't want to risk—"

"That was last summer! And it was a stupid work thing! I never should have trusted Kevin of all people to know what counts as a tree nut, but I'm not so stupid you have to baby-proof your house for me."

"I wasn't— It was stupid, I know. But I was excited, and I wanted everything to be perfect."

"When we all live together, you and Jo are allowed to have peanut butter or whatever. You don't have to sterilize the place just because I'm walking into it. I don't want you to do that."

"I know. I took it too far." Nash draws a breath and prepares to shoot himself in the other foot. "But you should know, I already cut peanuts out of my diet. And umm, all the rest. Your allergies."

Teddy's voice rises dangerously. "Are you serious? I don't want—"

"I want to know I can kiss you whenever I want!" Nash interjects, too loud over the top of him. A condom slips to the floor, but he hardly notices. "I don't want to accidentally send you to the hospital because I wasn't paying attention. I don't want to have to stay away from you because of what I eat; I'd rather stop eating it. So, I'm sorry if that's upsetting, but it's my choice and I've already made it."

Teddy stares at him, his jaw working in silence. Lowly, he says, "You don't have to do that."

"I want to."

"We still have years before we can live together."

"I don't care."

With an annoyed grunt, Teddy flops back and says to the ceiling, "That's irritatingly romantic."

Nash hesitates, encumbered by his armload of condoms. "Are you still mad?"

Teddy sighs. "Not really." He sits up. "Don't go all purge again, though. I hate taking Jo's side when she blue-balls me."

Nash makes a face. "Maybe don't talk about my sister and your balls in the same sentence."

"Maybe don't give me reason to." He looks around the room and shakes his head. "Let's get this stuff out of here and we can stop talking about her altogether."

He reaches for the dropped condom and Nash doesn't quite succeed at masking his wince.

Teddy snatches it up and shakes it at him. "The wrappers

aren't latex, Nash!"

"No, I know. I'll just..."

Nash turns on his heel before he does anything to make this worse. In the kitchen, he dumps the condoms in the trash and Teddy follows behind with the few that he dropped and the bag of trail mix. He fights to keep his expression neutral as Teddy eyeballs him, searching for signs of discomfort.

Nash glances at the trail mix. "You can toss it."

Teddy lifts his eyebrows. "I think I'll leave it here in case Jo wants some when she gets back." He plops it pointedly on the counter and waits, as if in anticipation of an argument.

"Sounds good," Nash forces out after a beat.

Teddy eyes him. "I'm thirsty."

"There's—"

Teddy is already pulling open the fridge, waving Jo's No Fucking Zone like a flag of war as he shifts things around, no doubt taking inventory of the depths to which Nash cleaned it out.

The moment he's distracted, Nash fires off a text.

My Favoritest Person 5evr!!!
Feb 5th 6:31 PM

I hate you

Lol
You didn't like my homecoming gift?

I'm changing your contact for
this

You know I'll just change it back next time
you need me to find your calculator app

I hate you

MUAH! Have fun with your spwecial
widdol teddy beaw ❤★

Hate.

An hour passes in silence while he kicks himself and Teddy
violently irons the fresh-washed fabric Nash picked out for
their new quilt. There's an apology stuck in his throat, but
he's already dropped too many *sorrys* on Teddy's cold
shoulders. If he keeps it up, it'll only add to the pile.

The worst part is he can see Teddy struggling to get over
it. This isn't how either of them pictured their long-
anticipated reunion. They should be in bed, curled into each
other, refamiliarizing themselves with the other's dips and
curves, the heat and give of flesh over fat, muscle, and bone.
He hasn't been able to sleep for a week, too busy imagining
seeing Teddy again, of holding him, of just sitting in silence
together.

And now here they are sitting in silence and it's
miserable.

Teddy sighs and thumps the iron down on the ironing
board. "Would you quit it with that look?"

From his spot on the couch, Nash meets his gaze over the
ironing board.

Teddy stabs his finger at him. "Yeah, that one. I didn't know you could do kicked puppy this good."

"I'm sorry?"

He rolls his eyes. "I know, Nash. You've made it abundantly clear how sorry you are."

"I won't do it again."

"I *know*."

He buttons his lips and watches Teddy, waiting for a sign of what the hell else he's supposed to do if apologizing only earns him more ire. He can't *un-throw out* the peanut butter.

Teddy sighs again and scrubs his palm over the top of his head, fussing his curls. "Look, I'm not— It's fine, okay? I'm not— It's fine. I'll get over it."

Nash says nothing. If it was fine, then it would feel fine, and it doesn't. It feels like he's belly-down on the ice waiting for the cracking to stop or to give way and drop him to the deadly waters below. If it was fine, he wouldn't be sitting here scrounging for the right words and coming up empty.

With abrupt movements, Teddy flicks off the iron and pulls the cord from the wall by the TV. When he turns back to face Nash, he squares his shoulders and lifts his chin. "You said you had it all planned out. What are we supposed to be doing right now?"

Nash's voice comes out strained. "We were going to spend the day in bed 'n' just... be together." He averts his eyes. "But I fucked it up in the first five— Before you even got on the plane. We were— We've been looking forward to this for so long and now..."

"Nothing's ruined, Nash." Teddy steps around the ironing board and sinks to a squat until he finds Nash's gaze.

"I mean it. Sometimes the only thing that's wrong is that I need to get my head out of my ass." He tangles their fingers together atop Nash's knee. "Okay?"

"But I know I shouldn't have—"

"Forget it, okay? Let's just make it a good week. I want to feel good. I want to make you feel good. If stuff comes up that we need to talk about, then we can do that whenever, right? We talk all the time. This week should be about us just being together."

"I can't ignore it if you're mad at me."

"I'm not."

"Don't— Teddy, don't."

"I'm not mad at you," Teddy says, all earnest offense. "I'm upset, but I'm not mad at you, Nash. I don't like what you did, but you didn't do anything wrong. I don't want you to do it again, but—"

"I won't."

"I *know*," Teddy says, suddenly sharp. He breathes out. "I know. You don't have to— You can stop apologizing and looking at me like— I don't want this to be our whole week. The sooner we move past it, the better. You've done all you can to make it right and now it's up to me to get over myself. I'm sorry I'm not better about letting things go. I wish... I wish it was easier."

"I'm not any better."

"Then let's practice together, huh?" He tries on a tentative smile. "Can I kiss you?"

Nash thinks about it. He wants as badly as Teddy for things to be light and easy again, but he'll never get there if he's only ignoring the worry worming around the back of his mind.

"Not if you're mad at me," he says.

Teddy rises and boxes him in on the couch, eyes on his mouth. "It's lucky I'm not then."

And when Teddy kisses him, he tastes like cran-grape. And when he sighs sweetly into his mouth, the ice gives way and drops him onto freshly laundered sheets. And when their clothes have gone and Teddy asks if he can make him feel good, he says yes.

And now he's drowning, and Teddy is the one holding him under.

"You're so soft," Teddy murmurs into the pliable flesh of his inner thigh.

Nash's knees quake where they're thrown over Teddy's shoulders and he pleads to the ceiling, "Please—" His breath hitches as another feather-light kiss is bestowed on the opposite thigh, followed by a nip of teeth. "Please touch me."

"I am."

And he is. Teddy's hands are hot, one braced just above his knee, keeping his leg up where he wants it, and the other is splayed over his hip, pressing him firmly into the mattress as his lips continue their languid, meandering journey up his body.

He's gonna die here.

Teddy fixes his mouth on thin, delicate skin and Nash gasps and arcs back. He's hot and tight all over, too big for his skin, on the brink of fracture. He pants, trembling, as Teddy releases suction and soothes the resulting bruise with his tongue.

"Please. Teddy, please."

"So polite." He scrapes his teeth over Nash's hipbone and restrains him easily when he bucks. "Tell me what you want."

"Touch me."

"I told you, I am. Is there somewhere specifi—"

"My *dick*," he snaps.

Teddy laughs and rocks forward to kiss and nip at his stomach. "What happened to my polite boy? He was so sweet. The sounds he'd make…"

Nash moans and jerks his hands, but they remain fastened over his head where Teddy put them. "You're gonna kill me."

"Mmm, might ruin the mood." Teddy releases his legs.

Nash's muscles and bad hip strain after so long aloft, but he hardly notices as Teddy crawls up and throws his leg over his waist without so much as grazing what he desperately needs worked to completion.

Instead, Teddy takes himself in hand and looks down at him with glazed eyes.

"Christ, Teddy."

The desire to touch turns overwhelming. He jerks again against the silk around his wrists.

Teddy glances briefly at his hands but continues slowly stroking. "Careful, honey. Don't ruin my hard work."

"I need something, please."

"Don't worry, you're next." A dark flush creeps from chest to throat as his breathing grows harsh. "You're gorgeous like this. Chest or mouth?"

"Mouth." If he doesn't get to touch him now, he's not gonna make it to his turn.

Teddy rises to his knees and palms the headboard, frustratingly close to where Nash's hands are bound. He maintains his careful distance, only allowing Nash the very tip as he jacks himself until his rhythm falters with a choked cry, gasping, eyes unfocused, lost in the haze of climax.

He droops low enough for Nash to kiss his shoulder.

"Come here. Now, Ted. Come here."

Finally, Teddy does as he's bid, palms hot on Nash's cheeks as Nash licks into his mouth, tasting to the backs of his teeth. The kiss lasts precious seconds before Teddy turns his head with a gasp, chest still heaving.

"Easy, easy," Nash murmurs, nosing along his jaw, his throat. "Breathe for me, darlin'."

Teddy tucks his face against Nash's neck, breath hot in the juncture of his shoulder.

A faint whistle catches in Teddy's throat and Nash's breath stops up with a trill of fear. He yanks once at his restraints. He's not so securely bound that he couldn't rip free if he wanted, but it would take some effort and the headboard wouldn't survive it. But maybe he's okay. It wasn't a full wheeze.

"Teddy? Are you—"

Abruptly, Teddy nips the side of his neck and sits up. "Your turn."

He slips down, closes his hand around Nash, and finally, finally, white-hot pleasure sweeps in and purges all else.

Nash wakes to a chill. A sound of complaint escapes his throat as he reaches for the fleeing warmth, but a hushing sound and fingers petting through his hair assure him back to sleep.

The next time Nash wakes, it's to weak winter sunlight and a crick in his neck. With a muffled grunt, he stretches out until something pops, then he goes slack. It takes a few more seconds of working his tongue around his mouth to remember why the silence is strange.

He sits up and blinks in confusion at the empty stretch of sheets where Teddy should be slumbering. It's barely past dawn on a Sunday, far too early to be up and around, especially in the chill, but he doesn't hear anything in the bathroom so Teddy must be up, up.

Resolved to find him, he kicks away the covers and pulls on a pair of sweatpants. He's midyawn, rubbing his sore neck when he finds Teddy perched on the edge of the couch, frowning at the start of their new quilt.

"You're up early."

Teddy hums in response as he pins together two squares, taking pains to line them up exactly straight.

Unease creeps over Nash.

The living room is dim, curtains drawn as they always are, the lamp in the corner putting out not-enough light. They were both dissatisfied with the lumpy seams in their last quilt, so it makes sense that he's giving the new one his undivided attention. And everything was fine last night— great, even. They conked out cuddled together in a post-coital haze and slept the night through. Or, well, he did.

The point is, he can think of literally nothing he could've done to upset Teddy again unless he kicked him in his sleep, and considering how stiff he feels, he slept like a fossilized rock. But if he didn't do anything new, Teddy must be still upset about the peanut butter even though he promised he wasn't.

Whatever it is, an old instinct is putting up red flags and telling him: tread lightly.

Tentative, he pads over to the couch and sits between Jo's No Fucking Zone and Teddy. He watches him fit a last pin through the fabric, then breaches the quiet.

"You alright?"

Teddy's jaw goes tight as he frowns at the squares. "Do you—?" He shakes his head and tosses down the fabric on the table. "Nah, nevermind." He stands. "Breakfast?"

"What?"

He's already in the kitchen, opening cupboards and pulling out cookware. "I was going to try making eggs the way you like them, but I wasn't sure when you'd be up. You feelin' eggs?"

He's feeling it doesn't matter as Teddy takes the egg carton out of the fridge.

"Sure."

Teddy chatters as he cooks, a little bit of something about a lot of nothing, and Nash can't shake the feeling something has gone wrong.

CHAPTER THIRTEEN

The bout

They're here!"

Nash hurries to peel the last of the masking tape off the fridge. The couch and the table were easy to remember to clear, the rose petals swept up, the streamers pulled down, the candles bagged and stowed in his closet, but he'd forgotten about the random No Fucking Zone attached to the fridge.

"Is the roast done?"

"Almost." He wads the masking tape into a ball and tosses it in the trash. "Another ten minutes maybe."

He's still unsure what wild hair is up Teddy's ass. He *knows* he's avoiding him, but he's doing it by being completely casual and it's makin' Nash feel crazy. Maybe it's all in his head, but their conversations are shallow as Teddy skips from topic to topic without lingering into any depth, and a physical wall seems to have cropped up between them while he slept. Hell, the whole reason Jo is staying out of the house for the week is because normally they can't keep their hands off each other while they're in the same room, but Teddy hasn't initiated contact once and anytime Nash gets too close, some sudden chore sends him tearing conveniently into another room.

Nash has given up trying to ask if anything is wrong and instead is trying not to say the wrong thing. The perfect words to fix everything are somewhere, but he's never been any good at finding them. Maybe once they're through dinner and there isn't company on the horizon, Teddy will open up about whatever's bothering him. He ain't ever been shy about venting his feelings, so this dance is foreign and, honestly, exhausting.

"Do you need help with—"

"Nope!" Teddy puts down one of four drinking glasses with a solid smack against the table.

"Okay," Nash says, mild as he can manage. "I'll get the silverw—"

The next glass slams on to the table as Teddy snaps, "I said *no*, Nash."

The front door opens while Nash is still reared back and Teddy is curled over the table like a dragon defending his hoard.

Nash blinks several times, battling against the sick feeling in his stomach and the voice in his head telling him to smooth it over before someone gets hurt. He shuts his mouth and turns to greet Julie with a forced smile.

Except it's not Aunt Julie, but Jo stood in the doorway looking awkward.

"Yikes," she says.

Teddy slams down the last glass. "I'm going for a walk. You don't need to wait for me."

"Well, but—"

"Just stop!" Teddy barks at him. "Just... *stop*, okay?" He turns his back on him.

All Nash can do is stare as Teddy crams his feet into his shoes, then stalks past Jo and out of the house with only thin long sleeves and his heels hanging out the backs of his sneakers.

The door slams and the house goes quiet.

Softly, Jo asks, "Did I do that? I was just— It was a joke. I didn't—"

"No," Nash says quickly. "No, he... I don't know. He's been weird since he woke up."

"Did something happen last night?"

His skin turns warm. "I— Well, we— You don't want to hear about it, but last night was good." Doubt creeps over him. "I thought it was good. Maybe it wasn't. It seemed... good."

Jo is looking at him with an arch expression. "You are toeing the line, buster. I don't wanna hear about that stuff."

"Then you shouldn't have supplied the condoms."

"They weren't *usable*. Oh my God, you didn't—"

"No, God, no. If that— Then I'd know what's wrong."

"You haven't talked to him?"

Not since yesterday when Teddy promised he wasn't mad at him. Would he have lied? Would he have heard Nash say he didn't want to be intimate if he was angry and gone and touched him anyway while he secretly stewed in his mind? He doesn't want to believe it, but he can't stop the wondering.

"I've tried. He keeps... I dunno. He's made it clear he don't want to talk about it. Or at least, not with me."

The thought leaves a bitter ache in his hollow stomach.

"You better hash it out quick. You've got less than a week."

"Trust me, that's all I've been thinking about."

"You know..." She shoots him an apologetic look, then drops the bomb on him anyway. "This doesn't bode well for our plan."

"What d'you mean?"

"I mean," she says carefully, "if your relationship is going to be rocky when you're together in-person then we really have no business going in on a mortgage together. Know what I mean? I'm not trying to be mean, but... I think it's something we should keep an eye on. If you don't learn how to talk out issues as they crop up, then your relationship is doomed to fail, and we need to minimize the fallout."

That stiff feeling in his neck is back, tense and pulsing.

"That's cold, Joey."

"I know, and I am sorry." She puts her hand on his forearm and looks up all big brown sorry eyes. "I know how badly you want this to work, but it takes two." She pats him and falls away. "It has to take two."

"Nash, this is delicious."

Nash forces a smile for Julie and continues to chew,

chew, chew. Beside him in one of the shitty folding chairs they break out when they have company, Teddy has said all of three words since he came back from his walk. He was sweating and pink-cheeked when he returned, then shut himself in the bedroom to "get changed." When he came back out, he was in different clothes—but it took several minutes and his aunt's arrival to summon him out.

Across the table, Jo shoots Nash a pointed look, but Nash hasn't got the first clue what she expects him to do about this. It's all he can do to keep choking down his plate. His mouth is dry, his stomach is in knots, and his thoughts are tumbling in a panicked spiral. He doesn't know what's wrong, let alone how to fix it. Is Jo right? Is this how all of their problems will manifest? With Teddy putting up a wall and biting his hand every time he reaches across it?

He wants to say no. He wants to look back on the past year and comfort himself with the fact that this is an outlier, but the fact is, they haven't spent enough time in the same state to say whether or not this is normal. For all he knows, this is how Teddy responds to any upset or miscommunication when he can't get space by putting down the phone.

They're just stuck here. Together. Snapping and biting.

"Theo, how was your flight?" Julie asks over the relentless click of silverware on ceramic.

He shrugs and doesn't look up. "Fine."

Her eyebrows lift and she tries to catch Nash's eye, but he keeps his head down too and sticks another bite of meat in his mouth even though he hasn't managed to swallow the previous one.

Across from him, Jo spears a sprout like it requires all of

her concentration.

"Made it in one piece," Teddy adds when the silence lingers.

"Can I assume it was a happy reunion?" Julie's expression shows her doubt.

Nash's mouth is full, so he nods even though their happiness expired far sooner than he thought it would. It *was* happy though, at first. Before Teddy learned what he did. Before Jo's prank brought it all into the light. They talked. The fucking trail mix is still on the counter. Teddy said he wasn't mad, and he kissed him. Things were good enough for sex, even though Nash worried they weren't there yet.

But hate sex is a thing, right? Maybe that's what it was on Teddy's end of things. It makes the food in his mouth turn ashen to think it. That's not the kind of relationship he—

"You don't have to eat it if you don't like it."

Nash picks up his head and finds everyone looking at him, but only Teddy is scowling.

"Hmm?"

"Just don't eat it," Teddy snaps. "You don't have to change your whole life to suit me if you think it sucks."

He's tempted to spit the meat out onto his plate so he can ask Teddy what the hell he's talking about, but his manners got ingrained deep so he forces it down in one big swallow so he can croak, eyes tearing, "What the hell are you talking about?"

Teddy shoves back with enough force to slosh cran-grape out of his glass onto the naked table. Nash's bedroom door slams behind him.

Bewildered and upset, he turns to Jo. "What did I do?"

Her eyes flit between the closed door and Julie before she looks at him. "Sounds like he thinks you don't like your life with him."

"That's bullshit!"

She folds her napkin atop her half-finished plate. "You need to talk to him."

"I've been trying. He won't talk to me."

"Maybe he will if we get out of the way," Julie says graciously as she also drops her napkin atop her unfinished food. She takes Nash's hand and says to him seriously, "I know you care for my nephew a great deal, but don't fool yourself into thinking he's infallible. Sometimes you have to tie him up and badger the truth out of him to get to the root of the problem."

She pats his hand and then sets about gathering her coat and shoes.

Jo stands but pauses before leaving the table. "D'you think you'll make it to my bout?"

"I wouldn't miss it."

Her lips tick up in a small smile. "It's gonna be a bloody one. You sure you're up for it?"

"I wouldn't miss it," he repeats, steadfast.

She smiles fully and kisses his cheek. "Good luck."

"You too."

Nash sees them out to the driveway while they speculate on the upcoming bout and the Buford Hell Women's chances against the loathsome Oakdale Brutes— No, sorry, *Beauts*. He waves them off as Jo peels away from the curb and Julie carefully backs out of the driveway into the street. Then he's alone with the task of coaxing Teddy into a productive conversation hanging over his head. He sweats.

To his shame, he stalls a good fifteen minutes by packing away the leftovers and washing up the kitchen before he gathers the courage to knock on his own bedroom door.

"Busy!"

Wrong-footed, he hesitates, but recalling Julie's advice, he opens the door anyway.

Teddy is in pajama bottoms at one in the afternoon, cross-legged on the bed, computer in his lap, tapping rapidly on what seems to be a single key.

"What are you doing?" It's not what he came in here to ask, but it pops out of his mouth anyway.

Teddy doesn't look away from the screen.

"Playing a game."

A game? He's been sweating and churning through scenarios in the other room all while Teddy plays a game?

"I was hopin' we could talk," he says slowly.

"Not now."

"Okay... When—"

"Don't know."

He stands there feeling about as significant as a dead beetle in a gourmet soup while Teddy taps his little key and scowls at his screen.

Doomed, Jo said.

Tie him up, Julie said.

Well, maybe he shouldn't have to. Maybe Teddy should want to fix this as badly as Nash does. Maybe he shouldn't be holed up playing games while Nash is tearing a worry hole in his gut wondering about their future and what he did to jeopardize it.

Nash closes the door.

Suddenly alone, he perches on the couch and stares blankly at the black TV while he churns the past day in his head over and over and over. After a while, he gives up on Teddy coming to him when his game is over and turns on *A Rose Without Thorns* with the volume low.

The bedroom door never opens.

Nash limps across the parking lot of the roller rink, hip stiff after a sedentary day on the couch, and tries not to turn his wrist on the broken bits of asphalt that sneak under his cane.

He still can't quite believe Teddy didn't come talk to him. He'd been concerned that he didn't even come out for food after barely picking at his dinner until he remembered the energy bars and fruit snacks. Nash didn't see him at all until he'd laced his boots, ready to leave for Jo's bout without him. He grabbed his keys and, seconds later, the bedroom door swung open and startled him so badly he dropped them.

"You're leaving?" was all Teddy said. Demanded.

After he explained where he was going, Teddy wordlessly changed into a pair of jeans, tugged on a hoodie, and gestured for him to lead the way.

Now Teddy's striding ahead of him like they're racing.

Nash lags behind, too sore in heart and body to compete. Maybe it's him that's the problem. Maybe he overestimated how much he likes the storm. Could be he was right all those months ago in his bedroom when he told Teddy he's looking for more calm nowadays. Maybe all of this is his fault for letting Teddy under his skin just for them to tear each other down all over again.

At the door, he finds Teddy has already paid their way in even though George always lets him in free because of how much time he spends in this place cleaning up and shooting the shit while they wait for the regular crowd to shuffle on home and the girls to shower and change.

He nods at George behind the counter but can't work up a smile. He follows Teddy through the lobby to the banked rink where a crowd is gathered, hollering and spilling beer and burnt popcorn.

It's a big one tonight, as far as their little town goes. Not much else to do on a Sunday that ain't church. Got a few faces from Deliverance and not a small number have migrated their way from Oakdale to cheer on their ghouls—*girls*, sorry.

A few people greet him or slap his shoulder as he passes by, and the smile he dredges up in greeting is more grimace than anything polite. It's a relief to sink into a seat up near the wall where none of the regulars are likely to seek him out—them being the type to crowd the rail. Julie is one of them, smiling and laughing with a couple of her girlfriends, the pink in their cheeks talking to the beer in their plastic cups and the empties stacked by their feet.

It's the strangest bout he's ever been to.

The crowd is rowdy and boisterous, and the girls as ferocious as ever, but he and Teddy sit still and silent in the shadows by the wall. Removed from the fervor, watching it unfold below them like saints above an altar.

The bug doesn't catch him. Not with Teddy sitting frigid at his side and their week together a big question mark, neon lit in front of him.

The Buford Hell Women lose spectacularly—by which he means a fight breaks out the instant the final whistle blows, and everything goes to hell.

Nash is on his feet, moving for the rail without realizing it, and only breathes when he spots Jo sporting a bloody lip as she full-body hauls a kicking and thrashing Belladonna out of the fray.

He doesn't think. He doesn't look for Teddy as he pushes through the crowd to check on her. If she took a helmet to the face, that could easily lead to a concussion, and she shouldn't be wrestling her friends into compliance while concussed.

By the time he makes it out of the stands and into the little back hallway behind the Employees Only door, she's shut away with the rest of the team in the locker room. He lingers outside the door while the coach's voice thunders through solid metal and rings down the hall. Ten minutes pass before the door opens and finally, the girls stalk, slump, and strut out.

Jo brings up the rear with a black look and a swollen, scabbed lip.

"Are you—"

"Save it," she snaps and sweeps past him, equipment bag swinging. "Check on me tomorrow, would you?"

He hurries in her wake. "Just tell me if you're more hurt or mad and I'll back off."

"I'm fuckin' furious, Nash. They played nothin' but cheap tricks all night and they're gettin' a goddamn medal for it. You know what I'm getting for pulling my teammate out of the fight? Fuckin' *benched*. Twelve of us, benched! That means we're gonna all suit up and show up at the bout next week just to forfeit. Waste of everybody's goddamn time to teach us grown adults *sportsmanship*."

She spits, and it smacks the floor in a pink-tinged puddle. With her shoulder, she slams through the door into the cool, humid night and kicks a loose chunk of asphalt across the parking lot. The lot is clearing out quick and soon it'll be only his old Lincoln and George's little coup left. The sky's black with clouds and only the sparse lights overhead hold the dark at bay.

"You need a ride home?"

"To that shitshow you call a relationship? No thanks."

He stops, stung.

She carries forward a few steps before she puffs out a frustrated breath and turns to face him. "I didn't mean that."

"Naw, you did. Doomed, remember?"

Her expression flickers with bared teeth. "That's not what I—"

"What's doomed?"

They swing around in unison to find Teddy straightening from where he was leaned on the hood of the Lincoln, the distant lamps overhead casting sharp white light across his face. His expression is a twisted tangle of emotion too complicated to pick apart, except that he's angry. Of course, he's angry.

He steps toward them and asks, "Me and Nash? You told him we're doomed?"

"That's not what I said!" Jo pivots to face Nash, her expression urgent. "Tell him that's not what I said."

He stares at her. She wouldn't be asking him to lie for her, would she? Not over something serious. Not while him and Teddy are so rocky.

Her temper crackles back to life, and he wonders what in him is so broken that he surrounds himself with people who run so hot when he's so, so cold.

"Nash, that *ain't* what I said!"

"Then why's the word 'doomed' been echoin' in my head all day, Joey?"

Teddy turns on Jo. "Why the fuck would you tell him that? You know how he dwells on shit."

Nash rears back as though struck. "I don't dwell."

Teddy shoots him a look like *"stop kidding around"* and Jo doesn't even acknowledge that he spoke.

"All I told him is if you two don't figure out how to talk to each other, you'd be doomed. If you couldn't pull your head out of your ass long enough for a conversation, then you doomed yourself and I had nothin' to do with it."

"That's— What would you even know about—"

"It's my *fucking job*, Theodore! What would *you* know about it? As far as I've seen from you, the second things get complicated, you shut it all down and run."

"I didn't have a choice."

"Don't fucking lie! You coulda called any time in the near decade we lived in that house after you left. You made your choice every day you didn't pick up the goddamn phone and now you're back and you're pulling the same shit!" She steps in close and the bulk of her turns menacing as she hisses through bared teeth, "You break my brother's heart again and I'll break you to bits."

"I didn't— He—!"

Jo's single bark of furious laughter cuts him off.

"Don't y'all remember *anything* from last time?" She stabs her finger at Nash, but she's glaring up at Teddy from a breath away. "He followed you around like a planet around the sun and you"—she stabs her finger into Teddy's chest —"you let him and you *loved* it. Now he's trying to fall back into your orbit, and you're balking like a scared horse and don't even have the balls to explain to him *why*. How 'bout you do us all a favor and stay the hell away from him if you don't plan on makin' it work."

That's all Nash can take.

Lungs burning, his throat knotted and tight, he makes for the car. His keys snag his pocket and he nearly drops them, but manages to keep going.

"Nash..." It's Jo calling after him, all regretful. "I shouldn't have— Nash, I'm sorry."

He can't look at her, can't speak through the tangle in his throat even if he could find the words past the ringing in his ears. He ducks in the car and pulls the door shut behind him. Doesn't bother putting up his cane, just tosses it in the backseat, then tips his head back and gulps a breath that echoes strangely in the confined space.

How did everything unravel so quickly?

He thought they'd make it this time. He really did. He was gonna do it all right. He wasn't gonna give Teddy a reason to leave. He was going to keep out of his head and always put Teddy first and—and—

The passenger door opens and Teddy ducks down to see him. He can tell it's him, even though he can't stand to turn and look. Can't be sure the tears bottled up in his neck won't burst free the second he locks eyes with anybody, least of all him.

"Jo's going back to her friend's place," he says softly. "She said she's sorry and she'll call tomorrow after she's cooled off." He pauses, watching Nash, then licks his lips and asks, "Can I come in?"

Nash gestures vaguely at the passenger seat. He's hardly gonna leave him here alone in the dark. He sets about freeing the car key from his house key and work locker key without succumbing to the tremble in his fingers.

Everything is coming undone. He thought this time he wouldn't be left to pick up the pieces. There weren't supposed to *be* pieces. It was supposed to work. He was supposed to make it work.

By the time Teddy has his seatbelt fastened, he finally fits the right key into the ignition and cranks it over.

"I can drive if you—"

Nash shifts out of park and begins the arduous crawl back to his side of town, painfully cognizant of Teddy beside him and his frequent glances under the sliding shafts of light. He's never been more grateful for how dead their little town is on a Sunday night. He doesn't breathe until they're safely parked in the driveway.

He shuts off the engine, and a thick silence takes its place.

"Nash," Teddy starts, all hesitation and uncertainty like he hardly never is, "we need to talk."

He's going to suffocate in here. It's too small. It's too quiet. It's too—too—

He opens his door and gets out. Behind him, he can hear Teddy doing the same, but he doesn't look at him, doesn't turn around to get his cane from the back, doesn't look away from the keys as he picks out the one for the door and fits it into the sticky lock that would be easy enough to replace should he ever think to do so.

And then they're inside, and it's not any better than the car. It's still too quiet. Too dark. Too —

He can't.

If it's all ending tonight, he's going to keep himself together long enough for Teddy to finish walking away. He's not gonna fall apart on him. He won't let him see. But to pull that off, he needs to pull himself together.

He won't take the bedroom — Teddy's made it clear that's the room he's most comfortable in — and he won't infringe on Jo's sacred personal space, so he bypasses both for the bathroom. As he flips on the light, the exhaust fan overhead whirls to life.

"Are you going to talk to me?"

That's rich coming from him after today. After the past twenty years.

Twenty-one years.

Nash would love to talk to him. He'd love to have talked to Teddy this morning and this afternoon and every day since they were twelve like he promised. But if Nash opens his mouth now, he's not sure what'll come out except he's fairly certain it won't be words. Wails, maybe — if he's lucky. Whimpers if he's not.

He shuts the door and cranks on the shower 'cause he's got that tickle in his nose and his throat aches from holding it all in and because the white noise pairs well with the buzzing in his head. He's beyond the limit of how many humiliations he can muster through in a day. There's no strength left in him for taking chances.

The keys are still clenched in his fist. He drops them in the sink and sits on the toilet with his head in his hands, willing his mind blank and for his emotions to tuck away somewhere they won't rear up and overwhelm him before he can get through this next bit.

Doomed, Jo said.

And Teddy... Teddy's the same as he's always been. It's his own fault he convinced himself that's a good thing. He fooled himself into believing this time it wouldn't end with heartbreak. No, worse, he thought it wouldn't end at all. He thought, like Walt and Spence, they'd be together until their bodies gave out and then they'd get put in the ground side-by-side—in death, a mirror of life.

Stupid. He's getting his heart broken all over again because he woke up one day and decided to be an idealist without ever once thinkin' better of it.

A knock at the door breaks him from his thoughts. "I need to pee."

Naturally.

His chest heaves, but he chokes everything down. He wipes dry cheeks, takes a handful of humid, steadying breaths, steels his spine, and opens the door.

Teddy plants a hand against it and blocks the doorway, pressing into his personal space. "I lied, but please don't shut me out." Something wild is in his eyes. "I know I deserve it, but please. I handled this all wrong."

Nash steps back, surprised by the sudden proximity and his intensity as Teddy squeezes into the bathroom. He presses the door shut behind his back, eyes wide and pleading.

"You don't have to talk if you don't want to, just listen," Teddy says, too loud over the hum of the exhaust fan and the crash of the shower. "This has gotten really messy, and I never meant— Look, that stuff Jo said? She was right."

Nash turns away and squeezes his eyes shut. He won't cry in front of him. He won't.

Teddy is right at his back. Palpable in his nearness. "She — I mean, she could have said it nicer, but she— The main points were all there. I should have called back then. I should have— It's my fault things turned out how they did. I had all the control, and I didn't do anything with it. I'm sorry. And what she said about how I'm acting now, she had some fair points, but she's *wrong* about us being doomed, okay? I— Are you hearing me? Could you look at me? Please?"

He's still braced for the hurt to hit, he realizes. More hurt. The worst of it.

Slowly, he turns, but he can't bring himself to look Teddy in the eye. He'll lose the fragile hold he has on his control, he knows he will, but he doesn't have to look at his face to see Teddy's in fight mode: feet set apart, shoulders squared and tense, his fingers in fists.

"What is going on in your head?" Teddy asks softly. "I hate when you stonewall me. You're too good at it."

Stonewall him? *That's* what he thinks is happening? That this is some childish cold shoulder punishment?

It's finally enough to ignite a spark and break through the barrier of noise in his head.

Lowly, Nash says, "You've been shutting me out all day, but I can't have ten minutes to get my head together?"

Teddy's expression pinches. "I— No. I mean, I shouldn't have—"

"I can't do this again," he croaks. "I can't— I told you, I— I was gonna do it all right this time. I... I dunno where I went wrong, but I'm sorry."

"Can't do what again, Nash? You have nothing to be sorry for."

A mad laugh bubbles up his throat, but he chokes it back. "Then what was today about?" he demands as his vision turns watery despite his best efforts. "If I didn't do anything to deserve you jumping up my ass about every little thing I said, why did you?"

"That's what I'm trying to say! *I* fucked up. I got all in my head and couldn't figure out how to talk to you or—"

"Couldn't figure out how to talk to me? You cut me out! You holed yourself up and played video games so you wouldn't *have* to talk to me. So you wouldn't even have to *think* about me."

"That's not— I was trying to get into a frame of mind—"

"Jesus Christ, Teddy. A frame of mind? You can't just talk to me? You have to— What is it then? What's so complicated you couldn't just say it?"

Teddy's jaw goes hard. "You're pushing me, Nash. I'm trying not to lose my temper but—"

"Fucking— Spit it out! When have you ever held back from me and why the hell would you start now? Quit makin' me guess and say what you mean."

Teddy flaps his arms against his sides and narrowly misses the sink. He's far too loud now as he shouts, "You're erasing your life and making it all about me!"

"What *life*? Take a look around, would you? There's nothin' to erase! D'you expect me to apologize for makin' you a bright spot?"

"That's not true. You have hobbies. You have—"

"I have Jo and I have work and I thought I had you."

"But quilting—"

"The quilt was work, Ted! It was the first one I'd ever made, and I only did it because Maureen couldn't. I get it that I'm too much, okay? It's too much for Jo too, so you don't need to feel bad for not wanting it. *Nobody* wants it except a bunch of old folks who can't get attention from anybody but the weird obsessive guy who takes people and makes them the center of the universe."

His fight gutters out under a wave of resigned melancholy. "So— So quit tryin' to make it go down easier and say what you need to say."

"Nash—"

Teddy reaches for him, but Nash flinches back.

"D-don't. Just—just spit it out. Just say it."

Teddy shakes his head. "Say what, Nash? I already told — Do you think I'm breaking up with you?"

"Aren't you? Haven't you been gearing up for it all day?"

"What? No!"

He steps closer, but Nash matches it, near knocking into the wall to keep from being touched while Teddy's angry at him.

Teddy curls his fingers into his palm and lowers his hand. "Nash, I can promise you, if we break up, it won't be me that ends it. Now that I've got you back, I'm not letting go without a fight."

A wet breath punches out of him. Behind it, the rest of the wave is cresting. He turns away and grinds the heels of his palms into his brow. Words are so difficult. He's never been any good at this, but usually he at least knows what book to look at, even if he's never found the right page.

"Then what's going on?"—his voice warbles dangerously —"I don't understand—"

He freezes as tentative arms wrap around his waist. When he doesn't pull away, Teddy cinches tight and his forehead presses between his shoulder blades.

"I love you, remember? I love you and I'm not going anywhere and even if no one else does, I want it—everything you've got. If Jo doesn't, that's her loss, but I need you to understand that I do, so we can work this out. I'm not giving up on us and I love you and I... I need your help. We went off the rails today and I know how it started, but I don't know how we got so far off so fast. Can we— Can we take a minute? And then will you help me figure this out? Please?"

Nash releases a shaky breath. Dimly, he realizes his hands, still pressed into his face, are trembling and damp.

"Okay."

Teddy must hear the single croaked word because he breathes out, hot against his skin, and relaxes into him without loosening his embrace.

"Do you believe me?"

He swallows delicately. "About?"

"That I'm not giving up on us and I love you." Teddy turns so it's his cheek pressed into his back, grounding him with his body heat and steady grip.

Slowly, the panicked itch that's been under Nash's skin all day eases into a profound exhaustion.

"I love you too."

"I know."

He breathes through the ebbing tide as his cheeks dry and his hands continue to tremble and Teddy remains a warm, solid weight holding him through the receding flood.

"Let me know when you're ready to talk. Take as long as you want, but I'm not going anywhere."

CHAPTER FOURTEEN
The truth of it

The living room is cold and weirdly silent after the cramped quarters of the bathroom. Or maybe Nash is cold because Teddy's no longer wrapped around him. He moves automatically for his usual spot, but Teddy beats him to it and sits with his back to the armrest and one foot on the floor. He holds his arms out.

He thinks maybe he should balk at the way Teddy is coddling him, but the truth is he's had a shit day, and this tender offering of affection is too compelling to resist. He sits between Teddy's legs and lays his head on his shoulder as Teddy folds around him.

He closes his eyes as Teddy drops a light kiss on his temple and hugs him tight.

"I thought you were leaving," Teddy says softly. "Earlier,

I mean. When you were getting ready for Jo's game."

"I was."

"No, I thought you were *leaving,* leaving. I thought I took too long."

"You did, Ted. You took way too long."

"If Jo hadn't gotten in your head with her talk about doomed relationships—"

"Don't blame her. I was already— I didn't know what was going on. All I knew was something was wrong— something I did—and you wouldn't tell me."

"I'm sorry. I should have— I don't know."

He stiffens. "What do you mean you don't know? You should've *talked to me.*"

"I didn't want to until I'd cooled off. I didn't want to yell at you about something that wasn't even really wrong of you."

"Wrong for you counts as wrong 'n' I wanna know about it."

"I get that, but— It's the— I know I have a temper. And I know how your dad was, and I don't ever want to be like that to you. It's really important to me."

Like his daddy? Teddy's worried about being like his *daddy?*

"You don't— If you're worried about that, you don't know—" Nash sits up enough that he can meet Teddy's eyes. "You got it all wrong. My daddy wasn't an angry man, Ted. He was violent, but that violence was a source of joy for him. You couldn't be like him even on your blackest day, even if you tried. D'you really think I could be with someone I thought was like him?"

Teddy searches Nash's face, judging his candor for

authenticity. "I thought... It's something I worry about."

"You're *honest*, Teddy. I never have to guess where I stand with you. If you're angry, I know it, and usually I know why. I don't have to watch over my shoulder, wondering if something's waiting to take a bite outta me. I've always valued that, and I don't want it to go away."

"Are you saying you like it when I lose my temper?"

"I'm saying I like knowing where I stand with you, but today you hid it from me, and you lied and put on a show, and I hated it. If you're pissed about somethin', I don't care how small or stupid you think it is. I want the truth of it. Don't mess my head around because you think it's kinder."

"I'm sorry. I— This sounds stupid in hindsight, but I was"—a sheepish smile lights Teddy's lips—"I was afraid of blowing things out of proportion."

Nash snorts and when Teddy reaches for him, he leans into his touch.

"I know," Teddy continues. "I'm an idiot. But I just... Everything was stacking, and it was stupid little things that wouldn't have bothered me before yesterday, so I was— I thought if I got myself under control then you wouldn't have to deal with it. Obviously, that didn't work out."

Nash shifts so he's sitting on the couch properly to see Teddy without craning his neck. The new position gets Teddy's knee digging into the small of his back, but it's a good, grounding pressure that keeps him present, not stuck in his head again.

"What was the first thing? The one that started the stack. It was the peanut butter, right?"

"Yeah." Teddy frowns. "I don't want to be treated with kid gloves, ever, by anybody, but it really got to me that it was you. You never— Even when we were kids and I couldn't go two steps without needing my emergency inhaler, you treated me like I was just as capable as anyone else, even though you were the one stuck hauling my ass back home whenever I pushed too far. And then I couldn't stop looking at everything you were doing like you were doing it because you thought I needed special treatment."

"I don't think you need special treatment, Ted, but I wanna treat you special. Because you are. To me."

"I know. That's what made it so difficult to talk to you. What kind of asshole gets all bent out of shape about his boyfriend treating him right?"

"I can pull back. I know I can be—"

"I don't *want* you to pull back. I *want* to get over myself."

"Well, I'll pull back until you figure out how."

"No! I don't—" He sits up. "Nash."

Nash meets his eyes.

Emphatically, Teddy enunciates each word. "I don't want you to hold back from me."

Nash lowers his gaze. "You don't— I don't think you understand the scope of what you're saying."

"What are you talking about? What scope? What—"

"About *this*. About us. About— about peanuts! About how—" He realizes he's got his hands clenched too tight against each other and makes a concentrated effort to relax.

"Jo was right," Nash says to his hands. "I keep trying to put people at the center of the universe and— That's why I went for my CNA, you know? Jo— The state took her, and I was... I had some dark years, but Lori, the one who made the sleeve for my cane, she was a bright spot. But then she went, and I knew I'd get bad again if I didn't find something to replace— Not replace, but to— to fixate on. Something I could put up in the middle of the room as the thing everything else works around. I thought if it was a job, nobody could complain. Nobody could— could leave. I mean, they all leave, but it's okay because they're supposed to and there's always someone else...

"And then this past year with you has been... I felt that fixation shift toward you again, tryin' to move everything to work around you and— Part of me knew you'd hate it. You've never liked being taken care of, but I— I wanted to. So I let it happen and I'm sorry. I shouldn't have. I believe you that you want me, but... parts of me. The easy parts. You don't want all this mess."

"That's not true," Teddy says softly. "You're not a mess."

"I'm supposed to have goals and ambitions—stuff I want just 'cuz I want it—but I don't. Everything I have, I wandered into because I followed someone else. I don't— I just— I latch onto people and I take the things that they want or that they like and I build a life out of it. I don't even know what I like or want."

"That's not true," Teddy says again.

"Would you quit tellin' me what's true or not about my own self? I think I know a thing or two more of it."

"Okay, fine, I believe you that you don't know what you like, but *I do*. Do you want a list? I'm pretty good at lists. Top of the list: moist eggs."

He shakes his head. "That ain't—"

"Small things count. They have just as much value as the big things, sometimes more." Teddy ducks to meet Nash's eyes. "And you're different, so what? I've always liked that about you. The world could use more different. It'd be a damn disservice if you watered yourself down because I'm an asshole."

"Jo calls it my smother hen mode. It's annoying."

"You're not annoying. That's never been an issue, not for me. Can I show you everything I did to get ready for this trip? I think it'll help."

"What do you mean?"

"Let me get my laptop. I'll show you."

Unhappily, Nash sits up and allows Teddy to wiggle his leg out from behind him and bound out of the room.

He's back in a heartbeat, laptop open and propped on his forearm as his fingers skitter across the number pad.

"Okay, so—" He sits against Nash's side and settles his laptop where their knees touch. On reflex, Nash puts his arm around his shoulders and Teddy huddles close. Excitement colors his tone as he double-taps one of many green icons on his desktop. "So I did the bones of this on the flight over for — You know, the first time. For the funeral."

A color-coded spreadsheet opens, loaded with tiny text. Nash squints at it. He's never been any good at computer stuff. At the very top it says "Buford Hills" in a large font on a blue rectangle, but the rest is a jumbled wash of itty-bitty boxes and symbols.

"What is it?"

"This column here lists different places around town and these columns mark whether they serve food I can eat, if they properly handle their allergens, if they're kosher—spoiler alert: most aren't—and if I can walk there without my asthma kicking my ass. Originally, I had the hotel as the central point but I updated it to here a while back. Although," he pauses, "I probably don't need that column anymore since you've got The Boat."

"What're all these?" Nash points at the bottom where there are dozens of little tabs, shrunk too small to fit more than the first few letters.

Teddy clicks into one. It seems to hold the same data as the tab for Buford Hills. The header reads, "WD, SD".

"This is for a little tourist town me and Luke vacationed in once." He clicks another. "And here's St. Cloud."

It's got more rows than the first two put together, a painstaking catalog of everywhere Teddy can go in his home city and what kind of accessibility he can expect to find there.

"I don't have the luxury of spontaneously going places. Everything I do is planned ahead with contingencies for if the team wants to spend the whole day at a roller rink that only sells pizza. Or what if the hotel's fridge breaks and I need to find food in town that won't kill me or break kosher? Or will I be able to get home if I can't find a ride?

"So it's— That's why it grates when people act like I can't take care of myself. I'm actually very good at taking care of myself. I know my limits and, yeah, I like to push them and sometimes it doesn't work out, but I'm not naive or in denial. I just... I've got a life to live, you know? I try to keep the burden off of other people, because it's a lot, I know it's a lot, trust me, I'm living it, but here you are trying to take up a portion of it anyway.

"So I mean it, you're not annoying. You're just... You're bumping up against some long-standing hang-ups I have about letting people help, but Nash, I like the attention. I've always liked the attention."

"But then, how're we gonna fix it?" he asks. "You don't want me to change, fine, but I still wanna know everything I did that bothered you. This ain't going away on its own, so I need to know what to do next time."

Teddy stays thoughtfully silent, his fingers sedentary on the keyboard.

Slowly, he says, "We could make a list and go through it. Decide what was okay and what was over the line. And then next time you'll have a reference point. *I'll* have a reference point, so I know when I'm being particularly stupid."

Nash looks at him in dismay. "There's enough for a list?"

Teddy smiles. He kisses the underside of his chin and Nash's heart stutters. "There's always enough for a list, babe. I like lists."

"I'm getting that."

"I have kind of a sensitive question."

Apprehension finds a home in his gut. "Alright. Shoot."

"Have you ever dated before?"

Nash looks away with a wince. Shrugs. "Not really."

"It's a yes or no question, I think. What does 'not really' mean?"

"I've gotten close a time or two, but... I... It's not just Jo that finds me too much. I don't do halfway very well, and most people don't like jumpin' into a new relationship with both feet."

"You mean like how we agreed to move in together before we agreed we were dating?"

He snorts and meets Teddy's stare. He's smiling softly and Nash finds himself mirroring the expression. "Yeah, somethin' like. What about you?"

"A few girls. A couple guys. Never really made it to the serious stage. Probably why I'm not very good at this."

"How come it didn't work?"

"They weren't what I wanted."

"But I am?" He doesn't succeed in keeping the doubt out of his tone.

"Ever since I left Deliverance you've been in the back of my head, the measuring stick everyone falls short of." Teddy leans close, stare fixed and earnest as he says, "I've never met anyone like you."

"That was a long time ago, Ted. What if I don't measure up either? We've changed."

"You haven't," he says with feeling. "You're the same stubborn, loyal pain in the ass I remember, and I'm not gonna fuck it up this time. It'd suck to wait another twenty years for a third chance."

"But you'd wait?"

"For you? I'd wait lifetimes."

His heart leaps into his throat. He can't possibly mean that, but looking into his eyes, all Nash can find is open, honest belief. The lump of emotion turns too hot to touch while he's this raw. He swallows twice before he can breathe without breaking down all over again.

Teddy searches his face. "I need to talk to you about something."

"Haven't we been?"

"This is unrelated. Nothing bad, just something me and Jo have been talking about."

"You and Jo?"

"Yeah, we uh—" He turns almost shy. "You know how I said I know what you like? I'm serious about making that list, by the way. But umm, also, you know how you told me and Jo to figure out our living situation? Well…"

On his laptop, he clicks the very last tab. The header at

the top is a soft yellow and reads, "Vervain Creek". Below it, there are three tables: one labeled Theo, a second Nash, and the third Jo.

"I thought you guys were lookin' at Liberty."

"We were, but... A few months ago— Well, we talked about it and you said you trusted us to pick something you'd like and— We thought it through. It makes sense if—"

"What're you trying to say, Ted?"

"Vervain Creek is here. In Tennessee."

Nash wrenches his head back to look at him.

"I know, it's not what we agreed, but— This is your home. I can't take you away from your home. And besides, Aunt Julie's here, and Uncle Darren. It just makes sense."

"But your friends, Luke, the team."

"I can get on a video call with them whenever I want, and I can join another team and make new friends, but I can't get Tennessee on the phone for you. I've thought it through, okay? I've been prepping the guys and— Well, Luke is thinking about moving along with me. His parents passed in high school—that's what kind of cemented us together—but he doesn't have anyone else."

"Does he want to live with us? We could—"

Teddy scoffs. "I love you for asking, but no. Dorm living nearly killed him, and I mean that so literally."

"Alright."

Nash stares at the spreadsheet without taking in any of the data. His mind whirls. For over a year now, he's been bracing himself to leave. He's been building up his resolve and collecting little things he likes about Minnesota and the North in general—little assurances that once he's there, once it's his reality, he'll have something to hold on to. Aside from

Teddy, that is.

Teddy ducks forward, and his eyes sweep over his face. "What's going on in there? What are you thinking?"

"I... I thought... Why leave Buford Hills then? Why—"

"Jo wants out. She wants—"

"Lights on after nine. I remember," he says musingly. "So this new place... I haven't heard of it. It's a city?"

"Technically," Teddy says, "but it's a little one, basically a large town. It's central, nearer to Knoxville than Nashville, but a good ways away from both. We're looking at neighborhoods on the edges and some homesteads outside the city limits that are still close enough for Jo's preference. Those are more expensive, but I think... I think you'd be happy there."

"I could learn to be happy in Minnesota?" He means it to be a statement, but it curls into a question.

Teddy shakes his head. "I've seen you here and I've seen you there. There's a clear difference. And maybe with enough time you could be happy there, but I'm sick of waiting on happiness. I want you happy now."

"But I am happy now."

Teddy carefully closes his laptop. "What I'm trying to say is, when you're with me in Minnesota, you're happy so long as I'm in the room. You don't like the winter there; it's dark, it makes your hip worse, and let's be honest, winter's half the year. And when we go out, you get quiet. When you have to talk, everyone always fawns over your accent, and you get quieter. I don't mind the quiet, Nash, I really don't, but there's a difference between the quiet here and the quiet there. I want you to be quiet because being quiet is comfortable, not because you're making yourself small. And

I... I don't want to be your sole source of happiness. It wouldn't be right."

"But if I lived there—"

"Would it honestly be better? Think about it. Yes, you'd have a new nursing home and maybe it'd be just as good as Cherished Hope, and Jo would be there so long as she's not traveling for work. What else? I can't think of anything, and I've been trying for months."

"Well, what else is there? Here, I mean. I can't think of anything."

Teddy's eyes near bug out of his skull. "What— There's the fucking— the *mountains*, first of all. Do you really not realize how often you look out at them and get this peaceful little smile? No? Okay, fine, sweet tea. First thing you ask for at any restaurant is sweet tea and they never make it right."

"Well, if they'd just stir in the sugar while it's still warm —"

"And add about a pound more," Teddy says in an eerie approximation of his accent. He drops the act. "Tennessee isn't all sunshine and daisies, but it's— There's a way of living that's unique to this place. It's all checking in on the neighbor because you heard a weird noise, then making sure she's stocked on sugar because you're there. It's learning how to quilt to give a gift to someone you've never met even though no one asked and no one was expecting it. It's— It's *you*. You *fit* here. This place is just as much as part of you as you are of it, and I'd be committing a crime by taking you out of it."

Teddy is lookin' at him, waiting for his reaction, his face all a mix of his emotions. For Nash's part, he can't for the life of him think how to articulate the echo of his heartbeat whispering *seen, seen, seen, seen*. He doesn't know how to verbalize that relief feels like a weighted blanket—comforting and thick. He doesn't know how to parse apart the gratitude mixed with a deep and binding affection for the man who, despite claiming him impossible to read, can see straight through to the tender bleeding heart of him.

"Fuck it," Teddy says. He flicks open his laptop. "I'm making the list."

"Which one?"

"All the things you like and all the things you want, and then maybe you'll see what I see."

Nash reaches across and gently closes it. "I'm sorry."

"For— For what? I swear, you haven't done anything—"

He walks his fingers to the back of Teddy's neck and smooths his thumbs over his cheekbones. "For thinking for even a second that you'd walk away when you've been doin' all this for me. I'm sorry."

Teddy's shoulders slowly come down from his ears. He circles his thumb and finger around Nash's wrist and searches his eyes. "Nash, I love you."

"I know."

"You know?"

"Yeah. I see it."

Teddy closes his eyes and leans in until their foreheads bump. "So next time I act stupid, you're not going to assume it's because I want to break up?"

"I fear if you ever decide that's what you want, you'll have a helluvah time convincing me you mean it."

Teddy laughs. His grip squeezes tight, then relaxes. "That's good. I'm still going to make the list, though."

"Good. I want all the lists."

Teddy looks up to grin all crooked at him, dark eyes dancing. His usual sharp, daring grin is entirely absent. In its place, a subtle shift of features—a luminescent glow. Beautiful. His.

Teddy's gaze sinks to his lips. "Man after my heart."

And then they're kissing and Teddy is in his lap and he's not sure where the laptop went, but it hardly matters because Teddy is here and he loves him enough to stay and to fix things when they break.

Nash has only just got his hand up the back of Teddy's shirt when Teddy sits back abruptly. "How come you're shaking?"

Teddy reaches for Nash's wrist and, to Nash's surprise, he finds a fine tremble in his fingers. He clenches to a fist and lets it go lax, but the trembling doesn't go away.

"It happens sometimes when I get upset." Normally, he has very steady hands, something the nurses like to comment on, but when his emotions build up like they did today, it shows in his hands.

"Are you upset?" Teddy asks, concerned.

"No."

"What have you eaten today?" His face turns dour. "And don't say pot roast, because we both know that's not true."

He thinks, then answers, "Eggs."

Teddy's expression pinches. "I'll make my lists after we eat. What do you want?"

"Leftovers are fine."

Teddy's jaw turns stiff. "I'll pitch those. What do you like?"

With care, Nash asks, "Why? They're perfectly good. I thought you liked—"

"*You* didn't like it. Watching you try to choke it down at lunch was miserable. You don't have to eat the same stuff I do. We can—"

"Teddy, I like pot roast. It wasn't—" His face turns warm as he admits, "I have a hard time eating when I'm stressed and I…"

Teddy's shoulders slowly unbunch and his expression turns contrite. "And I was stressing you out. Fuck, I'm sorry. I thought—" Teddy climbs off his lap and collects his computer from the floor. Rubbing the back of his neck, he says, "I guess we don't have to put that one on the list."

Relieved this bump was so easily smoothed out, Nash doesn't even mock him first. He stands and kisses Teddy's temple. Teddy leans into it and aims an apologetic smile at him after.

Then Nash mocks him. "We're putting it on the list so we can have on record what a fool you are." He links their fingers and tugs him toward the kitchen. "Food will do us both good, I think."

They stay up late, huddled around the kitchen table with Teddy's laptop centered upon it, picking at plates in between typing and arguing about what counts as a want versus a need versus a simple pleasure. It don't matter much what's called what, it all ends up on the list and by the time they retreat to bed it's with easy touches and simple kisses and not a speck of unhappiness between them.

The old ice cream parlor is long-since closed down and boarded up, waiting for someone to buy the plot and demolish the old rotted corpse atop it, but old habits die hard and the wooden picnic table out back hasn't fully crumbled yet. Nash rounds the building with his hands in his pockets and Jo is already there, perched atop it with her filthy shoes on the remaining bench. She stands as she sees him and hops down to the spongy earth without a care for the mud that squelches around her sneakers.

She holds her hands out at her sides. "You have every right to be mad."

He shoots her a queer look and steps past her onto the bench to take her seat on the table and fit his muddy boots overtop the prints she left behind.

"I ain't mad, Joey."

"Well, you should be!" She jumps up and drops heavily beside him. "I was way outta line. I should've never gotten in the middle of you guys."

He shrugs. "Sorta glad you did. Finally got him talkin' at least."

It's always amusing to watch the war on her face between saying whatever funny thing popped into her head versus the serious thing. This time, the worried downturn of her lips wins out, and he finds himself sorry for it.

"You talked?"

"Yup. Worked it out. Worked out how to handle it better next time." He pulls a face. "You wouldn't believe the spreadsheets involved."

She barks a laugh but stifles it with her palm. "Spreadsheets? Christ, what kinda talk— No, no. I shouldn't — Nevermind."

"There were lists and... and promises. Ones we mean to keep this time 'round." He looks at her sideways and hopes the funny thing will win out this time as he says, "So, thanks for kickin' us in the pants."

It does.

"You really shouldn't thank me for being a raging cunt. You're gonna send me down a path the church ladies'll be clutching their pearls over." She squints at him and he realizes he's smiling. "You promise you're not mad? Last night you were fuming. I don't think I've ever seen you like that."

"I wasn't mad." He shoots her an apologetic look. "Humiliated, yeah. And... devastated. The way you were talkin' and the way Teddy'd avoided me all day, I thought it was all over."

When he looks again she's frowning hard at her clasped hands between her knees.

"I'd rather you were angry."

He hums and looks to the distance where bumps of blue round out the horizon. "Never much cared for bein' angry."

She rocks against his shoulder. "I know." She blows out a breath that fogs in front of her and tips her chin up to the clouded-over sky—gray and blue, even after last night's rain. "D'you think I turned out like Daddy?"

"No," he says, too sharp at the surprise of being asked the same thing two days in a row by the people he's closest to in all the world. "You're nothin' like him. Don't think it for even a second."

She turns to him all concern and illness. "That can't be right. You never yell or lose your temper, but me? There's this ball of fury at the back of my throat and I can't cough it loose no matter how hard I try."

He sucks his teeth, then says, "I'm gonna tell you the

same thing I told Teddy last night." She rears back, surprised, but he doesn't give her the opportunity to comment. "You get mad because you care. Daddy got mad 'cuz he liked it. He liked the violence of it. The fear. Trust me, you're nothin' like him."

"Teddy asked you —"

"Yup." He manages a half smile. "C'mon, you can't be that surprised. The pair of you have always worn your hearts on the same sleeve."

She wrinkles her nose. "Since when are you into poetry?"

"Just sayin' what I see."

She huddles further into her coat. "Are you sure, though? I hardly remember —"

"I remember."

The details are foggy — nearly three decades'll do that to memory. Could he recognize his father if he passed him on the street? Probably not. He left so long ago his face is nothing but a blur of time, but he remembers the things Daddy'd say to him. The excuses. The beatings he disguised as lessons. The anticipation in the lead-up, and the satisfaction while he, Nash, was curled up sobbing at his feet.

"I remember," he says.

Jo links her arm through his and leans into him. "I'm sorry."

"It's alright," he says softly. "If me remembering means you can forget, then I'm happy to."

She rests her head on his shoulder. "Have you considered you do too much for me?"

"A time or two. Then I got bored."

She snorts a laugh but sobers quickly. "Kinda weird to think Teddy and me fret about the same stuff."

He worries his lip, then says, "Not that weird considering all the talks you've been having behind my back."

She sits up to look at him, concerned. "We haven't—"

"He told me about Vervain Creek."

Her concern collapses as she rolls her eyes. "It's hardly behind your back, considering you told us to keep you out of it. And it makes sense to stay here, so don't even think of kickin' up a fuss. The higher minds are made up. There's not a thing—"

"I'm on board, Joey. You don't gotta browbeat me into doin' the thing I want."

She turns curious. "Is it what you want? Teddy was real sure, but... I dunno. You never seem to want for much."

He and Teddy stayed up well into the night working with his spreadsheets, making lists. The first: a series of embarrassments for one or both of them—every little thing he did that made Teddy feel like he was being swaddled in bubble wrap for his first day of preschool. Some, they agreed were overreactions while others they flagged as things for Nash to curb going forward. The second: a list of wants, his wants as defined by Teddy. It grew longer than he thought possible and contained things he's certainly not going to repeat to his little sister, but it got him thinking.

Maybe the problem isn't that he doesn't want anything, but that his wants are either small and simple or nebulous and undefined with few in-between, so he never recognized them for what they were and certainly never thought to ask for them.

"I want you to come with us," he says. "I know you've got your concerns with the stability of our—"

"Nash, if you say it's fixed, I believe you—especially if there're spreadsheets. Every good relationship is based on well-organized spreadsheets, that's what all the magazines say." A prideful little smile lights her lips as he snorts a laugh, but it fades quickly. "Seriously though, you're not leavin' here without me and you'd be hard-pressed to try. We're gonna need a bigger house, though. I need space for when you two're bein' all..." She makes a grossed-out face and shudders.

"That's up to the two of you to sort out." He bumps her with his elbow. "We good?"

She bumps him back. "We're good."

"Ice cream?"

She looks at the dilapidated building in front of them. "I fear they're fresh out, hun."

"I told Teddy where we were meeting and he asked me to bring him back a sherbet. I didn't have the heart to tell him about the state of the place."

She sighs and hops to her feet. "Well, if your precious teddy bear wants it, we better deliver."

He rises and steps gingerly to the ground. He left his cane in the car so he wouldn't have to clean it, but the squashy ground leaves a little something to be desired regarding stability.

"You know he says the same shit about how I am with you, right?"

"But it's cute when it's me because I'm the darling baby sister." She twirls in a clumsy pirouette.

He laughs, "Sure it is, dorkling," and shoves the back of her head.

"Hey!"

They slip and slide through the mud all the way to the parking lot, rough housing and snickering, and he couldn't possibly want for a thing more.

Their second attempt at dinner with Aunt Julie goes much better than the first. She comes over early to help with the cooking and Teddy sits on the back of the couch cracking jokes until Jo arrives to contest him for the comedian throne and they devolve, as always, into bickering.

He doesn't realize he's smiling until Aunt Julie pulls him into a one-armed hug and tells him how good it is to see him happy.

The rest of the week passes in a pattern of quiet moments, cheesecake-sweet kisses, and rushes of activity. They visit Cherished Hope and Nash lets the residents fawn over Teddy and beg him to bring back his hockey friends to spice up the monotony. At the roller rink he skates responsibly, hand-in-hand with Teddy — their arms extended to keep skate and inline from colliding — and stops well before his hip takes a beating. Just the two of them go on a day trip to Vervain Creek to sleuth out the old-timiest ice cream parlor to replace their old haunt from childhood, then they spend a solemn morning at the cemetery with Jo, Aunt Julie, and Uncle Darren. When they leave there are four new stones placed atop his headstone.

And on their last night, Nash and Teddy make the ATV ride to the top of the world to spend their final hours in each other's company under the stars with the wind and their sycamore tree, per tradition.

Nash has said a lot of goodbyes in his life, but kissing Teddy in front of God and everybody at the airport hardly feels like one. It's *fly safe*. And *call me when you land*. And *I'm gonna miss you like hell*. And *see you again soon*. And *I can't wait*.

TWO YEARS LATER

Nash steps through the doorway and, as he has every day for the past three, he stops to take it in and marvel that it's all his. The hardwood gleams under the thick rays of Tennessee summer sunshine that pours through the front windows. Jo is already complaining, saying they let in too much heat and are too irregularly shaped for curtains, but he's finding it difficult to be as practical. He's never lived anywhere this light.

They've spent every day since the day they arrived painting over inoffensive gray walls, and every night sleeping in a motel away from the fumes while their moving trucks sit on the curb and rack up a bill. As he keeps telling Teddy, it's worth it to have the luxury of making the space exactly what they want before they fill it.

There's so much house he needn't have worried about agreeing on colors. Jo claimed the den, Teddy insisted on secrecy as he outfits the little sunroom on the back corner,

284

and together they agreed Nash should get jurisdiction over the kitchen since he's the only one with any competency there.

He chose a nice buttery yellow, and it's aglow in the sun.

"Teddy?" Nash's voice echoes strangely in the empty space. He steps off the patch of tile that marks the foyer and makes for the back of the house. "We're about to unload. Don't think you're getting out of helping. The guys'll be here any minute."

They flew in this morning and are jumping straight from the airport to the house to help out. Or, well, that's the plan. Nash has his reservations about how helpful they'll actually be. A wild pack of dogs might be better behaved than the hockey team, but they've got two trucks to unpack: a big one from Buford Hills, and a much smaller one that came all the way from St. Cloud, Minnesota.

He's still having trouble believing there'll be no more airport goodbyes. Teddy's staying. And *he's* staying. Here, in this beautiful home. Their home.

It's gonna take a while to sink in.

"I'm almost done," Teddy calls back.

Nash pauses beside the ajar door of the half bath. It's the farthest he's allowed to go.

"Can I come in?"

"Not yet!"

He shakes his head and wanders back to the sun-filled rooms at the front of the house. The kitchen bleeds into a sitting room complete with a gas fireplace, stone mantle, and a box of logs he hopes the previous owner wasn't actually burning in the thing. Jo insists the fireplace will be nice on cold, wet nights and if it means she'll be around to use it, he'll happily keep it maintenanced and ready to light up at a moment's notice, but they are *not* putting wood logs in a gas fireplace.

Atop the mantel is a welcome basket from Ivory Hall Senior Care Center that the three of them have spent the past few days picking apart, so now only the tangerines are left. Once they have the silverware unpacked, they'll be able to peel them without repeating Jo's unfortunate incident.

Anyway, her eyes are fine now and it was kind of them to send even though he has a couple weeks to get settled before he starts. He tries not to dwell on it too much. Teddy is sure he'll fit in just fine, but... Well, it was a rough start at Cherished Hope, to say the least.

He already visited, of course. Teddy did his online investigations and made a list of contenders, then, while Teddy was in-state, they spent a couple of days together hopping around to see how they measured up in-person. Ivory Hall didn't win top marks, or even second-best, but despite its short comings in technology and that atrocious receptionist, it felt the most like a home. The staff seemed close-knit and were kind and familiar with the residents, but also respectful and capable. Nash felt it was the closest to what he was looking to replace. Maybe even a notch better. He only hopes he can fit neatly into the fold.

And besides, receptionists come and go like bad fads. They'll probably have a new one by the time he starts.

"Ready!"

Nash retraces his steps, passes the half bath, hangs a right at the sliding glass door that leads to a narrow porch overlooking a breathtaking view down the backside of the mountain, and stops at the glass-paned door that encloses the sunroom. A pleated white curtain blocks the view inside.

"I can come in?"

"Yes," Teddy says, all impatience and untempered excitement.

Nash opens the door and loses his breath.

He wasn't sure about the rust-colored paint Teddy chose for this room, but it looks good illuminated by the curved glass overhead and contrasted by pops of green from the few potted plants strategically placed around the room. But it's the forget-me-nots that catch his eye and hold it.

They're planted in a long wooden trough that spans the length of the window. There are only enough blooms to fill the center, but uncovered soil is freshly watered and in his mind's eye he can see the whole thing spilling over with dozens upon dozens of delicate blue flowers.

"You built this?"

Teddy rubs his cheek with his wrist. His fingers are dusted with dirt and a ratty, three-day-old bandage circles his thumb.

"See the hose in there along the side?" he says. "That's the irrigation system. They don't need watered much, so I worried I'd forget now that they won't be in my face every day, and rigged it up to be automatic. Took a while to nail down the timing, but I've got the math in a spreadsheet if you're interested. Probably gonna take some fine-tuning because they're definitely going to get more sun here, and I'm a little worried they won't take to the new soil, so we'll have to keep an eye on them, anyway."

Nash runs his fingers along the smooth wood of the trough. Below it is a long, shallow plastic basin to catch any drippings.

"You made this for me?"

Teddy looks at him and loses the critical frown. "Yeah. I mean, I promised, didn't I? I don't know how you found the only florist in the state that'll bother with wildflowers, but—"

Nash cuts him off with a kiss—palms over cheeks, boots threatening socked feet. Against his lips, he murmurs, "Thank you."

Teddy loops his fingers around Nash's wrists and smiles into the kiss. When he pulls back, his eyes are dancing. "I take it you like it?"

Maybe it's the excitement of all of their plans finally coming to fruition combined with the drain of the past several weeks of nonstop move preparation more so than Teddy's surprise flower trough, but he's sopping with happiness as he presses their lips together again. Nash wants this forever. He wants to curl up in this feeling and never leave it. He wants sun-warmed floorboards and wildflowers and the love of his life, his best friend, and—

He rips back so suddenly, Teddy stumbles into the place he used to be.

"Can I see your laptop? I have another want for the list."

"Now?" Teddy demands. You know Jo's gonna come stomping in here to yell at us if we take any longer." Despite his warning, Teddy wipes his hands on his jeans and fetches his computer from a shaded corner.

Nash waits for him to pull up the correct spreadsheet from the sea of green icons on his desktop, then accepts the computer when he hands it over.

One-handed, tongue between his teeth, Nash painstakingly types in his latest want by hunting and pecking out the letters. Teddy never fails to mock him for the way he types, so he finishes as quick as he can and then turns it around for him to read.

It's probably not accurate to call it his latest want. It's his longest want. The one that's been in the back of his mind, formless and yearning for as long as he can remember. Only in the past few years did he find the words for it, and now, finally, he has the gumption to put them all together and share them.

Teddy is already reaching to close the computer as he skims his addition and is saying, "I can't believe you're thirty-five and still—" He freezes midmotion and his breath hushes past his lips as he forms the words on the screen, as though to check that they say what he thinks they do. Then he wrenches his neck and looks up at Nash with wide eyes.

"Yes," he blurts. "Holy shit, yes. When?"

Teddy abandons his laptop to teeter on the corner of the flower trough and Nash laughs, bubbling and irrepressible as they tangle their fingers.

"Hadn't gotten that far. We'll have to find a place, a nice church or a synagogue or— I don't really care where. We could do it right here in this room."

"Nash," Teddy says, all intensity and heat. "How long have you been thinking about this?"

"Umm, forever, I think." He moves a lock of hair from Teddy's forehead, only for it to spring stubbornly back into place. "I remember the first time I saw you and part of me just knew if I let you too close, I'd spend the rest of my life wanting to be near you."

"You remember that?"

"Mm-hmm. You were crying."

He rolls his eyes. "I was six, my parents had just died,

and I had to move to a new state. I'd like to know who wouldn't be crying."

"You were crying, but you were looking at all of us like you were daring us to say something. First thing I did was vow to stay far away from you."

"You did?"

"Yup. Failed immediately, of course. What was our teacher's name? Mrs. Rainer? She made us bus buddies and after I walked you home that first day, you bullied me into playing Pokémon with you, remember? I was gone on you after that. Couldn't ever stay away. I don't think I realized how deeply I felt until years after you'd left."

Teddy ducks under his chin and rocks into him, arms cinching tight. "Your parents didn't do us any favors, did they?"

Nash holds Teddy close. "We made it anyway."

"The greatest losses of my life brought me to you both times. Almost like an apology."

Nash keeps quiet and strokes along Teddy's spine. Theology is a topic they discovered early on not to delve into. Not necessarily because their beliefs are in conflict, but because Teddy likes to pick at things and ask complicated questions that don't have real answers, and the way Nash figures it, it's all a moot point and not worth fussing over. He's doing all the good he can with what he's got. Either that's enough or it's not, and he won't find out which until he's too dead to do any different.

He's stirred from his thoughts by a faint trembling under his hands. Then Teddy snorts, and a giggle slips free. He looks up, and he's luminescent as he says, "We're getting married."

Nash is helpless to do anything but kiss the words from his lips.

"For fuck's sake!"

He flinches back and finds Jo in the doorway.

She plants her hands on her hips. Her hair is cropped short for summer and is bound up in a stubby ponytail that drops strands to hang around her neck whenever she moves. In a paint-stained tank top, khaki shorts, and an old pair of boots, she's ready to work.

"I leave the two of you alone for two minutes and you go and get engaged? Can I trust you to behave while I get the first box, or will we be expecting a baby by the time I get back?"

It shocks him, the ferocity of the want that grabs him. Nash has never considered before that he could make a family of his own. It was always going to be him and Jo 'till the very end. He hoped he might get to keep Teddy—keep him close, keep him happy, bask in the brilliance of him—but he never looked beyond that. Never thought he'd make it far enough for there to be more to wish for.

Now, though... They've got the space, inside and out, a whole mountain to explore and learn and a good creek that cuts across their property—not too deep, perfect for a couple of kids to get wet and muddy and track it home.

He looks down and finds Teddy watching him, a familiar energy about him that he recognizes and knows.

"Look at you," Teddy says softly. "Should I get the spreadsheet back up?"

Nash licks his lips. "Yeah, I think so."

Teddy laughs and pulls him down for a kiss that's spoiled by the smile on his lips.

"Would you two slow down?" Jo whines a bit desperately. "I'm not ready to be an aunt."

"Aunt Jo," Nash muses. "It sounds right, doesn't it?"

She wilts. "Well, when you put it that way."

"Should we hold off on adding me to your bank account?" Teddy asks. He looks at Nash. "Maybe I should add you to mine instead."

"What?" Jo squawks. "And leave me on my own? No way. We already decided, and this changes nothin'. We're sharing expenses. It don't make sense to have a bunch of different accounts."

"But a baby, Jo... Kids are expensive. Are you sure you —"

"You think I don't want to financially support my little niece or nephew?" A strange look comes over her face. "Niece," she says. "You have to have a girl."

"It's not like shopping for a puppy. And we haven't even talked— Maybe we want a surrogate. Or— There's all kinds of things to consider."

She turns to Nash. "Promise me. I can't be the only girl. Promise."

"Yeah, okay."

"Ha!"

"Nash!"

"What? You know I'm a sucker."

Teddy thumps his head once on Nash's shoulder, then pulls away to collect his laptop. He hands it over with a stern, "No more baby talk. Marriage first, then—"

"Or how 'bout we unload these trucks first," Jo butts in. "I don't wanna step on your ever-blooming relationship, but if we have to pay for another night because you two got all gooey, I'm gonna blow a gasket."

"Alright, fine. Trucks first."

Jo leads the way out of the sunroom with Teddy on her heels as they argue logistics on which truck to tackle first, what needs to wait for the muscle to arrive, and should they track dirt through the house carrying everything to its proper room or pile it all in the front to be dealt with later?

Nash lets them fade away as he opens the computer and finds his spreadsheet still pulled up. He clicks the box below, "will you marry me?" and types "baby girl." Then below that, "parenting classes." His folks didn't do him any favors, but he doesn't have to be more of the same. He'll be everything they should've been and everything he wishes he had.

"Nash?" Teddy's voice echoes through the house. "Where'd you—"

He pokes his head into the sunroom and, upon spotting him with the laptop, softens.

"You good?"

"Yeah. Really good."

"Meet us out front when you're done? We're going to start with my truck. Make sure we can turn in at least one before they close."

He shuts the computer. "I'm ready now." He sets it back in the shaded corner where the sun won't cook it, and as he turns around, Teddy catches him by the waist.

"Hey," Teddy searches his face, fingers flexing against Nash's ribs, then says, "I'm really happy. I think this was the right move."

Nash bumps their foreheads and says, "I'm really happy too."

"We've got a lot of good stuff ahead of us, don't we?"

More than Nash ever expected. More than he dared hope for. When he's old and his body and mind aren't what they once were, he intends to look back with nothing but joy and satisfaction. He's going to savor every second, starting with this one. He doesn't want to forget a thing.

Also by Sarah B. Elisa

Wildflowers of Deliverance
Red, like my bleeding heart in your hand
Blue, like don't forget about me
Violet, like these delights (Coming soon)

Watch for more at SarahBElisa.com

About the Author

Sarah B. Elisa (she/her) grew up in Iowa with one foot in the city and the other on the back highway that leads to the small town where she was born. She writes stories centered around character growth and relationship dynamics—both romantic and platonic. She has a particular love for the queer and the working class, and finds joy in breathing fresh air into old tropes.

Watch for more at SarahBElisa.com

www.ingramcontent.com/pod-product-compliance
Lightning Source LLC
Chambersburg PA
CBHW052021240626
47153CB00006B/1900